THE REMNANT

THE REMNANT

BY MONTE WOLVERTON

Published by CWR press, an imprint of Plain Truth Ministries, Pasadena, CA

Library of Congress Cataloging-in-Publication Data

Wolverton, Monte, 1948
The Remnant / Monte Wolverton

p. cm.
Includes biographical references and index.

Cover image ©123RF Stock Photos/Cosma Andrei, and Marv Wegner—PTM

ISBN-978-1-889973-19-7

1. Fiction
2. Popular works
3. Christianity—Miscellanea
I. Title

Contents

PROLOGUE—
DATE 2063

On the eastern coast of Tunisia, overlooking the Gulf of Hammamet and the Mediterranean Sea, sits the Great Mosque of Monastir, a place of prayer since the ninth century—but no longer. In the year 2062, a cataclysmic global war prompted the World Federation to ban all religion.

Now, less than a year later, a high-level meeting was being held here in the mosque, repurposed like many former places of worship as a museum and site for seminars and forums. Ironically, the subject of this particular Federation conference was religion.

The men and women entering the cavernous hall were clearly familiar with making decisions, issuing orders and receiving respect. Some wore military dress uniforms, others wore dark suits that spoke of power. Chatting and posturing, they seated themselves in black leather chairs flanking a ridiculously long, polished ebony conference table.

In front of each chair was a name card, an agenda, a water glass and a smaller glass, which waiters filled with the attendee's choice of strong coffee or Tunisian mint tea.

As ushers gently closed the ornate doors from the outside, a middle-aged man with wavy black hair, a blue-grey Italian suit and Mediterranean features called the meeting to order. His deep voice echoed through the hall. "Welcome, everyone of you, to the first meeting of the Religious Directive Implementation Council."

"Let's hope it will also be the last," quipped a portly gentleman in a military uniform. The group laughed, until they noticed the glare in the eyes of the chairperson.

"Continuing," said the chairperson, "you have been asked to serve on this council because you each represent key interests in business, industry, natural resources, intelligence, security, academia, judiciary and media. Let me remind you that the directive is a done deal for the entire world—proposed by the Foremost Council and ratified by the Grand Council. Our question is not *whether* but *how*."

Heads nodded in agreement.

"To set the stage," said the chairperson, "as you all know, our objective is not, nor has it ever been, to obliterate religion from the memory of humankind. We are merely altering our perspective. Religion has become a useless, disease-prone appendage. It is a part of our collective history, to be sure, but the time has come for it to be decommissioned. Unfortunately, many will insist on hanging on to dangerous superstitions. Citizens of the Safe Zones must comply. Those who choose not to comply must be resettled, yet happily, they can become a valuable resource for the Federation and for industry. A sort of win-win situation."

Some members of the group listened attentively, while others gazed at the architecture, stealing quick glances at other attendees to check their reactions.

"Religious professionals present a challenge. Pastors, priests, prophets, imams and rabbis must be dealt with first so they don't stand in the way of our plans. We will offer them—um—extensive reeducation and indoctrination in the Federation Values. A best case scenario is that they can become walking testimonials for our system and can continue to preach—but preach Federation Values. Early results have been positive. Those who don't work out will be dealt with on an individualized basis."

"Any comments so far?"

There was silence, except for a cough that echoed through the great room.

"Fortunately," continued the chairperson, "a majority of citizens, according to the latest polls, are soured on religion, and agree wholeheartedly with Federation policy. This, thanks to the cooperative efforts of our propaganda people and the entertainment industry. Most citizens are ready to get rid of glassy-eyed religious nincompoops and their snake-oil sales force with their ridiculous frocks and silly hats."

Laughter reverberated and trailed off.

"Very well then," said the chairperson. "Dr. Gantassi, can you offer some perspective from the standpoint of the Ministry of Information?"

A tall woman in a cobalt blue suit cleared her throat. "Our primary challenge here is to avoid the perception that this is some sort of pogrom—a religious cleansing—and that those who persist in their religious delusions are being sent to concentration camps or work camps against their will. While that may be accurate, it is also a destabilizing construct. Accordingly, as we implement this directive, we should at all times emphasize the freedom of choice these individuals are being offered. We all serve the World Federation, to make the planet a better home for humankind. These individuals, by persisting in their beliefs and practices, are freely choosing to serve the Federation in a unique and important capacity. That's the way we want everyone to think of it."

"Oh good grief!" said the portly man, as he tugged on the collar of his medal-bedecked, starch green jacket, and puffed out his chest.

"Where did you work? In a New York ad agency or a PR firm? Maybe as a political speechwriter? What's with all the psychology? Just let my security forces round these people up, load them into boxcars, and send them where they need to go."

"General Feki, with all due respect," said the chairperson, "we understand how your approach might seem to be more—um—*efficient*. Yet it would be preferable to accomplish this task without the Federation being perceived as jackbooted Nazis, and without multiple insurrections. It's always better if we can manipulate—or I should say *encourage*—people to cooperate voluntarily. Thank goodness we live in an age where the masses are easily brainwashed by well-crafted PR tactics, disguised as advertising and entertainment. And yes, before the war, Dr. Gantassi's services were often in demand from major American advertising agencies, PR firms and politicians—back when there *was* a USA."

Muffled guffaws swept through the room. A small man in a black uniform addressed the chairperson.

"Secretary Bougatfa, if I may offer a brief summary of our plan for managing religious practitioners, the Council may find it helpful."

"By all means, proceed, Director Kleinschmidt," said the Secretary.

"Thank you, Secretary. This program relies heavily on surveillance, as does all law enforcement of course. Our contractors have redoubled their efforts to provide us with drone technology to carry the plan out in each and every Autonomous Region, to peer into every citizen's living room, workplace, bedroom—anywhere and everywhere. Indeed, many of you sitting here have been under surveillance already."

The Secretary chuckled, looked around the group and winked at a couple of people. Some shuffled uncomfortably.

"Now you may ask," continued Director Kleinschmidt, "'How can you surveil someone's faith?' Well, I suppose it is *possible* to keep one's faith internal. Yet in my experience, religion almost always includes visible components—icons, books, rituals, trinkets, clothing, food, bizarre habits and customs—the list goes on and on. There's always something.

"In any case, when our surveillance teams have gathered sufficient evidence that a subject is practicing religion, they will transmit it to the Compliance Division, which will issue a series of notices to the subject. If the notices are not acted upon, we will send a final notice of relocation, followed by a visit from an agent, who will secure the subject for relocation."

"Quite smooth," agreed the Secretary.

"And," continued Kleinschmidt, "in keeping with Dr. Gantassi's excellent advice and directives, we will never use the words *arrest, violation, crime* or *prison*. We will treat subjects in a courteous, businesslike manner. If subjects are reluctant or need convincing, our agents are trained to reassure them and further sell them on the program. Our prototypical tests in Charlotte, formerly North Carolina—with a higher than average Christian population—have yielded 91.3 percent compliance. Likewise, Varanasi, India, on the

Ganges, a traditional center of religious activity, has yielded 85.2 percent compliance."

"*Sell* them on the program?" scoffed General Feki. "And what if they *don't* comply? What then?"

"As I was about to clarify," said Director Kleinschmidt, "armed security officers will accompany each agent, which of course encourages compliance. Noncompliant subjects will be quietly and efficiently dealt with through other procedures. I will not elaborate on those at this time."

General Feki sighed, his chubby fingers drumming the table, his eyes staring upward at the fresh paint covering the old Koran passages on the ceiling. "Mmmhmm. People will see right through this nonsense. They will comply because they *have* to. Not because they are *sold*."

Secretary Bougatfa pretended to ignore General Feki's comments. "Thank you, Director Kleinschmidt. A wonderful plan. Ms. Stavros, your agency is handling processing?"

"Yes, Secretary. Upon the issuance of the second notice to a subject, our systems will identify their abilities and determine how they would be most useful to the Federation. Upon arrival at a processing center, we will perform a medical scan, issue uniforms, rescan for contraband, give a brief orientation and place them on a bus or train to their destination facility. And of course in the process we will weed out the remaining non-compliants."

"Excellent!" smiled Secretary Bougatfa. "This should reassure those of you here representing industry. Thousands of work camps around the world are under construction as joint projects of the Federation and private enterprise. We will provide the finest, problem-free labor. A well-oiled machine! And of course the Federation will direct and manage the labor force, while private enterprise reaps the benefits. Not entirely dissimilar to the exploitation of inmates under the privatized American prison system in the 21st century. A remarkably good deal, I would say."

Business representatives smiled broadly and nodded. A couple of them applauded.

"Now, on the academic side, Dr. Zhao, would you give us a quick perspective?"

"Certainly, sir. We are producing a series of holoseminars for educators who teach social sciences and history at the university level. Elementary and secondary school educators will follow. New textbooks are in the works. We are also planning a coordinated effort with our media associates across the table here. Finally, we are working with municipalities and local scholars to transform houses of worship and temples into museums, where we will offer programs to educate the public and orient them toward the Values."

"A massive undertaking! Splendid work! You know," mused the Secretary, "if we are to be truthful with ourselves, we are actually doing away with superstitious metaphysical religion, and replacing it with the one and only pragmatic religion that has successfully improved the condition of humankind, and to which all, both small and great, rich and poor, bow the knee— good old-fashioned, unbridled, materialistic *capitalism!*"

Attendees grinned and laughed. A couple of the business and banking representatives applauded.

"And finally, General Feki," said the Secretary, "I know you have been *anxiously* waiting to grace us with a word about the removal and disposal of religious texts."

"I thought you'd never ask. I will grace you with two

words: *nearly done*. We have covered all the Safe Zones and almost all Wilderness areas worldwide. Bibles, Korans, Upanishads, Talmuds, whatever—we detect and disintegrate them on the spot. Of course we will have to continue our vigilance for decades, but the initial phase is almost complete."

"Marvelous," beamed the Secretary. "Well, that should give you a brief overview of the program as it now stands, and..."

A man at the far end of the table spoke up. "Secretary, it seems as if this is all a *fait accompli*. Can we make suggestions at this point? While we certainly all agree that religion should be abolished, considering its role in the war, there are significant issues here involving due process and compliance with Federation law..."

"Excellent question, Justice Daya. Your suggestions are welcome at any time. Just send me a holovideo. But please know that hundreds of thousands of hours—perhaps millions of hours—of work, planning and testing have already gone into this system, not to mention the fact that major parts of the world economy are predicated on the forthcoming labor force."

Justice Daya nodded and raised the palm of his hand in assent. "I certainly appreciate that, but I..."

"Justice Daya," interrupted the Secretary, "you are here for the express purpose of seeing to it that the Great Court and the judicial branch of government in general *interpret* the law where necessary in order to make this all happen. If you feel we need to tweak the law or constitution in some way, let me know and we will take the appropriate measures in the Grand Council."

The room was uncomfortably quiet for a moment. Scanning the whole group, the Secretary added, "And really, all of us are here to learn about the system so that the various agencies and enterprises we each represent can fall into line and give it full and enthusiastic support." He smiled. "Do we all agree?"

All heads nodded.

"When a man is denied the right to live the life he believes in, he has no choice but to become an outlaw."
—Nelson Mandela

Part I: Escape—
Date 2131

1.

The tunnel was barely big enough for one lean person to crawl through at a time. Grant Cochrin gritted his teeth and clawed his way forward, a small flashlight duct-taped to his hat illuminating the next five feet. Everything beyond was pitch black. Gravel dropped around him as his backpack scraped and caught against the crumbling ceiling. He felt his claustrophobic panic rising. As a petroleum geologist he had always worked in the great outdoors or in a comfortable lab. He had never been any good in closed places, and he couldn't imagine one much worse than this. But for the sake of his family and friends crawling behind him, he couldn't say a word. He had to keep moving and stay positive.

The smell of damp dirt centered him, in this case, the aroma of glacial deposits laid down twenty-two thousand years ago in the Late Wisconsin Glacial Episode. Grant's geological training always kicked in when he was close to dirt. He loved dirt. If he could keep thinking about the dirt, maybe he could kick the claustrophobia.

"How much longer?" From behind him came the voice of his wife, with a clear note of desperation. He couldn't let her know he was feeling the same way.

"Not long. Just about ten more minutes for this part of the ordeal, honey. One step at a time."

"One step?"

Dana could be a dead-serious critical thinker at times when Grant didn't think he needed critique. And now, ten feet underground, she was trying to be a comedian. Which was, as always, exactly what he needed.

"Okay," laughed Grant, "one bloody knee-scrape at a time." In spite of the fatigue and claustrophobia that he and certainly everyone else was fighting, he guessed this would actually be the safest part of their journey. But he didn't want to scare his family and friends any more than they already were—with the possible exception of his fearless friend Bryan, who had helped plan the escape and who was more aware of the risks than anyone. As Grant struggled along, he found himself muttering, "Please! We could really use some help now— and even more after we get to the end of the tunnel!"

"Say what?" asked Dana.

"Nothing," answered Grant. "Just pushing some dirt out of the way." This whole thing had been Grant's idea. He had worked hard to convince Dana and the kids and his friends that it was well worth the risk. Now, only minutes into the reality, he found himself wondering if his family and friends (besides Bryan) were up to the challenges that lay ahead.

Grant thought back to his discovery of the entrance to the tunnel behind their kitchen sink years ago while fixing a drain, well before he had any thoughts of escape. He had accidentally poked a hole in the wall with a pipe wrench, and was surprised to find a vertical shaft dropping about eight feet, complete with a polyester rope ladder. At the bottom there was a tunnel large enough to crawl through. Perhaps foolishly, he had braved his claustrophobia, and explored the tunnel by himself. He found that it continued horizontally for about 300 feet, gradually ramping deeper underground, passing under the footing of the work camp wall, finally emerging into an old drainage cistern. From there, a large concrete pipe led about a quarter mile under one of the streets of the abandoned and deteriorating city of Minot, opening along the bank of the Souris River. Why and how the tunnel got there, Grant did not know, but now it seemed like a Godsend. Some enterprising inmate must have spent years digging it. Who knew how many inmates had used it to escape—or had died trying?

But today, there was no going back. It was a one-way trip down the tunnel and out the other end. If all went well, Grant and his gang would be at least a mile down the riverbank before any of the guards or coworkers at the work camp noticed they were missing. The guards might never discover how they had escaped. Bryan, the last person down the shaft, had carefully replaced the bottles of detergent and brushes under the kitchen sink and re-secured the paneling with screws from the back before descending the rope ladder into the shaft. He had also set bug and drone disabling devices to block any surveillance by the guards, who probably weren't awake anyway.

Grant's attention was yanked back by Dana. "Are you guys still behind us?"

"Well, yeah," Grant heard his sixteen-year-old daughter Lissa answer. "Where else would I be? Are we almost there?"

"Wuss!" came the voice of his nine-year-old son Tadd. "This is totally cool! I want it to go on forever!"

17

"Tadd," said Dana, "show some respect for your sister. We're all in this together."

"Just a few more yards, honey," called Grant to his daughter. "I've been here before, and it doesn't go on forever. Sorry, Tadd."

Grant never wanted to do it this way. He would have preferred it if Warden Davis Grimhaus had just let them walk away. The Wilderness—anywhere outside the work camps, the big city Safe Zones or transportation corridors—was near suicide, according to Grimhaus and his guards. So why not just open the gate and let them go? Grant suspected that the Wilderness wasn't such a dangerous place after all. He was banking on that. And in any case, the further they crawled, the more committed they were. Once anyone, citizen or inmate, set foot in the Wilderness, there was no coming back, according to Federation law. The Feds might kill you, they might let you live, but you could never return to Safe Zone civilization or the work camp again, dead or alive.

Grant had been the only petroleum geologist in the Minot Work Camp, the hub of oil drilling and pumping operations in the still-productive Bakken Formation, stretching from Minot in the former state of North Dakota northwest into what had been Montana, Saskatchewan and Manitoba. Grimhaus really couldn't afford to let Grant go. It would be next to impossible for Grimhaus to offer a big enough salary to score a citizen petroleum geologist to work out here. An inmate with Grant's abilities? One chance in a million.

Both Grant and Dana had spent their lives in the work camp. Although he had no academic degree, Grant had learned geology from his father who took great pains to give him the equivalent of a BS in geology, including a foundation in the other sciences. His father had been incarcerated at the age of fifteen along with Grant's grandmother and grandfather, a university geology professor sentenced to the camp in the religious purges following the Final War in 2062. That was 69 years earlier. It was now 2131.

The Final War, along with environmental disasters and pandemics, had left the world's population at about a tenth of what it had been. The World Federation had dissolved national boundaries and reorganized the earth into Autonomous Regions. With law enforcement personnel at a premium, citizens were restricted to governable and heavily defended Safe Zones surrounding the cities that survived. Everything else—the vast amounts of sparsely inhabited territory in the world—was Wilderness. It was off-limits to citizens (allegedly for their protection) and the Safe Zones were certainly off limits to anyone from the Wilderness.

Had the Cochrins not stubbornly persisted as Christians, they would have been released from the Minot Work Camp long ago and sent back to the comforts of Safe Zone civilization. But the Federation, from its magnificent capitol in Carthage, Tunisia, had declared religion taboo. It had sent all who practiced religion, and who refused to sign an Affidavit of Renunciation, to work camps—like the one in Minot—that dotted Wilderness areas around the world. Camp inmates served the Federation and industry by extracting resources—oil, coal, timber, minerals, metals, geothermal, water and wind energy.

Camp inmates weren't starving. They had roofs over their heads, places to sleep, friends and families and free healthcare. They could practice their faith. They were protected from crime. In rare off-hours, they could even enjoy holovideos, entertainment and of course propaganda from the big Safe Zone cities.

They were not being punished, per se. They were here to work, and smart wardens wanted a sustainably productive workforce that would stay put and not try to escape.

However, inmates worked long hours, sometimes seven days a week. There were no vacations, little self-determination, and no communication with people outside the camp (except occasionally through bootleg channels). Protection from crime didn't cover abusive guards or unethical wardens, although Federation inspectors officially frowned on such things. In a nutshell, inmates had plenty of security, a lot of isolation, but little freedom.

The unremitting, oppressive environment slowly but surely convinced Grant that he had to persuade his family and friends that freedom in the Wilderness was worth the uncertainly and peril involved in their escape. So now here he was, crawling through a muddy, dark tunnel and risking his life and those of his loved ones in search of something better somewhere out there in the Wilderness—a group, a community, a church or an institution of some kind that followed a man named Jesus. Grant had gone from hoping and dreaming that such a group existed out there—to certainty.

At last, Grant's flashlight revealed a dark opening. He swung his feet over the edge and stepped down onto the wet floor of a dank concrete cubicle. His flashlight beam flitted around the hundred-year-old tank as rats scattered.

One by one the rest of muddy escapees emerged from the tunnel. Dana was first, then Lissa and Tadd, all with big eyes. Grant shined his flashlight up the tunnel. The next one out was a grinning but disheveled Sara Davenport.

"I hate to say this," said Grant, "but right now you don't look anything like a former professor of religious history at New Harvard University."

"Right now I don't feel like one," laughed Sara.

Owen Fenbert appeared in the tunnel entrance, his dark, smiling face framed by white hair. "Hi, folks. How about a little help? This is just too tight for a big guy like me to turn around." Grant and Dana held up his tall, muscular frame while he slid his legs out and onto the ground.

Bryan Hantwick, fit and thirty-something, energetically hopped out, his khaki vest pockets bulging with electronic gadgets, tools and dangling wires. "What a rush!" He pulled a small gadget from a pocket and poked at it a couple of times. "And nobody knows we're gone yet. What's next?"

"One more leg to go," said Grant. "Down this conduit for about a quarter mile and we'll be at the river. At least we don't have to crawl anymore." They entered a seven-foot wide hole on the opposite side of the tank, and trudged into the darkness. Every sound reverberated, including the skittering of rodents, which were occasionally illuminated by Grant's flashlight. After a few minutes they began to see dim natural light—not bright, as it was only 5:30 in the morning.

As the light increased, they noticed bits of vegetation growing on the floor—and something else—chunks of white and yellow. As he saw larger pieces, it dawned on Grant that these were bone fragments. As they neared the end of the conduit, the bones became more numerous. The group rounded a curve and stopped in their tracks. A jumble of bones lay to the side, as if deposited by flowing water. They stared in horror as they recognized intact human skeletons with gaping skulls, some with shreds of clothing still attached.

No one said anything for a while.

"Ew!" commented Lissa.

"Cool!" exclaimed Tadd, trying to be macho in spite of his fear.

"You know," said Grant, "these were real people, who lived sometime within the last seventy years. Likely they fled in here from Federation drones, but the drones got 'em anyway. Could have been right after the war. Could have been one of the later sweeps of the city to keep Wilderness people away from the camp."

The skeletons were a graphic reminder to Grant of the danger they were in and would continue to be in. Federation drones were just as lethal as they always had been.

The group continued for a few more yards and emerged into daylight through a wall of prickly bushes onto the bank of the Souris River, which flowed through the center of the old city. They turned and surveyed what they had traveled under—the crumbling city of Minot, and the wall of the work camp, peeking in the distance over a half-collapsed brick building.

"Thank God that's over," said Sara, pulling thorns from her jacket. "We did it! We're out!"

"Yeah, thank God, but it may be a little too soon to celebrate," cautioned Grant. "We still have a way to go before we're beyond the camp's peripheral surveillance. And even then…"

"The more distance we put between the camp and us the better," interrupted Bryan. "For now we head east—along the river bank." He activated a small device on his wrist that projected a map in the air in front of him. "And I suggest…"

"Dad!" interrupted Lissa, "I think I dropped my iCap back in the first tunnel!"

Grant remembered the day he had acquired the device for his daughter's birthday from one of the truckers who brought supplies to the camp. He didn't really like the idea that it transmitted video and audio directly into Lissa's visual and auditory cortex. But other teens in the camp had them. They were wildly popular in the Safe Zones and Lissa had always wanted one.

"Can we go back and get it, Dad? Pleeeeze?"

Tadd rolled his eyes. "Universe to Lissa: We're escaping from prison! Forget your stupid iCap!"

Lissa looked at her brother as if he was an annoying insect. "Dad! It's got all my music in it! *All* my music!" She began to cry.

Grant put his hands on both his kids' shoulders. "Tadd, this is not merely a prison break. We're leaving the place that has always been our home—like it or not. There's stuff in your backpack you wouldn't want to lose because you'll look at it and remember growing up in the camp. And your sister just lost something valuable to her. Go easy on her, okay?

Grant turned to Lissa. "You know, honey, we really can't go back in there. We'd risk getting killed—or worse. We can't replace you, or anyone here, but we can replace the iCap. Somewhere down the road, there'll be some way we can get another. Okay?"

"Okay, Dad," blubbered Lissa.

"You spoil those kids," Dana whispered.

"I know," said Grant. "Now what were you saying, Bryan?"

"I was saying that we need to stay under the cover of whatever trees and vegetation we can find. We've disabled the implants, but on the slim chance they manage to get around what I've done to the system, they can still find us with satellites and drones."

Not only had Bryan disabled the locator implants

on each person, he had uploaded a program into the work camp system that simulated the typical daily movements of each member of the party, so it would appear that the implants were active and the escapees were still in the camp. The guards would be clueless until a coworker missed one of the escapees. That might not happen for hours. At least that's what they hoped.

Further, Bryan had hacked into the satellite and drone communication systems so they would not register traveling groups of people. The systems would continue to perform normally in every other way. Then he encrypted his system alterations so that only he could unravel them. If he had covered his bases, it would seem to the warden and the guards that the escapees had simply vanished.

Back in the work camp and its outposts, the Federation Net was available. Inmates were connected, with a variety of devices, to news, entertainment and the same propaganda as any other Federation citizen. In the Wilderness, outside the camps, there was no Internet, and none of what used to be called "cellular service." Bryan's wrist device, however, was able to scan and garner information from the full spectrum of radio signals, and it would serve them well on this journey.

Within a mile of trekking along the river, the party came to a railroad bridge, where oil tanker trains crossed every other day. The railroad was part of a Safe Corridor, connecting the Minot camp and the oil fields with refineries and cities in the east. Sensors and lasers guarded the corridors. Any human who passed into a corridor from the outside without properly coded devices or implants, or at a designated corridor crossing, would be zapped. Some corridor borders were littered with corpses of Wilderness inhabitants who had ignored the warnings and tried to cross over.

Grant squinted at the bridge, and then at Bryan. "Tell me again that this is actually going to work."

Bryan was poking at his wrist device. "Look—we have to cross this corridor at some point if we're headed southeast. The closest designated crossing is at least ten miles away, which would expose us more on the camp side of the corridor. So for us, this is definitely the least lethal place."

Dana grabbed her husband's arm. "Grant...*least* lethal?"

"It's okay, Dana," said Grant. "We'll get through it. Just tell us what to do, Bryan."

"Okay. I tried to hack the corridor system but I couldn't. Then I realized since stuff floats down the river all the time, if we keep our hoodies on and stay under water as much as possible, the system probably won't recognize us as human or as a threat, because it scans for human faces. We're all going to walk out into the river until it gets over our heads. We'll be moving with the current. About ten yards or so after we pass under the bridge, we can walk back up on the bank— the one on our right."

Dana looked doubtful, but Grant nodded his head reassuringly, and motioned for her and the gang to follow him out into the slow current, first walking then floating toward the center of the stream. They ducked their hooded heads under water, trying to hold their breath as long as possible, popping up for a gulp of air when they felt like their lungs would explode. So far so good.

Directly under the bridge, Sara took a quick breath and dropped underwater. Suddenly a pencil-thin shaft of intense blue light stabbed down from above, missing her by inches. Three more bolts followed in rapid succession, leaving bubbles, steam and a dead fish on the river surface. She balked, and Dana reached over to pull her forward.

Soon everyone was moving faster through the muddy riverbed. Now they were afraid to surface at all. Grant surfaced long enough to see another blue bolt near where Tadd had been only seconds before.

About thirty feet past the bridge, they crawled out on the other side of the river, gasping. Grant looked for Dana and Tadd, who had surfaced unharmed.

"Thought they were gonna get us there for a second," said Grant.

"The heat from those things is intense, and my shoulder feels a bit sunburned—but I'm okay."

Meanwhile, Tadd was doing his own headcount, his wet, blond hair whipping across his cheeks as he looked upstream and down. His brows wrinkled. "Dad, where's Owen?"

A full minute went by while everyone scanned the river behind them. Suddenly, with a splash, Owen popped up several yards downstream. Heads rotated.

"Owen! What are you doing down there?" called Bryan.

"Well I sure as heck wasn't gonna stick around with all those zapps comin' down!" said Owen.

Sara stared, absentmindedly applying pressure on her shoulder. "How on earth did you do that?"

"Learned to swim when I was five—back in Pittsburgh right before The War." Owen stared off into the distance with a smile. "Learned to hold my breath underwater when I was workin' on rigs up at Fort Peck Lake. You never forget skills like that."

"Alright, we need to keep going," said Grant. He didn't want to risk any more zapps if they could help it. "As I recall we should climb the river bank here and head south."

"Yeah—straight down until we hit Highway 2, and then we dogleg east over to the 52 and head southeast for about two hundred seventy miles to Fargo," said Bryan, matter-of-factly.

Lissa had been silent up until now, "two hundred seventy miles?! That's like…forever of walking!"

"That'd be about two weeks, if we walked 20 miles a day," Bryan responded.

Lissa looked like she might get sick. "How far are we going, anyway?"

"We talked about all this weeks ago, Lissa-prissa! Or were you zoning out with your iCap?" Although Tadd was several years younger than his sister, he took an edgy pride in his awareness of things scientific and the world around him.

"I don't know how far we'll go yet, Lissa," said Grant, putting his arm around his daughter. "Maybe Fargo will be it. Maybe further. In any case, we're all in this adventure together."

The 52 was not a smooth road. Maintenance happened only as needed to carry the trucks between the remote pumping and drilling sites and the Minot Work Camp, and that was mostly on the other side of Minot. Grant had traveled the Bakken formation for decades—first when he was apprenticing with his father and after he inherited his father's position as geologist. He had not been very far this direction, though.

For the time being, the gang took care not to walk directly on the road, but next to the sparse trees and bushes, so as not to be obvious to drones or the predatory motorcycle gangs that roamed the Wilderness.

About three hours after they started down the 52, Bryan's watch detected a small aircraft moving northwest at about five thousand feet. It was barely visible. "Looks like somebody has discovered we're AWOL.

They probably don't know what direction we took, so they're probably scanning all the roads out of Minot." Of course it was too late to hide. If they could see the drone, their drone could see them. "Here's the big test. If that things start circling around, we're toast. If it keeps flying northwest, my fix worked."

"Question is," said Grant, "how much time and effort do they want to spend finding us? Hopefully, we're not worth it."

They stared helplessly at the black speck cruising silently overhead. Grant gritted his teeth and waited to see which way it would turn,

"It's changing direction, Dad. I can see it!" said Tadd. It was true. The speck had veered slightly to the right, apparently following the road north out of Minot. The gang watched until it faded into the northern sky.

They let out a collective sigh—then looked at each other and gave uncomfortable laughs—half to shake off their fear and half out of relief they were still alive.

Grant pondered—*they might encounter all sorts of other troubles and trials, but the first big hurdle was over. They had officially escaped from the Minot Work Camp, thank God. If they weren't detected and zapped, if they weren't attacked by thieves or motorcycle gangs, if they didn't succumb to disease or malnutrition, they would likely live out their physical lives along with the millions of other non-persons who were residents of the Wilderness. Maybe they would find the community they were looking for. Maybe not.* Now Grant was beginning to feel the full weight of the journey that lay ahead.

2.

Just a couple of years earlier, neither the Cochrins nor any of their friends would have given escape a second thought. Not that life in the camp was easy. It was pretty much all work—forced labor tends to be that way. It was a bleak, industrial existence in drab, grey buildings.

Inmates and families were confined to the camp, with no forays out onto the prairie unless their jobs took them there (as Grant's did, nearly every day, along with the ever-present guards). The Cochrins were crowded with their kids into one of about two hundred slum-like one-room apartments, with communal latrines and showers. A small staff maintained these shabby quarters. Inmates who cared ended up doing most of the electrical, plumbing, painting and carpentry repairs themselves in what little spare time they had.

Guards' and wardens' quarters were far nicer, of course. Residences, offices, commissary, school and infirmary were all enclosed by an inner wall. An outer perimeter enclosed industrial warehouses, machine shops and ranks of oil tanks, storing crude for transport to refineries. The entire complex was designed to keep Wilderness outlaws out as much as it was to keep workers in.

The crumbling city of Minot was right next door, but there were certainly no bright lights and busy streets. It was home to only a few nomadic Wilderness residents. Occasionally one of the many motorcycle gangs—called raptors—would try to set up headquarters there, but not for long. The camp guards would periodically "sanitize" the city for security reasons, calling in armed Federation drones. After decades of this, the town was little more than bombed-out ruins.

Yet despite the hardship of camp life, inmates were safe and protected. They were free to marry, raise families and conduct business among themselves. They were paid modest salaries—not in Federation *dinar* (the Tunisian unit of currency now used worldwide) but in work camp scrip. With company currency, they could purchase their own provisions and possessions from the commissary, as well as a few black-market extras.

And Warden Grimhaus was not a tyrant. He was a jaded bureaucrat who wanted nothing more than to keep the camp productive for two more years until he retired and moved back to civilization and his favorite golf course (if he could find a golf cart big enough to accommodate his ever-expanding girth). He didn't want to hear about problems and unrest among inmates.

The guards kept necessary order, but spent most of their time hunting, fishing, drinking beer and wagering on the next North American Autonomic Regional Football League game—(still the king of sports in what used to be the USA. Former Canadians had their hockey, and soccer ruled overseas). Guards served for five years and were rotated back to civilization. They had little or no investment in the Minot Camp as their home.

Troublemakers in the camp were punished, to be sure, but the goal was always to get them back to work. The idea was not so much to punish or to reform inmates, but to keep the camp running.

In the Minot Work Camp, the inmates pretty much ran the show as far as the oil business was concerned. Many of them had worked in the industry back in civilization, and were schooled in the latest hydraulic fracturing technology, designed to squeeze every last drop of oil and whiff of gas out of the Bakken formation. Inmates planned the work schedules. They operated the rigs. They maintained the equipment. At remote drilling and pumping sites, the guards were there as much to protect the operation from raptors as to keep inmates from escaping. Unstaffed pumping sites and tanks were guarded by Federation-proprietary automatic particle-beam weapon systems, and Wilderness inhabitants with any kind of brains kept their distance.

So—escape from the camp? Why? For sane people, that simply wasn't an option. The only viable way out of a camp was to die or to abandon your faith. Why risk the unknown horrors of the Wilderness when you had a job, food on the table, family, friends and a form of religious freedom? That's something "free" citizens back in the big cities didn't even have.

When he was working at remote sites, Grant was too busy to pay much attention to his Wilderness surroundings, beyond the geological features. He had seen inhabitants of the Wilderness from a distance—silhouettes on a ridge—an old jeep kicking up a plume of dust across the prairie, or a gang of raptors speeding down a road on motorcycles.

One time when Grant was working at a remote drilling operation, some Wilderness people ventured too near. They appeared to be carrying weapons. The guards, who had been eating lunch, killed them without batting an eye and returned to eating their sandwiches. Grant was horrified, but if the Wilderness people were as dangerous as they said, he was thankful for the guards' protection.

Grant had never seen a Wilderness inhabitant up close, let alone spoken with one.

Until he met Bob Kroener.

It was one of those coincidences that made Grant believe more than chance was involved. Grant had been working with mud loggers (technicians who gather geological and other data at drilling sites) about twenty miles northwest of the old town of Dickinson. They had set up a lab to service several sites, and Grant was stationed there for a few weeks to analyze data and make recommendations. Only two guards were assigned to the lab, and this afternoon they were both sleeping off a few beers. Work crews hadn't put up fences yet and the perimeter sensors were yet to be installed. There were no inhabitants to speak of in the area anyway— or so they thought.

Grant was the only one in the lab that night. He needed a pair of pliers, and stepped out into the freezing air to get them from the large tool shed. The shed was unlocked, not unusual where there were little or no security issues. A heater warmed the shed enough to keep fingers nimble. Grant was thankful for that as he rummaged through a drawer, trying to find a small set of needle-nose pliers. He heard a rustle coming from the racks of shelves in the back.

"Hello? Somebody there?" The guards were still asleep and the two mud loggers were in the dorm, watching a holovideo and eating dinner. Maybe it was an animal.

"Hello?" Grant switched on the light in the back of the shed. He peered around a shelf. Standing between two racks of shelves was a thin, middle-aged man in a tattered leather trench coat.

"I just wanted to get in out of the cold," said the man, looking fearful. "And borrow a couple of your tools. I promise I'll bring 'em back."

"You shouldn't be here" said Grant. "You're from the Wilderness, aren't you?"

"Yeah. What are you gonna do, zapp me? Fire away." The man raised his hands in mock surrender.

"No, no, no—I'm not going to zapp you," answered Grant. "But if the guards see you they'll kill you on the spot. You better get out while you can."

"You can zapp me but I'm not budging until I'm warmed up and I have the tools in my hand."

"I'm not going to hurt you. See?" Grant opened his lab coat. "I have no weapons. Not even a butter knife. I'm not into hurting people. What's your name?"

"My name is Bob. Bob Kroener."

"Alright, Bob. I'm Grant Cochrin. You stay right here and I'll get you a cup of hot coffee. I think we have some extra sandwiches in the fridge, and we'll see about the tools. But then you have to go. Okay?"

"Okay," mumbled Bob, seeming somewhat grateful.

Grant ran over to the lab building and into the kitchen. This was bizarre. In his entire life, he had never had a chance to talk with someone from the Wilderness. *Maybe I should keep him around long enough to ask a few questions*, he thought. He glanced toward the guard room. Both guards were kicked back in their chairs, snoring away—empty beer cans and chip bags scattered on the floor. Grant poured a cup of coffee and grabbed a ham and cheese sandwich out of the fridge, being careful not to make any noise.

Back in the tool shed, Grant dragged two stools into the space between the stacked shelves. Bob gratefully sat on a stool, took a long slurp of hot coffee and munched into his sandwich.

"I'd like to ask you a few questions," whispered Grant. "First, why are you here?"

"Because it's warmer in here than it is out there. Also, my truck broke down about a mile away on the 85. I saw your lights and headed over."

"You own a truck? In the Wilderness? Where do you get the fuel?"

"I carry stuff between Regina and Rapid City—and other places if need be. If nothin' else I scavenge recyclables and sell 'em to merchants or workshops. Got a few friends along the way who sell me biodiesel."

"You mean—people do *business* out here?"

33

"Of course we do. How else can you live?"

"But how do you keep from—I mean, is it safe?"

"Safe as anything. Been doin' this for twenty years. Only had to use my gun twice in all that time."

"How did you end up out here?" asked Grant. "Why wouldn't you want to live in a Safe Zone?"

"Ha," snorted Bob. "Like I'd have a choice? My great granddad made the decision to stay out here after the war when the Feds tried to round everyone up. After that, no one could leave the Wilderness. I don't reckon my family or I would want to live in the Safe Zone anyways."

"So, you have a family?"

"Yup. Down in Rapid City. Wife and three kids. And my crazy brother-in-law, Ernie."

"I've always been told that the Wilderness is dangerous—that I wouldn't last more than a day or two out there—that it was total anarchy. Roving gangs of armed raptors on motorcycles—disease, radioactivity, mutants, zombies and…."

Bob burst out laughing. "Zombies? I suppose there's a few folks out there who could pass for zombies. But do I look like one? Heck, the Feds *want* everyone in the Safe Zones and work camps to believe that so they can keep 'em there. Yea sure, there's a few places in the Wilderness you wouldn't want to go, and you gotta watch out for them raptors. But it's not all bad. There's plenty of people who step up to keep some kind of order. We take care of ourselves."

Grant thought for a while. This was surreal. A Wilderness inhabitant who seemed to be functional—and beyond that, reasonably intelligent. "You have kids—how do you teach them? Do you have schools?"

"There's schools in a few of the bigger towns, but mainly we just teach 'em ourselves. Teaching ain't that big of a deal. There's plenty of old textbooks around.

I've scavenged more than a few of 'em from old libraries."

Grant and Dana taught their kids as they had been taught by their parents. Warden Grimhaus had started a small part-time school in the work camp. If the kids didn't give up their religion and leave, he knew they would eventually become his workers (or whoever succeeded him), and he wanted intelligent workers. It seemed like education in the Wilderness was not much different than in the camp.

"Tell me this," Grant scooted his stool closer. "Are there Christians out there?"

"Christians? Oh, yeah. I ain't much for religion, but there's a few down in Rapid City. And another, bigger group over in Fargo. There's also Muslims, Buddhists, Hindus and what have you. You can find pretty much anything in the Wilderness if you look hard enough," Bob answered.

"You're telling me that there's a group of Christians over in Fargo? They meet openly?"

"Of course they do. Why wouldn't they? It's not like the Feds care about what we do out here, as long as we don't get any big ideas about inventin' particle beam weapons or takin' over the Safe Zones. Anyways, I don't know a lot about that group in Fargo but I hear they're okay. Met a couple of 'em once on my way through there. Maybe a little—peculiar. Well, to tell you the truth I usually drive on past. But they're not the only ones—there's others in towns all over the Wilderness. Seems like the further south and east you go the more there are."

Grant could no longer chance the guards waking up. He gave Bob the few tools he needed, along with another sandwich, thanked him and watched him head out onto the cold, dark Wilderness prairie.

3.

Days later, back at the Minot Work Camp, Grant told Dana about the encounter with Bob Kroener. Dana was incredulous, "You actually *talked* to someone who lives in the Wilderness? That's a little hard to believe, honey. I mean—you actually carried on a coherent conversation? And he didn't try to hurt you or trash the lab?"

"No. In fact he seemed to be a pretty decent guy. And intelligent."

"Intelligent? How is that possible? Wait—you didn't catch anything from being in the same room with him, did you? Are you feeling okay? Maybe you better get checked out at the infirmary!"

"I'm feeling fine physically," said Grant. "But it's really starting to bug me. We've been lied to our whole lives—and our parents were lied to. Things out there are not as horrible as they've told us. There are real people out there. There are Christians just like us who are free to worship openly. Probably with real Bibles."

A real Bible, Grant mused. *That's what I'd really like to see.* Grant wanted this, not because he thought the book itself was somehow magical, but because it would give him more information about God. What Grant knew and believed to date was pretty much bare bones, no-bells-and-whistles.

His mother and father had told him about a man who lived a couple thousand years ago named Jesus, and some of what he taught—how he rubbed the religious and political leaders the wrong way—how he was executed—how it turned out that he was really somehow God in human form—and how we could see and learn from Jesus that God is for us, not against us. That was it. Grant didn't grow up with a lot of details or dogma.

Which is not to say that he wasn't curious about what details and dogma might be out there.

Before Grant's father died, he had given him an amazing gift—a *remnant*—a fragment of a page from an actual Bible, with some of the sayings of Jesus. Grant imagined that someone, maybe his grandfather or grandmother, had held onto it while the Bible was being ripped out of their hands. On one side, it read:

...for they will be shown mercy.

8 Blessed are the pure in heart, for they will see God.

9 Blessed are the peacemakers, for they will be called children of God.

10 Blessed are those who are persecuted because of righteousness, for theirs is the kingdom of heaven.

11 "Blessed are you when people insult you, persecute you and falsely say all kinds of evil against you because of me.

12 Rejoice and be glad, because great is your reward in heaven, for in the same way they persecuted the prophets who were before you.

13 "You are the salt of the earth. But if the salt loses its saltiness, how can it be made salty again? It is no longer good for anything, except to be thrown out and trampled underfoot.

14 "You are the light of the world. A town built on a hill cannot be hidden.

15 Neither do people light a lamp and put it under a bowl. Instead they put it on...

On the other side, it read:

... marries a divorced woman commits adultery.

33 "Again, you have heard that it was said to the people long ago, 'Do not break your oath, but fulfill to the Lord the vows you have made.'

34 But I tell you, do not swear an oath at all: either by heaven, for it is God's throne;

35 or by the earth, for it is his footstool; or by Jerusalem, for it is the city of the Great King. 36 And do not swear by your head, for you cannot make even one hair white or black.

37 All you need to say is simply 'Yes' or 'No'; anything beyond this comes from the evil one.

38 "You have heard that it was said, 'Eye for eye, and tooth for tooth.'

39 But I tell you, do not resist an evil person. If anyone slaps you on the right cheek, turn to them the other cheek also.

40 And if anyone wants to sue you and take your shirt, hand over your coat as well.

41 If anyone forces you to go one mile, go with them two miles.

42 Give to the one who asks you, and do not turn away from the one who wants to borrow from you.

43 "You have heard that it was said, 'Love your neighbor and hate your enemy.'

44 But I tell you, love your enemies and pray for those who persecute you,

45 that you may be children of your Father in heaven. He causes his sun to rise on the evil...

That, of course, was the closest thing he had seen to a real Bible. When Grant, Dana and their friends got together, sometimes they would carefully extract the *remnant* page from its leather sleeve and read it. They would also recite portions of the Good Book that had been passed down orally.

Sara would weigh in on what she could remember from having once read a file of the entire Bible. Hidden in the university archives, the file had escaped the postwar purges, and her curiosity had driven her to read the whole thing. They would talk about what the passages might mean. They would talk about what might be in the verses before and after: *Who* will be shown mercy? God causes his sun to rise on the evil *what*? And *why*? Does he want to burn them?

They would talk about how the faith that kept them in this work camp could be acted out in love for each other and their fellow human beings.

While most inmates of the work camp were there because they held on to various cherished Christian traditions and observances (or to a lesser extent, those of other religions), the Cochrins and their friends were unique because they took an interest in Scripture, or what little of it they could piece together.

Grant's musings were interrupted by his wife answering him. "Okay, Grant, first of all, you're *upset* because the government *lies*? As if you were expecting the government to tell the *truth*? Seriously? Are you *sure* you're feeling okay? That doesn't mean anything. We still don't know for sure what's out there. Could be worse than what we've heard, could be better. And second—this is just one guy you talked to—a guy who walks in off the prairie and gives you a story so he can get a sandwich and a cup of coffee and rip off some tools. You can't confirm that *anything* he said was accurate—I thought you were supposed to be a scientist. So, where are you going with this?"

"I don't quite know. I have to think about it."

They were both silent for a while. "Grant, I'm sorry to be so critical, but it kind of sounds like you're ready to jump over the wall and take us with you, based on this one chance encounter."

Grant put his hand on Dana's. "I'm not going to do anything that we don't agree on 100 percent. But I think we need to keep thinking and praying about this. I wonder if the encounter with Bob Kroener was merely chance."

Dana was not entirely reassured.

As the months went by, Grant thought and prayed about the meeting with Kroener and his description of life in the Wilderness. He thought about it from the time he got up until the time he went to bed, and then he dreamed about it. He talked to a few of the truckers and they seemed to confirm some of what Bob said. But even the truckers had never ventured out of the safe corridors, as far as Grant knew. And if they had, they wouldn't tell anyone. Grant also feared that asking too many questions would alert Warden Grimhaus.

Grant and his family were stuck in a secure prison—not unlike the kind of security the Israelites had in Egypt, according to a story his mother had told him. But freedom was out there in the Wilderness. The idea of finding a larger, perhaps more knowledgeable group of Christians where he, his family and friends could openly discuss their faith appealed to Grant more and more. It didn't just appeal to him. It *tugged* at him.

When they got together with their trusted friends, Grant began sharing a few of these thoughts. Sara, Bryan and Owen seemed increasingly interested, although Dana continued to worry. Gradually, over the weeks, the idea of actually venturing into the Wilderness emerged. When it sounded too much like plans were being laid, Dana had had enough. After one meeting concluded, and the kids were out of earshot, she sat down with Grant in their kitchen.

"Are you really intent on doing this?" she said barely above a whisper. "I feel like you're going to drag us all out into a world that we know nothing about. This really scares me, honey."

It pained Grant to see Dana fearful. But it was true that he was gradually becoming convinced that leaving the camp was what they needed to do—maybe somehow what God was calling them to do. Like every adult at the camp, Dana worked. She worked full days at the commissary while the kids were in school. She wasn't happy about their tiny, dingy apartment. She could see on holovideos how people lived in the Safe Zones—tree-lined streets, big houses, stylish clothing, cars, boats, parties, sports. Yet she didn't want wealth— just a decent home for her family. She wouldn't renounce her faith for that. But Grant believed there was a place somewhere in the Wilderness where she could have a physical and a spiritual home.

"You're right," said Grant. "We really don't know for sure what it's like out there. But I still can't help thinking there's a community somewhere that would welcome us—where we could settle down, have a decent home and be free to follow Jesus the way he intended."

"You mean *intends*, and how do you know what he intends?"

"Well, we have the Bible to guide us…"

"Actually, all we have is ourselves and a few other inmates who have memorized a few passages the way they were taught. And our *remnant*. And the last time I checked, Bibles are still forbidden, so we have no way of verifying what we think it says."

"So what are you saying?"

"I'm saying that it seems to me you're looking for something you don't even know exists, based on criteria we don't have! If we stay put and do our jobs, don't you think God can take care of us? You say you trust God, but sometimes I wonder…"

Grant didn't know how to respond to that. So he agreed. "Okay. Okay, fine. There's no question that we should examine our faith from time to time. I just think it's pretty clear that the Federation's policy is not to exterminate religious people, and Christians specifically, but to keep us separated from others who share our faith—and therefore powerless."

"That goes without saying," responded Dana. "It's a fact of life under the Feds, and there's nothing we can do about it."

"No, not if we just accept it and stay in our little boxes. The only way we can ever make a difference is to connect with people who believe like we do. I know there are other Christians here in the camp, but it seems like most of them are only interested in hanging on to traditions. I know there's something more. There must be Christ-followers out there. We need to find them. We need to learn from them. We need to join them. We need to work with them—maybe even to change things for the better! The only way we can do that is if we get out of here."

Dana stared at Grant with knitted brows. On one level, she found herself wanting to buy into what her husband was offering. A fresh start? A revitalized faith? A nice home? A friendly community? Freedom from the Feds? But on another level, this didn't seem to be a give-and-take discussion—no weighing of risks versus benefits of moving ahead with this possibly delusional undertaking. This idea was looking to her more like a manifesto. Grant's manifesto.

"You know, the more I think about it," continued Grant, trying to talk through the grave concern emanating from his wife, "what if God led us to a group of people who are *really* following Jesus? What if we could settle into their community—maybe live in an actual house with a yard or some acreage—maybe they have a school there and maybe our kids could grow up with other Christian kids."

Grant could see a glimmer of possibility in Dana's face. "You know, I think Sara, Owen and Bryan are willing to join us. If they do, we'd have a group equipped to face the challenges of the journey. Sara taught at New Harvard and studied Christian and religious history. Bryan is a technical genius—he was heir to the Feds' biggest surveillance technology contractor. MIT grad—traveled all over the world—until his brothers ratted him out for looking into Christianity. Owen has the best mechanical mind I've ever seen, and he's one of the wisest men I know. These are good, faithful friends. They stick with us, no matter what."

Dana stared at the floor. A picket-fence home in an idyllic little town? It was actually beginning to tempt her, but it still felt too storybook. Grant had built up this vision in his mind to the point that he was ignoring the huge risks involved. Yet, the idea that their friends were leaning toward Grant's vision made her want to give it a chance. Maybe.

"Grant, I worry that you're offering stuff you can't deliver. It's dangerous—for our kids, for us and for our friends. You need to consider what's driving you. I think we need to discuss the realities with our friends. Then, unless you're thinking about an escape, which I hope and pray you aren't, you need to discuss it with Grimhaus, and see if there's even a remote chance that he'll let us walk out, which there probably isn't."

The debate continued for weeks. Sara and Bryan had lived most of their lives in a Safe Zone, and were inclined to opt for freedom. Owen had lived a long life—what was one more adventure? The kids were a little antsy but game. The Wilderness seemed exhilarating compared to their drab little school, where they were often conscripted to do miscellaneous jobs for the camp. Dana was still reluctant, but conceded that if they were going to do it, the least dangerous scenario would be for Grimhaus to let them walk out.

4.

"What the heck!? You've *got* to be kidding!" The corpulent warden sat behind his disheveled desk, red-faced and neck veins bulging. "You want me to just up and let you walk out into the Wilderness, never to be seen again? I suppose now you're gonna tell me you're—who's that old guy the Jewish inmates are always talking about? Moses! That's it. You're gonna tell me you're Moses and you're gonna send plagues. Well, send me all the plagues you want, but you're still the best petroleum geologist we've ever had around here and you're not goin' anywhere!"

Grant answered, "Yes, sir. I understand, sir. But eventually we will need replacing. I'm just suggesting that you replace us sooner rather than later."

Grimhaus regarded Grant from over his reading glasses and under his shaggy grey eyebrows. "C'mon, Grant. I'm not ready to replace you and you're not ready to be replaced. I'll leave that to my successor. And don't get any ideas about sneaking out. You won't get a mile from here before drones see you and zapp you. And you sure as hell don't want any of your family to get hurt, do you?"

"Certainly not, sir."

"I don't want that either," Grimhaus continued. "The crazy thing is, you'd do this because of that Jewish nut case from a couple thousand years back. Heck, no one knows if he really existed!" Grimhaus laughed and shook his head. "You religious people are all alike! I've put up with you for nearly three decades, and it's a wonder I'm not looney. Believe what you want, but pleeeeze—don't jeopardize the operation here. And your family! Your family!"

"I understand your position, sir."

Grimhaus rotated his huge leather chair and gazed out the window at rows of oil storage tanks and a railroad siding with tank cars stretching into the distance, waiting to be filled.

"Grant, old buddy. We've worked together in this facility for decades. I've known you since you were a little tyke. I remember you playing with your blocks on the carpet here in my office while your dad and I talked. When you grew up and took over from him, I knew you were capable of big things. In fact, if your granddad hadn't been sent here you mighta been my boss. You're a smart guy. You and I have built this into a world-class facility."

The Warden motioned to a framed award on his wall signed by the current World Federation President, Mehdi Kazdaghli. "You should have that award hanging in your apartment, Grant. You earned it for us. This is your life's work. Your contribution to the Federation and the world. Your dad and granddad would be proud. You and your family should be proud."

Grant felt a wave of nostalgia and guilt. He knew that Grimhaus was laying it on thick, desperate to keep Grant here any way possible. The only thing not thick in here was the thinly veiled threat of being zapped if they decided to escape. *But probably not one he would follow through on, thought Grant. He wants us alive and working...or would he, after we try to escape?*

Dana received the news of Grimhaus' reaction with some dread. Once her husband got an idea in his head, it would be hard to dissuade him. Neither of them said anything, but they both knew that from this point forward, Grant would be quietly, carefully and systematically planning an escape. He would be accumulating supplies. He would be selling off some of their meager assets a little at a time to other inmates. He would be saving the only form of currency they had—work camp scrip. He would work with other members of their small gang because they had already bought into his fixation. And in spite of Dana's fear, she found herself imagining freedom, stability and community somewhere down the road. This was going to happen.

Anti-semitic overtones notwithstanding, Warden Grimhaus had raised the Exodus metaphor. And even though he hadn't heard much about Moses, Grant was beginning to think of him as a role model. Of course he hadn't mentioned anything to Grimhaus about taking Sara, Bryan and Owen with him.

"Not all those who wander are lost."
—J.R.R. Tolkien

PART II: THE ROAD TO SOMEWHERE

1.

For Grant, his family, and his friends, the first few days on the road were hard. A group can go only as fast as its slowest hiker, and hikers are slowed by things like blisters and overtaxed muscles. Grant knew they needed to go gently until they became more fit and grew thicker calluses on their feet. On the fourth day they covered twelve miles. After more conditioning they hit their stride of twenty miles per day, stopping to rest every four miles or so.

They encountered no vehicles, and no raptors, thank God. Only a few foot travelers headed north, and they passed without so much as a "howdy."

Periodically a silver ship would fly overhead. Some were barely visible at high altitudes, others were lower. Yet others, Bryan discovered, were entirely invisible at any altitude. He would consult his watch to see what kinds of signals were emanating from the crafts—to determine if the group was being scanned. Although the group seemed to be in the middle of nowhere, this was a constant reminder that the Federation was only seconds away.

One evening Bryan broached the subject of what

47

they should call themselves. "You keep calling us a *gang*," said Bryan to Grant. "Every time you use that word, I think we should all be riding choppers and wearing leather jackets with pointy rivets and chains."

"Don't forget the tats," said Lissa. "We could all get some at the next town, if they have an ink shop."

Dana sighed in exasperation.

"Seriously, though. What are we? Are we a gang? A group? A congregation? A band of Christian warriors?"

Grant chuckled. "I don't know. You're right. *Gang... band...* those sound sort of militant to me. What about *team?*"

"*Team?*" asked Tadd.

"Yeah. It implies that we all have a common goal, we all work together and everyone has his or her job. And of course there is no *I* in *team*."

"Right," said Tadd. "But there's *me* if you rearrange the letters. And *meat* if you're hungry."

"Good one, Tadd," Bryan said with a laugh.

"Don't forget *mate*," added Owen. "We're all mates, aren't we?"

Grant rolled his eyes and gave a lopsided grin. "Okay, okay! So are we a team?"

"Yes," the team chorused, in a unison that would become less characteristic as the journey went on.

Dana, Lissa and Tadd had never been out of the work camp. They were in shock at the vast expanse of wide open prairie. Dana was still troubled by the loss of security, but she felt herself being enticed by this new experience of freedom—even though it promised hardships and dangers.

Grant and Bryan had planned the escape for mid-spring. Game was plentiful, temperatures were moderate and days were longer. When it rained they broke out their ponchos and continued. As night fell, they looked for secluded places, and avoided campfires so as not to attract attention. They used small backpacking stoves they had acquired over a period of months from camp supplies for field workers.

Bryan, whose pre-incarceration hobbies included guns, had acquired a Ruger Single-Six .22 revolver with a nine and a half inch barrel from one of the truckers. Not too noisy, so it wouldn't attract much attention. Nearly every other night the team enjoyed some kind of small game for dinner—jackrabbit or even pheasant and quail, although Bryan found bagging the latter two challenging with only a .22.

In the evenings, Grant would carefully extract the *remnant* from its protective leather pouch and read through it for clues as to how he might meet the challenges of the journey, and clues as to what kind of man Jesus was and is. He pondered how fortunate—how blessed—they were to have something like this. And he wondered what the story was behind this fragile scrap of paper, printed with such powerful words.

2.

Sixty-eight years earlier in the Columbus suburb of Westerville, Ohio, Max and Joyce Cochrin and their fifteen-year-old son Leon sat at their kitchen table, drinking coffee and anxiously waiting for the knock on the door that was sure to come this evening.

In the nineteenth century, Westerville had been a stop on the Underground Railroad, where escaped slaves were hidden as they moved toward Canada and freedom. Even in this slavery-free state, many escapees were caught here in Westerville and "sold down the river" by opportunistic Ohioans. Later, Westerville had become the center of the prohibition movement, leading to the ill-fated eighteenth amendment. This pleasant, affluent suburb had more than once been a center of controversy and unrest. For the Cochrins, that tradition would continue tonight, except now *they* were the ones going into slavery—no matter what the Federation called it.

The dinner dishes had been washed and put away. Their most important belongings were crammed into five suitcases, waiting by the front door. Joyce had cleaned their home of twenty-five years until it was spotless, just because she liked to leave things that way.

"So what do you think it's gonna be like in North Dakota?" asked Leon. "Will it just be all work—or will they let us have some fun? Will we have some kind of house, or will we live in a cell or something?"

Max stared at his coffee. "Son, you know about as much as I do. This is all new. It won't be the life we have here, I'm afraid, but I'm keeping my hopes up that it won't be like a Nazi concentration camp. I believe the idea is not to exterminate religious people, but to banish them to the periphery, to use them to advantage. And I think they want Minot to be a stable, productive operation."

Joyce raised her worried eyes to Max. "I wish I could be that positive."

"What other choice do we have, Joyce?"

Dr. Cochrin's twenty-five-year tenure as Professor of Geology at The Ohio State University ended abruptly. He would have retired eventually anyway, although this was not at all what Joyce and he had planned. They could hardly complain, however, considering that about a year ago, most of the people in the country and the world had lost their lives in a horrific war that lasted only minutes. Columbus was one of several American cities to be spared, somehow. The Cochrins still had their lives and health. Their freedom was another matter.

An authoratative rapping sounded at the door. Joyce flinched and spilled coffee on the table. "Oh, dear!" She grabbed a napkin and began to wipe furiously.

Max stood up, tugged at his shirt, adjusted his collar, strode confidently to the door and opened it. Outside stood two soldiers with rather large weapons, and a woman wearing a suit with a Federation ID tag. "Good evening," said the woman. "Are you Dr. Max Cochrin?"

Max straightened and answered, "I am."

"Is this your wife and son—let me see…" The lady consulted a small tablet. "Joyce and Leon Cochrin?"

"That is correct," answered Max.

"I'm Agent Norris," said the lady, with a smile. "As I'm sure you are aware from our earlier notice, it has been determined that you are choosing to practice religion. You have chosen not to sign an *Affidavit of Renunciation*. You have also declined our invitation to attend a *Values Indoctrination Course*. Accordingly, I'm authorized to help you and your family relocate to the Minot Work Camp, where you'll have a new opportunity to serve the Federation in a way that comports with your unique abilities. Don't worry about your property. It will be placed in probate and a Federation judge will determine its disposition among your relatives, if any. Please bear in mind that you may choose at any time to sign an *Affidavit of Renunciation*, and join in a *Values Indoctrination Course*, whereupon you will be eligible for reevaluation. The Federation wants above all to be fair and equitable, and to protect the freedoms of its citizens."

"We understand," said Max. His wife and son stood grimly behind him, still in a state of shock. They had discussed their "choices" repeatedly after receiving their final notice. They had been Christians all their lives, regardless of where they attended church—or if they attended church. Church buildings were in the process of being demolished or turned into museums and Federation meeting houses. But the Cochrins would not give up their faith. They would accept the consequences, although they were uncertain as to what those might be.

"You can bring a reasonable amount of personal belongings with you, and I see you have already taken care of that. My associates and I will inspect your baggage and electronic devices for security purposes. Please remain in the room while we do so."

The Cochrins sat back down at their table while Agent Norris and the two soldiers opened their luggage, dumping things on the floor. They scanned the contents of all electronic devices. They searched everything else to reveal possible contraband, such as printed paper.

One of the soldiers showed his tablet screen to Agent Norris, who nodded, produced a knife and cut the lining of one of the suitcases. Out fell loose pages of a Bible and a leather cover. Joyce put her hand to her mouth and gasped.

"Ma'am, we'll have to confiscate these items," said Agent Norris perfunctorily. "You're ready to go."

The soldiers piled all the other things back into the luggage and motioned for the Cochrins to carry their bags out the front door. Agent Norris slipped the Bible pages and cover into a plastic envelope, closed the door behind them and attached a special padlock. The Cochrins, dragging their luggage, boarded a bus filled with other religious practitioners. They looked out the bus window in tears as their home, neighborhood and city disappeared behind them. Their next stop would be a processing center, and from there they would be transported by rail to the Minot Work Camp, where they would live out their lives in service to the Federation.

But the Cochrins still had themselves, their faith—

and something Agent Norris' instruments had failed to detect in another part of their luggage lining: a single page of the Beatitudes that would become an integral part of the Cochrin family legacy.

3.

It first appeared as a *fata morgana* mirage hovering over the road as it topped a low ridge about ten miles northwest of the mostly abandoned town of Carrington. As it came closer, its clattering diesel engine became audible. It made the team stop in their tracks. They looked first at Grant, then at Bryan, waiting for a reaction.

"Right off hand, I'd say we don't have to worry about it being Federation technology," said Bryan. "And I don't think any self-respecting raptor would ride something like that."

When it got within about a hundred yards, Owen identified it as a John Deere 950 tractor—manufactured around 1979. The tractor was towing a trailer filled with something that smelled like cow manure, according to Owen, the only person in the team ever to have experienced that aroma.

In the driver's seat was a grey-bearded man in his sixties wearing faded overalls, a dirty sweatshirt and a tattered North Dakota State Bisons cap. He looked like a twentieth-century farmer who'd been extracted from a cryogenic chamber, along with his one-hundred-fifty-two-year-old tractor.

Finally, the tractor rolled to a stop in front of the team, engine still idling.

"Afternoon, folks!" said the man.

"Good afternoon," they responded cautiously.

"Where did you get this machine?" Owen asked as he walked around the tractor, eyes wide, mouth gaping, inspecting every part. "This is unbelievable! My great-grandfather had one just like this. I saw a photo of it once when I was a kid."

"Well," answered the man, "I found 'er in the back of the barn at the farm I moved into about thirty years ago. Whoever owned the place had drained the oil and diesel, put 'er up on blocks, removed the tires and wrapped 'em in polyester covers, then sealed the whole kit an' kaboodle off in a special room. I put 'er back together, cranked 'er up, and she ran like a scalded cat. Been drivin' 'er ever since."

"Where do you get fuel for it?" asked Bryan.

"I got my sources," said the man, squinting at Bryan. "You ain't the kind o' folks I usually see walkin' down this highway. Come to think of it, I ain't seen anyone walkin' out here in quite a while—and the ones I seen then were packin' vintage assault rifles. I think they was probably raptors whose bikes broke down. Don't get as many of 'em up here as they do around Fargo. But two less raptors are two less raptors. So I took care of 'em just before they took care o' me!" He motioned to a Colt CM901 hanging off a hook welded to the tractor seat. "Old tech, but it kills 'em just as dead as those new-fangled Federation gizmos. What're you folks up to, anyways?"

Grant had anticipated this moment since his encounter with Bob Kroener nearly two years ago. This guy seemed a bit more dangerous than Kroener. He had a weapon and apparently no compunctions about using it to defend himself.

What would he say? He couldn't very well admit that they were escapees from the Minot Work Camp, as and risk being turned in for a finder's fee. Or maybe not? Wasn't everyone out here an escapee of sorts?

"We're Christ-followers, on our way to Fargo. We escaped from the Minot Work Camp a few days ago,"

Grant heard himself blurt. Everyone looked at him in disbelief. He had never been any good at lying—and this old-timer didn't seem like someone who could be easily fooled.

"*Christ-followers* eh? Hot dang! If I ain't a Christ-follower muhself!" yelled the man. "Where's my manners? I'm Durward Alder." As the team introduced themselves, Grant wondered how a person who was so nonchalant about killing human beings could identify himself as a Christ-follower. But then this was the Wilderness, and likely there was all sorts of ethical and moral confusion out here.

"You folks look like you could use a ride, some vittles and a warm place for the night. Or as many nights as you want to stay—long as you lend a hand with a couple o' chores."

The team looked at the manure-filled trailer.

Durward chuckled. "Not the most sanitary mode o' transport, but it sure beats hoofin' it, I'd say."

"Okay," said Grant. Each member of the group grabbed a perch on the trailer's rim, barely wide enough to sit on. Tadd wasted no time planting himself on the right wheel guard of the tractor and Owen sat down on the left.

"Looks like you two fellers are interested in how this contraption works," said Durward. After a brief explanation of tractor basics, the short trip was underway. Tadd watched Durward depress the clutch and shift the gears by hand. Owen was mesmerized by the ancient technology, devoid of any electronic readouts or sensors that were so taken for granted with modern equipment. After an hour and a half of trundling down the cracked and potholed highway, Durward turned off onto a progressively bumpier dirt road. Lissa nearly fell backwards into the manure, just before they rounded a small hill to see a huge, weathered red barn and white farmhouse—two stories with a veranda on three sides. A large vegetable garden flanked the house.

"Welcome to Alder's Acres. About three hundred of 'em last I figured. Don't matter 'cause there ain't many surveyors and lawyers out here. And I don't use all that land anyways, 'cept for huntin'."

Grant, Owen, Bryan, Sara and Tadd pitched in to help Durward unload manure near his massive garden. "My friend back up the road, Marilyn, has dairy cows. We trade manure for veggies," explained Durward. "A lot o' trading and barterin' goes on around here. We got a little network of folks who look out for each other. You do what you have to just to get by. And I get by pretty well, long as we keep the occasional raptors away."

Grant and Dana glanced at each other. They had come from an environment where professional law enforcement was taken for granted. Out here, you were on your own. What did that mean for a Christian? Grant hadn't quite thought this part through.

After helping Durward with a few other chores, the team took turns using his indoor shower apparatus. He had managed to keep the plumbing functional in the old place. Heating oil from his unnamed fuel source fired a water heater and a small furnace on cold nights to supplement his fireplace.

Bryan and Dana helped out in the kitchen to prepare vegetable stew. Durward seemed delighted with his visitors, and delighted that he was getting so many things done that had long gone undone. Over dinner, with a fire crackling in the stone fireplace, Grant asked Durward about his faith.

"Oh, yeah," Durward replied. "I like that Jesus feller. He didn't put up with no guff from no one. My favorite

Jesus story is the one where he's walkin' down the road and a big gang o' teen skinheads start givin' him flack, pokin' fun at him on account o' his long hair—an' Jesus up an' calls three grizzlies out o' the woods an' they rip those smart-ass teens to pieces and eat 'em all right on the spot! My kinda guy, that Jesus!"

Tadd and Lissa had stopped eating and were staring wide-eyed at Durward, who winked back. They lowered their eyes and continued eating.

Is he kidding—or is he testing us? thought Grant.

"That's fascinating!" exclaimed Sara. "I'm not familiar with that particular narrative..."

"Hmm. I think I remember a similar story, but...tell me, where did you hear your stories about Jesus?" asked Grant.

"Oh, here and there. My ol' grandma used to tell a few Bible tales. She was around before the war—before they got rid of most of the Bibles an' such."

"'*Most* of the Bibles?' You know someone who has one?" asked Bryan.

"Not around these parts. But you folks are headin' down to Fargo. A couple years ago I heard some feller down there had one. Runs some kinda school there. His name was somethin' like Norman...Norton...*Nordwyn*. That's it—Nordwyn."

"Thanks! We'll look him up," said Grant.

"You mentioned your friend Marilyn up the road?" asked Sara. "Were you ever married?"

"Married to Marilyn? Ha! Wouldn't *that* be a disaster of nuc-u-lar proportions? Nope—the crusty ol' gal is nothin' more than a friend. Gettin' hitched would ruin it."

"No—I'm sorry. I meant were you ever married to anyone?"

Durward put down his spoon and leaned back in

his chair. The sparkle seemed to leave his eyes. "Yup. That was a long time ago. Laura and I worked side by side fixin' this old place up. We were happy here. And then *they* came."

"Who came?"

"The Feds and their crazy flyin' contraption. It came over that low hill to the south of us. Just floatin' along with no sound. Seems that a gang o' raptors had tried to hi-jack an oil truck somewhere south of the Minot Camp. They were headin' south with it on the 52. Feds swooped in and zapped 'em with that thing that kills people but don't damage anything else. But some o' the raptors got away.

Meanwhile Laura was out mindin' her own business—walking down the road with a big bag of chickens she'd just traded up at the Mulligans' place. The Feds don't care—they just zapped every human on the highway and a hundred feet to either side. They got Laura. I buried her out behind the house."

"I'm so sorry for your loss," said Grant.

"I think about her ever' day—ever' hour. The Feds didn't say a dang thing. No apology, no nothin'. They don't give a rip. We're non-people out here. At least when you was in the work camp you had a number and a name. Out here you're nothin'. Hope you realize what yer gettin' yerselves into."

"Maybe we don't," said Dana, looking at her husband. "Why don't you fill us in a bit more, Mr. Alder."

Grant tried to remain expressionless, and reached for another slice of bread.

"They's three reasons why people live here in the Wilderness," continued Durward. "One—they was born here, because their families chose to stay out here when the Feds moved everyone into the safe zones. Those people knowed what they was gettin' into. No law and order, 'cept what a community can get together and agree on. No guvment. Every man for himself. That idea suited some people just fine. And it still does.

"Two—they chose to up and leave the Safe Zones later. The Feds just let 'em go. Even if they was wanted for some crime, the Feds don't care. Three—they escaped from a work camp, like you folks. One thing's fer sure: once you're out here in the Wilderness, there ain't no goin' back. The Feds don't want anyone in the Safe Zones to know things ain't quite as bad out here as they say. Oh, they's plenty o' bad fer sure—but also plenty o' good. That's just the way it is when you got freedom.

"But I guarantee you—if they really wanna find you they'll find you and zapp you—unless you did somethin' to interfere with their spyin' machines." Durward raised an eyebrow at Bryan. Bryan shrugged.

"This isn't too reassuring," said Dana, becoming increasingly agitated. "We don't know whether a Federation ship is going to come cruising over the hill tomorrow and zapp us all to kingdom come, whether we're going to be robbed and killed by raptors or whether we're going to starve to death. Seems to me this freedom thing is overrated."

There was an uncomfortable lull in the conversation. Owen tried to break the tension, "Well, we're certainly not starving right now. I don't think I've ever tasted any vegetable stew as fine as this." Others nodded in agreement. Durward was sitting back in his chair with a slightly bemused expression, waiting for Grant to react to Dana's comment.

Grant cleared his throat. "I think what Dana is trying to say is that we're braving some big risks for the sake of our quest."

"Quest?" asked Durward.

"Yes—I think that's a good way to describe it—to

find a community that's maybe like the church in the days of the apostles—the way God intends it to be. I realize we're still in a state of shock—out of our familiar environment and in a challenging new setting. But I also know we're going to find what we're looking for."

"Wow," said Durward, wiping his mouth with a dirty red handkerchief from his overalls pocket. "You got a tough row to hoe there. I don't blame Dana for feelin' a little antsy about it. You got yerselves any sidearms or anything like that?"

Grant shook his head. "Nothing but Bryan's .22 for hunting small game."

"Well, they ain't no guards out here to keep order like in your work camp. They ain't no law 'cept in some of the towns. You pretty much gotta look out fer yerselves or you'll be roadkill. Or worse, depending on which raptor gang gets you."

"Worse?" asked Bryan.

"Yup. Ain't so bad around here or even around Fargo. But the fu'ther south you get, so I hear tell, the bigger chance you'll run into slaver raptors—human traffickers. You gotta carry some respectable weapons to protect yerselves. I think the good Lord at least expects you to do that."

Grant didn't necessarily agree, although he'd never been in a situation quite like this. His grandfather had identified himself as a *pacifist*. Grant's father had inherited that perspective and passed it on to Grant. Beyond that, in the *remnant* he carried in his backpack, Christ commanded his followers to love their enemies. Grant took that at face value.

On the one hand Christians were to treat enemies well, even pray for them—to do them no harm—no violence. Jesus also said, "do not resist an evil person." While Grant often pondered exactly what non-resistance meant, he pragmatically concluded that Christians didn't have to allow enemies to harm them, and that Christians could and should do what was necessary to avoid violence. But was it really necessary to carry a powerful lethal weapon to avoid violence? To Grant's way of thinking, that didn't comport with loving one's enemy.

"I appreciate that perspective," said Grant, diplomatically, "but we trusted God to get us out of the work camp, and we'll trust him to get us down the road." Owen and Sara nodded in agreement. Dana frowned. Bryan stared at the fire, and laid his spoon down. Tadd and Lissa turned to Durward, waiting for his response.

"Suit yerself. I got an old AK-101 and a couple o' Baby Glock 26s that might come in handy. Or you can look around fer somethin' more to yer likin' in just about any town out here. But you'll have to trade somethin' fer it. Whatta ya got?"

"I thought I just said we wouldn't need any firearms," said Grant.

"Yup, that you did," said Durward, "but I ain't sure all o' yer friends and family here are buyin' it."

"We have work camp scrip," said Bryan,

"Then yer in business. That stuff is pure gold. You can use it perty near anywhere—any of the corridor truckers will take it. That's the way we get stuff out here that we couldn't get otherwise. Well—*one* of the ways."

Grant wasn't sure what Durward meant. If truckers couldn't go outside the safe corridors and no one from the Wilderness could cross in, how was this trade happening? Apparently things weren't as airtight as he had been told. But he didn't ask about it. He had bigger fish to fry—this issue of lethal force wasn't going to go away, and he wasn't happy with where his friend Bryan seemed to be headed.

4.

They stayed at Alder's Acres for two more days, helping with repairs to his barn and other odd chores. In return, Durward equipped them with provisions. He hauled them out to the highway on his tractor-trailer. "Might as well give you a good send-off," he said.

Back on the highway, Alder looked into each of their faces. "Y'know, if I was a couple of decades younger, I'd join you, but I'm perty happy where I am. And I'm just too orn'ry to join up with whatever group you find on down the line. In any case I think the Good Lord'll take care of me right here.

"Think on this—most o' you have lived yer lives up to now in a perty closed-off situation. You need to ask yer-selves—are you really ready to live in a world o' freedom? Well, I guess it's a bit late fer that, 'cause here you are! When you were back in the work camp with ever'thing decided for you, freedom sounded like something you wanted, leastwise most of you," he said, glancing at Dana. "Now you got plenty of it and it's a scary thing."

"But aren't the people back in the Safe Zones just as much in prison as we were?" asked Tadd.

Alder grinned. "Smart kid. That they are! They just don't know it. Myself, I 'druther be free even with all the dangers. You folks take care o' yerselves now, and I hope you find whatcher lookin' fer. Come back and see me if you can. Yer always welcome here. Godspeed."

"Just one more thing," Durward added, placing a hand on Grant's shoulder and looking him straight in the eye. "Be real careful, folks, 'cause people out here ain't always what they seem to be."

The group of pilgrims said their goodbyes and headed down the road. Durward watched them until they disappeared over a rise. Then he drove home, unlocked his desk drawer, pulled out a small electronic device, and sat down in his well-worn leather easy chair.

As they walked, Grant commented to Dana, "Durward's a fine fellow, but I don't know if you could call him Christian. It seems like his ideas about Jesus are a little off the wall. Maybe it's because he hasn't had much contact with the groups down the road."

Dana only raised an eyebrow. It remained to be seen just how off the wall things could get.

Fargo was still about one hundred forty miles away—maybe seven more days if they made exceptional time and didn't have any injuries or setbacks. Durward had put a name with the Christian group in Fargo—*Nordwyn*. And he had said there was a school of some kind. That meant a community, with some kind of protection and security.

Dana found herself hoping, even believing, freedom could actually be worth the risks. She listened as the kids talked about what might be there. Stores, new friends, sports, a home with their own rooms. Maybe even a new iCap. Sara was wondering about teaching. Owen was wondering if they had cars to work on. Bryan was wondering about their technological capabilities.

They walked through the little town of Carrington, turning south where the 52 and 281 joined. They didn't see a soul on the streets, and most of the buildings were crumbling. But Grant noticed the tattered curtains in an upstairs window move, when there was no wind. Bryan was sure that he spotted someone ducking behind a fence. They walked a little faster, with the distinct feeling they were being watched.

On the open road again they encountered two weathered, muddy cars and a truck traveling north. No one stopped to say hello or ask questions. As they continued south, they noticed some large animals roaming the prairie in sizable herds. Owen identified them as buffalo—plenty of meat but not something Bryan could bring down with his .22.

Two days later, they sighted Jamestown in the distance, where the 52 merged with I-94 and turned west. Only a hundred miles to Fargo. Grant had no idea who lived in Jamestown. They could be walking into a den of thieves or a community of decent people like Durward Alder—or even Bob Kroener. The team had more than enough provisions to make it to Fargo, so Grant thought it would be safer if they followed the old road that circumvented the town.

Lissa changed that. "Dad, one of my shoes has worn all the way through and the other is close. I need to get another pair. Do you think this town has a shop?"

Grant winced. Lissa wasn't going to be the only one with that problem. It had to be attended to, otherwise they would risk a blister or foot injury. Aside from being painful for his daughter, it would slow the whole team down. Since shoes didn't show up on the road when you needed them, their only choice was to head through Jamestown and see if they could find something. Maybe they would be lucky enough to meet someone willing to trade work camp scrip for a pair of shoes that happened to be the right size.

"We'll need to take this road—the 281—to go through town," said Bryan, consulting his map-watch.

Once in town, they trudged down the street, flanked by old buildings with shattered windows and cracked walls. Some had collapsed entirely and were half-covered with prairie grass. At first not a soul was visible. Then, up ahead, they spotted a few beat-up old vehicles parked along the street and several individuals milling around a storefront. As they drew closer, they could read the sign: Art's Emporium.

Thinking out loud, Lissa said, to no one in particular, "I wonder what Art has for sale."

Articles of heavily used clothing hung on a rack outside the store. Propane tanks filled a locked cage. Weathered looking men and women sat at makeshift tables drinking dusty bottles of some beverage. "It looks like the kind of place that might sell shoes, but then I guess I don't really know what that looks like."

"We'll find out," said Sara.

"And maybe an iCap to replace the one I lost in the tunnel," said Lissa hopefully. "It's sooo boring walking for hundreds of miles without any music! You can't imagine what it's like!"

Grant laughed, "We don't have to imagine it because we all just did it."

"Well, yeah, but it's not the same when you're an adult," protested Lissa. "Everything's so boring anyway. I hope we get to Fargo soon."

Tadd rolled his eyes and made a snorting noise. He had not yet arrived at the age when adults seemed simple-minded.

By then the team was making its way through the little crowd outside the storefront. The crowd fell silent and watched them enter the store. Inside, Art's Emporium had a characteristic smell of worn wooden floors, candy and housewares that only Owen remembered. Even Sara and Bryan, Safe Zone city dwellers until some years ago, had not experienced this.

"My gosh! That aroma takes me way back," Owen said, eyes closed.

"Well, greetings friends!" boomed a voice from behind a dark wood counter. The voice was attached to a man of some girth, with a round face framed by wavy, disheveled brown hair, graying at the temples. Apparently, this was Art. "You look like you just arrived in town! What can I help you with today? Perhaps ice-cold bottles of Joy Juice all around?"

"We're looking for shoes," said Lissa.

"Shoes! Well you've come to the right place," said Art. "Or actually the *only* place this side of Fargo, unless you want to go over to Valley City, but our selection exceeds anything they offer. We have literally hundreds—perhaps thousands—of slightly-used shoes of every style you can possibly imagine, right around this corner. Would you help this fine young lady, Eleanor?"

A large, middle-aged woman, possibly Mrs. Art, shuffled through an open doorway behind the counter. As she walked out, rows of beads that hung from above jingled against her movement.

"Certainly, my dear." She turned to Lissa, gesturing toward the back of the shop. "Just follow me, honey."

As Eleanor disappeared with Lissa, and the others looked through the various types of merchandise, Art addressed Grant. "Well, sir, what brings you and your little flock through Jamestown today? On the road to somewhere are we?"

"Yes. To Fargo."

"You folks have come a long way, I take it?"

"From the north, yes," answered Dana, tersely.

"From Minot, judging from your Federation-issue jeans. You might want to trade those in for something more fashionable—and something that doesn't make you look like you just escaped from a work camp. The Feds might have a price on your heads, you know."

Dana looked uneasy, thanked Art, and began poking through a stack of jeans. Lissa was back with a pair of slightly worn walking shoes, and was testing used iCaps. Tadd was checking out soccer balls. Bryan was perusing electronic gadgets and firearms. Sara was rummaging through dusty old books. Owen tried on a leather wide-brimmed hat. Funds were limited, but that didn't stop them from looking.

Art continued talking with Grant. "Going to Fargo, eh? Just walking or do you have some other conveyance? Because if you don't, I can get you there far more quickly than the five or so days it would take you by foot! Not to mention safety from any raptors who might be lurking in the grass."

"I'm listening," said Grant.

"Art's A-1 Transport will get you there safe, sound and rested tomorrow morning, in the comfort of our coach, accompanied by two of our finest armed security guards."

"Okay. What's the fare?"

"What have you got?"

"We have work camp scrip," answered Grant.

"Oooh! That'll do nicely," beamed Art. Work camp scrip enabled Art to acquire commodities and services he couldn't acquire even with Federation currency. "1,200 dinar per person?"

"That's reasonable. Can we do it this afternoon?"

Art shook his head. "Oh, no no no. Our scheduled departure isn't until 9 tomorrow morning."

"Alright. And 'til then?"

"'Til then? Why, you'll be our guests, of course, right next door at Art's A-okay Accommodations. For a small fee, of course."

"Couldn't we just camp somewhere?"

"Well, you could, but I wouldn't recommend it. Raptors, you know. A far greater problem along the I-94 than anywhere north of here."

"Okay. Fine. We'll spend the night here."

"Excellent! I'll have rooms prepared. Dinner and breakfast are included, by the way."

5.

The tired wayfarers welcomed the prospect of any kind of bed, after several days of sleeping on the ground. Plus, dinner and breakfast? Why not?

Eleanor wasn't a bad cook. They dined around a big oak table. The fare was better than what they could get in the work camp and decidedly more abundant—pot roast, creamed potatoes, gravy with bits of sausage, green beans, green salad. They even served a decent Cabernet, much to the delight of Bryan and Sara, who had been aficionados of such things before being sentenced to work camp, where alcohol was available only if the guards were willing to sell it.

Despite his unassuming, robust, even macho demeanor, Bryan had been raised in an environment of privilege and power. Before the Final War, his great grandfather had been founder, CEO and largest stockholder of the biggest drone manufacturer in the world. Since then, Federation contracts had made the corporation—and Bryan's family—opulently wealthy. He would have taken control on the death of his father, but his brothers had other ideas. His curiosity about Christianity gave them an easy way to get him out of the picture.

Bryan had traveled all over the world, had hobnobbed with celebrities and politicians, and had visited the world's finest wineries and dining establishments. He had tried to maintain his mental and emotional health by putting it all behind him, but occasionally he had flashbacks to his lifestyle as one of the rich and famous.

Sara's background didn't involve great wealth, but her professorship at New Harvard came with an annual cycle of receptions, parties and dinners. She would admit that after living at the work camp for the last few years, she missed those moments of enjoying fine wine, food, and dressing to impress.

"You mentioned security guards earlier today. Is that how you keep your operation safe?" inquired Bryan.

"Security. Yes indeed. We have an excellent company of guards here to keep the town safe for travelers such as yourselves. Truth is, they spotted you well before you hit town. Apparently you passed their inspection, because you're still alive, aren't you?"

Bryan nodded. "That would explain our feeling of being watched back in Carrington. We were pretty sure someone was lurking, but they didn't say anything."

"Of course they didn't." Art smiled. "You don't have any weaponry to speak of. You're on foot. Wearing work camp clothing. And of course your general demeanor. You presented no threat."

"What demeanor?" asked Sara.

"Well—I guess I'd say you folks seem antsy, uncertain, not street-smart, just-fell-off-the-turnip-truck. That's fine with my guards and me, but elsewhere you might be seen as easy marks—low-hanging fruit—a snack for human predators."

"Turnip truck? You raise turnips?" asked Tadd. Owen snickered and choked on his green beans.

"A figure of speech," explained Art. "And you make my point. Whether they're from the big city Safe Zones or from the work camps, I can tell 'em a mile away. They've been overprotected, kept in the dark and told what to think. They're naïve. In the words of that old songwriter, *You know something's happening here, but you don't know what it is, do you, Mister Jones?*"

Bryan had been around far more than any of the others, including Art. He smarted at the bumpkin implication, but he also understood that he was a bit clueless when it came to the Wilderness. He decided to remain quiet and listen.

"Jones? Our last name is Cochrin," corrected Tadd.

"It's the lyrics to a classic hit from the 1960s, son," said Grant, attempting to regain his standing. "What things do you think we could stand to know?"

"Well, for starters, if you want to survive out here, and I presume you all do, I would suggest that you need to develop a more effective game face, and perhaps carry some respectable weaponry. Secondly, may I offer a small history lesson, from my perspective?"

"We're all ears," said Sara.

"I perceive that you may be on a religious pilgrimage of sorts," began Art. "Work camp escapees are either hardened thugs or religious zealots, and you are obviously not the former. Tell me, do you know how religion—or some religions—became anathema?"

Sara answered. "The official story is that religion has historically been the greatest source of war, violence, hatred, bigotry, oppression and opposition to scientific progress. So after the Final War, which was deemed to be caused by religion, the World Federation declared religion illegal and replaced it with its own moral code—The Values—designed to maintain civil order and protect and promote commerce."

"Very well put, Ms. Davenport," said Art. "Like a propaganda textbook. You should be restored to your professorship. And I agree wholeheartedly with the part about organized religion. It's a crock." The team cast uncomfortable glances at each other. "However, the Final War was not directly caused by religion, *per se*."

Grant shifted in his chair and frowned. They were coming face to face with more Federation revisionism. "Okay—What caused it then?"

"Consider the religious state of world just before

the war. Extreme Islamic and Hindu factions had forced most Christians to leave India, Southeast Asia and the Middle East, with the exception of Israel, whose economy back then was based on Christian tourism. The nominal state religion in Europe continued to be Christianity, but most citizens had become Islamic or atheist. The Americas became the last bastion of Christendom. The Vatican even established a New World Campus in Mexico City."

"They sure as heck didn't tell the story this way in MIT," said Bryan, shaking his head.

"Well of course not," laughed Art. "Consider the physical and economic state of the world just before the war—reeling from eco-disasters, food shortages and diseases—Russia, China and India faring the worst. But somehow, Mexico, Central America and most of South America were spared. Argentina and Brazil had become wealthy through agribusiness. Mexico had developed the most productive agricultural system ever. They were exporting food and charging outrageous prices. The Russians had enough of that. They infiltrated Mexico and staged a bloodless revolution, turning it into a virtual Russian province. Now Mother Russia had her pudgy hand on the throttle of power through control of the world food supply. Pope Francis III happened to be residing in Mexico City at the time, and spoke out against the coup in the strongest terms. The Russians responded by putting him under house arrest."

"I don't know," protested Sara, removing her glasses and rubbing her squinting eyes. "I am aware that a lot of the material I learned and taught at New Harvard was propaganda and revisionism. But really—this is more than hard to believe. It's absolutely crazy!"

"It gets crazier," said Art. "Now Catholics were riot-

71

ing all over the Western Hemisphere, demanding the release of their beloved Pope Francis. The United States was compelled to act. It trained its particle beam weapons on Moscow, demanding Russian withdrawal from Mexico, and the release of the Pope. The Russians accused Americans of caving to religious fanaticism, and risking the death of billions. Claiming they had little choice, the Russians trained their weapons on American cities. Europe, Canada and Australia sided with the United States, focusing weapons on Russia, as did South Korea and Japan. Israel and the Arab countries focused their weapons on each other, as usual. Meanwhile, China and India, along with the wealthy countries of South America, watched to see which way things would tilt. The standoff continued for a week. In Tibet, the Dalai Lama defied his Chinese overlords and went on a hunger strike for peace, prompting millions of Buddhists to follow suit, shattering fragile economies all over Asia."

Everyone at the table had stopped eating, enthralled with Art's account, except for Lissa, who was in her own world, experiencing a music video with her new iCap.

"Who knows how the standoff would have resolved itself? But as it happened, the outcome depended not on human will, but on a faulty neutrino relay in an American warcraft stationed one hundred fifty miles above Moscow. That little relay unleashed a particle beam and evaporated the entire city in an instant. Within seconds, Russia retaliated by destroying nearly all of the largest American cities and nearly all American weaponry.

"Europe responded by snuffing out remaining Russian cities and industrial centers, accidentally including cities in western China. China responded by taking out all the major European cities. Europe retaliated by vaporizing most of eastern China, with collateral damage to South Korea and Japan.

"After sustaining such heavy damage on their continent, Europe's shadow government in Northern Africa now took over, deploying massive aerospace warships hidden in undersea bases. They took out all other remaining warships, and within minutes, Euro-African warships were strategically positioned in control of the world. Central and South America had been spared major damage.

"From start to finish, the world war happened in less than ten minutes. India, the most powerful country not to have sustained major damage, quickly capitulated, followed by major Latin American countries and every other country whose government was still intact.

"The Euro-African government had suddenly become the World Federation. With European cities decimated, the Federation established its capitol in the ancient city of Carthage, in Tunisia. So there you have it, and here we are now."

"Again, compared with the official account we were given in college this sounds preposterous," said Bryan, calmly.

"Of course it's preposterous," laughed Art. "It's the world we live in. Always has been preposterous. In some ways not much has changed since the twenty-first century. Government is driven by the same pragmatic, global corporate and banking interests that were running the show then.

"And, oh yes, the Russians released Mexico, obviously, but since religion was declared illegal, Pope Francis III continued under Federation house arrest in Mexico until his death."

"By the way, you *do* know that the proscription

against religion is not quite enforced equally, don't you?"

"What do you mean?" asked Sara.

"I mean that, especially in other parts of the world, moderate Muslims, Hindus, Buddhists and Jews are more or less free to practice their faith as long as they do it very quietly, in the privacy—as though there *were* privacy in the Safe Zones—of their own homes. Don't ask, don't tell. Anyway, they're really not technically proper religions, according to the Feds."

"Well of course they are," protested Sara.

"You are misinformed, professor. They are *ethno-cultural heritages*. Which effectively singles out Christianity as a religion—and the one that the rest of the world would most like to do away with. That's why most of the people you knew in camp are Christian."

"Where did you get all this information?" asked Sara. "We realize the Federation account of the war has been propagandized significantly, but Art, your story is just…outlandish."

Art chuckled. "An appropriate word, considering. But I guarantee you I didn't concoct the tale. You know, out here we do have sources that don't exist in the Safe Zones, and certainly not in the work camps. Eleanor? Would you be so kind as to retrieve the documents?"

"Yes dear, I have them right here." Eleanor brought out a large leather folder and laid it down on a desk at the side of the room. She unclasped the folder. Inside, between sheets of clear plastic were several newspapers. The top one was dated August 26, 2062, and headline read, "Pope Held Under House Arrest in Mexico City Coup."

"The big American cities may have been wiped out," continued Art, "but for weeks afterward, many valiant small-town papers continued to print all the news they could glean from what was left of the Internet and satellite media, so their readers could stay informed. That is, until the Federation forces came in and tried to move everyone into the Safe Zones.

"There are thousands of abandoned libraries across the Wilderness. They had copies of those newspapers. As a merchant, over the years I've amassed a considerable collection that paints a picture of life before the war. The pages in this folder tell the story of the war—what I believe is the true story. Take a look this evening at your leisure—you'll find that it suports my story."

As everyone else read through the printed accounts, Grant asked Art more questions.

"Those libraries—and millions of abandoned homes. Surely there must be thousands and thousands of Bibles still in existence."

"When the Federation forces swept through after the war, they did their best to destroy any sacred book in any form, electronic or hard copy—Bible, Koran, Book of Mormon, Bhagavad Gita, you name it. Even commentaries about those books. But that was seven decades ago. You can be sure many of those books were missed and still exist in Wilderness areas all over the world, but nobody's going to admit it, in case the Feds decide to do another purge someday. Nobody wants to see armed drones floating in over the horizon, zapping everything that moves on the landscape. I just can't tell you how discouraging that would be." Art laughed sardonically.

"I guess that makes sense," said Grant. "But I've heard of someone in Fargo who may own a copy of the Bible. What do you know about a guy named Nordwyn?"

"Ahh, yes, my old friend Nordwyn." Art smiled wryly. "Or as he likes to be called, *Prophet* Nordwyn. He is…of some considerable influence in the area, especially east of Fargo. Not so much out this direction though. We have an agreement, and I occasionally perform certain—services for him.

"In any case, many have passed through here on their way to find him. And more than a few head back this way to get away from him! He interprets what news we get out here and says that Jesus will be returning any second now. He has predicted the exact time of Jesus' return maybe twenty times over the years, and he's not getting any more accurate. But his followers still think he's the greatest thing since controlled plasma photonics. Does that sound like the man you're looking for?"

"I guess it does." Grant was suddenly hit with a sinking feeling. Art made Nordwyn and his followers sound like a—what was that word his granddad had used for off-base religious groups? A *cult!* Grant had hoped they would have to look no further than Fargo for a community of true Christians. And he could already feel Dana's exasperation.

But maybe his judgment was premature. Maybe Art was just too cynical and materialistic to recognize a good Christian. Kroener had indicated that the group in Fargo was okay, if a little different. And even if they didn't decide to stay in Fargo, surely there was something they could learn from Nordwyn. Or at least see a real Bible. Grant would hold off on any conclusions until he met Nordwyn in person.

"There are two ways to be fooled: one is to believe what isn't true, the other is to refuse to accept what is true."
—Soren Kierkegaard

PART III: FARGO

1.

Jamestown was quiet at 9:00 a.m. The Cochrin team was awake, filled with breakfast and waiting on the curb, except for Dana and Lissa. Lissa was late because she, "didn't know we were leaving that early." But that was okay, since the bus was twenty minutes late.

As it clattered around the corner, Owen recognized a big, blue 2033 biopropane Van Hool coach. Emblazoned on the sides of the bus in less-than-perfect yellow lettering was *Art's A1 Transport*. It squeaked to a halt in front of the passengers. By then, a number of other customers had joined the group.

As they queued up to board the bus, Grant was dismayed to see Bryan toting some kind of impressive weapon. Bryan clearly seemed to notice Grant's uncomfortable glance, as well as Tadd's wide eyes and gaping mouth. "You like it? It's a Russian SR-6M Vikhr compact automatic assault rifle—about 2060 vintage, capable of firing 22 rounds per second. Art gave me a great deal on it. Based on what he said and on what Alder told us, I didn't think we could afford to be without some form of protection from here on. Hey, gotta listen to the experts. These guys live out here."

Grant said nothing. He was well aware that two knowledgeable Wilderness residents had advised them they needed to be better armed, but he still didn't like the idea. Wasn't God all the protection they needed?

Art himself turned out to be the bus driver. One armed guard took tickets and inspected passengers at the door. Another sat in the back of the bus, holding his weapon. They let Bryan on with no comment, other than "nice," and a nod at his Vikhr.

Owen eagerly grabbed the seat behind Art. He was interested not only in antique tractors, but in any vehicle, and especially those he remembered from his childhood.

In a few minutes they were underway. Tadd's mouth dropped open as he spotted an enormous buffalo standing on a rise not far from the highway—then he realized it was a statue.

"Off to your left," announced Art, "the world's largest buffalo. Been standing there for over a hundred and seventy years. We keep it propped up, as it attracts a few sightseers, such as there are in the Wilderness." Art deftly negotiated the frequent cracks, upheavals and breaks in the ancient freeway. At some places the road had deteriorated entirely and he had to guide the bulky bus over primitive dirt roads to get around the damage.

"Why are you driving the bus yourself?" asked Dana. "Don't you have someone else to do that for you?"

"Of course I do," answered Art, "but occasionally I have a bit of business in Fargo."

About an hour and a half into the journey, Tadd was the first to spot a gang of rough looking characters by the side of the road. They were heavily armed and standing next to a beat up Humvee.

"You see that, my friends?" asked Art. "That is what you avoided by taking my deluxe transport." Art and the guards waved at the men who waved back with their weapons, flashing crooked, partially toothless grins.

"Raptors?" asked Grant. "Why aren't they going after us?"

"We have an arrangement. They don't bother us, and we don't blow their heads off like we did with a couple of other groups. Additionally, every few days we toss them a generous crate of goodies—food, libations and—*ahem*—various substances. In return they do a masterful job of keeping away other gangs who could be much more dangerous. So you see, it's quite pragmatically civilized and good business all the way around."

Sara was paying close attention. She was beginning to get a glimpse of the network of tenuous truces and agreements that gave some political structure to the Wilderness. She recalled the studies of leaderless small groups that had been done in the mid-twentieth century. Even with no constituted leadership, some kind of structure always emerged to make the group functional. It was the same way here in the Wilderness, except that brute force was a much larger part of the equation than in legitimate government and institutions. *Or was it?* she mused. *Maybe it was pretty much the same, minus the thin and hypocritical veneer we call civilization.*

On a hunch, Bryan entered "Nordwyn" into his watch. He began receiving a scratchy audio signal of an urgent male voice saying something about the "last days." He listened for a few minutes and then turned the signal off.

Art navigated to the center of Fargo, where they

passed a couple of burly men who seemed to be wearing some kind of uniforms. Art pulled his bus to a halt near the former City Hall and let his passengers off. Three men were waiting and entered the bus as soon as the Jamestown passengers were off. Two of them were armed and one was handcuffed. Grant didn't ask why.

Art leaned from his open window and addressed the team. "Goodbye friends. In the immortal words of St. Paul, 'Walk circumspectly, because your enemy walks about as a roaring lion seeking whom he may devour, and never let yourselves be burdened again by a yoke of slavery!'" Art pursed his lips and thought for a moment. "I'm sorry, I believe that middle part was actually written by St. Peter. In any case, take care of yourselves and may the Deity in whom you trust keep you."

With a grin and a cheerful wave, Art, his bus, and his associates disappeared down the street to attend to whatever other business awaited. Once again, the Cochrin team was on its own in a Wilderness that seemed increasingly dicey. Dana turned to Grant. "Did I just hear him quote what sounded like Scripture?"

Grant stared at the departing bus. "I think you did. Don't tell the others I said this," Grant said in a low voice, "but every day we're out here in the Wilderness I'm a little more—well—bewildered. You think people are one thing, and then suddenly they're something else—like Alder said."

Art had let them off in the center of old Fargo. They could look across the Red River of the North and see the old city of Moorhead in what had been the State of Minnesota. There were only a few people on the streets, and they had no idea where Nordwyn was headquartered.

This was the biggest city the Cochrins had ever seen, and it was better preserved than Minot. Some of the buildings in the middle of town were dilapidated, others looked like they had been minimally repaired and maintained. Tadd counted eighteen floors on one tall structure. The sidewalks weren't crowded with people by any means, but a few figures walked here and there.

"Where to now, boss?" asked Bryan.

"Your idea is as good as mine," said Grant. "Let's see what this lady has to say." A small, elderly lady was hunched over a shopping cart as she wheeled it down the buckled sidewalk.

Owen stepped up. "Pardon me, but could you direct us to someone named Adar Nordwyn? We've heard that he lives here."

The lady stopped her cart and stared at Owen over her glasses, with one cracked lens. "Why, Prophet Nordwyn? Of course he lives here. Where else would he live? He could have been taken by the Lord, you know, but he remains here shepherding God's one true flock as they prepare for the Second Coming of Christ." The woman's eyes became wider as she spoke. "The Lord almost returned several times, you know, but we just weren't ready yet. Weren't keeping the Lord's Day the way it should be kept. Yes, and Prophet Nordwyn is showing us what we must do to get ready. To be acceptable to Christ when he returns, which could be soon—very soon. Behold—he is even at the door!"

Owen paused for a few seconds to regain his composure. "Well…that's just wonderful. Darn wonderful. But exactly where can we find Prophet Nordwyn? Right now, I mean."

"What's going on?" Lissa had disconnected her new iCap long enough to realize that the team was not headed anywhere at the moment.

"We're asking directions" answered Dana, patiently. "We'll know more in a few minutes."

The woman with the shopping cart was rummaging through her bags and finally got around to answering Owen's question. "Oh, the Prophet makes his home on the campus of North Dakota State University—now it's called Lastdays University. It's just a few blocks to the northwest," she said, pointing southeast. "Wait, is that this way?" pointing west, and squinting at a weathered street sign. "Whatever. Anyways, you can't miss it. It's like an oasis of—something—I can't remember—in a world of—something or other. You just head up kinda that way and ask anyone and they'll send you to Prophet Nordwyn."

"Well, thank you my friend," said Owen, with a smile. "We hope you have a…"

"Prophet Nordwyn always loves to receive guests," interrupted the woman, fidgeting with her bags. "Who knows? Maybe you'll become one of us." Owen tried to repress a wince. The statement reminded him of a line from a mid-twentieth century science fiction movie he'd seen once in the camp rec room, *Invasion of the Body Snatchers*…although he was sure the lady meant it in the best possible way.

"Hmm. Lastdays University," mumbled Bryan as he consulted his watch. The team proceeded over a mile to the northwest, arriving at Lastdays University campus. In spite of Art's opinion of Nordwyn (and the odd encounter with the shopping cart woman), Grant was still entertaining high hopes that they would not need to journey any further. Dana was scanning the tree-lined streets, imagining herself and her family living in one of the dilapidated but spacious homes (having fixed it up of course), with their friends living in neighboring homes. Maybe her husband's quest and the risks they had endured to this point would all be worth it. Perhaps God had brought them here after all.

2.

In stark contrast to the deteriorating streets and homes they had seen, the old campus was immaculately maintained. Tadd had already met a local Labrador retriever and was throwing a stick for him to fetch on a huge lawn punctuated with shady trees thick with white blossoms. While Sara, Bryan and Owen had seen similar things in their pre-work camp days, this was a new experience for all of the Cochrins. It was idyllic. Sara was thinking it might be a little *too* idyllic.

Grant was talking to a man who seemed to be a resident of the Lastdays campus. "Yes," beamed the man, "Isn't it breathtaking? Prophet Nordwyn has personally supervised the restoration of the entire campus. Probably much better than the way it was originally. We are truly blessed to live in this oasis as we await the soon-coming of our Lord."

"It is magnificent," agreed Grant, sniffing the aroma of flowering shrubs and freshly mowed lawn. He gazed at his son chasing with the dog around a tree. Then he reminded himself of the business at hand. "Can you direct us to the Prophet's residence or office?"

"Certainly sir! Just follow this path and the signs. He makes his home in the former university president's house. His offices are just across the street in the Administration Building, which they used to call Ceres Hall back when this was North Dakota State. If you have any more questions, I'm sure our campus security guards can help you."

The deeper the group walked into the campus, the more overwhelmed they became. Sara and Bryan were familiar with the great universities of the world, and this campus rivaled any of those, if not in size, in image. Neatly dressed people walked purposefully to wherever it was they were going. Women wore businesslike dresses. Men wore suits and ties. They smiled and greeted the visitors cheerfully and politely. Crews of gardeners and maintenance personnel scurried here and there, some driving small electric carts, to the delight of Owen and Tadd. Lissa had finally put away her iCap and was staring at everything around her in disbelief. "This is so awesome!" she gushed.

As the team approached Nordwyn's residence, they were struck by its mansion-like quality. Across the lane, as predicted, sat an imposing four-story structure that looked like it had been built around the beginning of the twentieth century.

A plaque over the entry read *Lastdays University Administration Hall.* Two security guards were posted in front of the structure. They didn't appear to be armed, but they were both nearly seven feet tall and in excellent physical condition.

Grant approached one of the guards. "Do you think Mr. Nordwyn is available? We've come a long way to see him."

The guard smiled, looked down at Grant, and surveyed the group. "Indeed, it does look as if you've been traveling." He assessed the Vikhr hanging from Bryan's shoulder. "That's a fine weapon, sir, and I'm sure it served you well in your perilous travels. We trust that you will store it while on campus, and we can provide a place in our armory for that. We expect no incidents, but we are quite well prepared for any. But for now, we ask that you leave the weapon with us while you are visiting the Administration Building."

The guards were cordial, but seemed like they could become much more insistent if they needed to. "Thank you," said Bryan, reluctantly handing his weapon over. "No target practice while I'm in the building, now."

"I am tempted," smiled the guard, "but I will abstain."

The guard addressed Grant again. "Why don't you all come with me and we'll find out if the Prophet can see you today. I think there's a good chance. He's always happy to welcome new people. And afterwards maybe we can find you a place to stay."

Once inside, the guard accompanied the Cochrin team in two elevator loads to the fourth floor of the building, where the executive officers were located. Again the Cochrins had never experienced anything like this. They had never been in an elevator. They had never stood on a thick, white plush carpet in an executive lobby. The closest Grant had come were his frequent visits to Warden Grimhaus's office, and that was primitive by comparison.

A businesslike lady sat behind a polished mahogany desk neatly stacked with papers. She peered over her reading glasses and smiled at the team. "Good morning!" she said.

"We have some weary travelers who would very much like to visit with the Prophet," announced the security guard.

"I think he may be available for a chat. I'll go see." She disappeared down a short hallway, apparently designed to protect the Prophet's privacy when his office door was open. In less than a minute she returned. "The Prophet is attending to some pressing business right now, but he will be delighted to meet with you in a few minutes. Please have a seat."

They carefully sat down on a thick, cobalt-blue couch and matching chairs. The Cochrins and Owen ogled their posh surroundings. Mid-nineteenth-century landscape paintings hung on the wall. Antique porcelain figurines rested on a shelf. A Mozart concerto played softly in the background. Sara's and Bryan's mouths were hanging open in surprise. They had been in similar environments, but in the Wilderness? Finally, a green light lit up on a device on the lady's desk. "The Prophet will see you now. Right this way, please." The team quietly filed down the short hallway behind her. Entering Nordwyn's office, she held her arm out as an invitation to come in.

As the team filed through the door, a grinning Nordwyn came forward to shake each person's hand with both of his. "Welcome! Welcome to Lastdays University my friends!" He had a round, friendly face with ample thick, grey hair—not one strand out of place. His grin appeared sincere and his eyes sparkled. In his early sixties, his stout body was decked in an impressive light grey tweed suit with a dark blue silk tie and a matching handkerchief. His wrist sported a large gold Rolex watch. "Please! Sit down! Tell me, what do you think of our campus?"

"We've never seen anything like it," answered Dana.

"Even New Harvard is no match," added Sara.

"New Harvard?" Nordwyn sat back down in a soft leather chair that enclosed his body like a glove. "Where do you folks hail from?"

"Um—up north—around Minot," stammered Grant. "We're in search of true Christ-followers."

"And a place to settle down," added Dana.

"Minot, you say," said Nordwyn. "That must've been a long, tiring trek, if you did it on foot. But I tell you what—if it's genuine, true Christianity you want, you've come to the right place. We don't add or take away. Here at Lastdays we just let the Bible interpret itself."

"Speaking of which, some say you actually have a Bible," said Grant.

"Yes I do, and I consult it every day. And I don't mean I just read it—I *study* it. Oh, yes! When it was revealed to me just *how* to recognize and interpret the thousands of hidden, coded prophetic messages in there, it began speaking to me in a way that it does not speak to others."

"Coded messages?" asked Sara.

"Thousands. Absolutely. In fact, just yesterday I deciphered a message that said seven seekers would come to visit me. And here you are!"

"That's remarkable," said Bryan, his brow wrinkling.

"Yes it is. And that's why I say you've come to the right place. Because you'll learn things here you won't learn anyplace else. And—you won't be caught short when it's time to leave."

"Leave?" asked Grant.

"Christ was ready to return a few years ago—but his people *weren't* ready. When they *are* ready, and just before he returns, he'll take us away so he can severely punish the world, or what's left of it. While we're there he'll give us our final training so that we can be prepared for leadership in the world to come. Surely you don't want to be stuck here when he punishes the world."

"Don't call me Shirley," interrupted Tadd, grinning.

Grant and Dana were aghast. "Tadd! Really!" scolded Dana. "Show some respect!"

Prophet Nordwyn's mouth dropped open for a moment and then it spread into a wry grin. "Haven't heard that one in a while."

"I'm sorry sir," said Tadd. "I was just trying to be funny."

Prophet Nordwyn chuckled. "That was a good one. But, you know, it just goes to show, you can't be expected to understand all of this in just five minutes. It takes time for God to reveal his will to us. So why don't you just be our guests for a while. You'll love it here, I guarantee. It's the happiest place on earth."

Before Grant or any of the visitors could respond, Nordwyn had pressed the button on his intercom. "Myrtle, can you find our friends here some nice accommodations somewhere on the campus? Make 'em good. These folks have been through a lot. It's time they had a taste of real abundant living."

"What's *abundant* mean?" asked Tadd. "Is it cool or is it gross?"

Nordwyn gave a jolly laugh.

"It's cool," Dana reassured him.

"We'll find out, won't we," mumbled Sara, under her breath. Only Bryan heard her, but he shared her concern.

3.

A well scrubbed, wide-eyed young man identified only as Rudy ushered them out of the Administration Building. Unlike many of the displaced people in the Wilderness, he seemed to be a native of the area, and spoke with a strong Midwestern accent. They strolled down a long walkway, past well-manicured flower beds and neatly trimmed hedges. Workers waved as they passed by, greeting them with a cheerful, "Good afternoon!"

Finally they came to an aging but carefully maintained brick building. Inside, a comfortable lounge was filled with young men and women, reading, talking and studying.

Rudy turned to the Cochrin party, "We're sorry there are no apartments big enough for your whole family, Mr. Cochrin. We have a small room for you and your wife, eh? And we hope your kids won't mind sharin' with students here at Lastdays. And of course, Ms. Davenport, Mr. Fenbert and Mr. Hantwick, we're sure you'll be okay with sharin' rooms with the other students, eh?"

Sara started to say something, But Grant interrupted. "I'm sure whatever you have to offer will be wonderful. We're grateful for your hospitality."

"Oh you betcha! There are over a hundred and fifty students livin' here on campus, learnin' about God's way from Prophet Nordwyn. Two years and they'll get a degree and go forth to preach the truth, or remain here on the campus to be used in the Work."

"The Work?" asked Sara.

"Oh, yeah. The Work of God," said Rudy with rising North Dakotan enthusiasm. "It's growin' by leaps and bounds, doncha know? You can see Prophet Nordwyn preach every day at noon on our iCap station. It reaches east as far as what used to be Milwaukee and as far south as what used to be Kentucky. We're even broadcastin' on old fashioned AM radio. A lot of folks still have those things. We offer literature printed on our own printin' presses on almost any subject. And little by little, we're workin' on restoring the old Fargodome so people can come and see Prophet Nordwyn in person. As time gets short, God'll be callin' thousands of people to follow his Prophet, and we sure as heck wanna be ready for that, doncha know?"

"You betcha!" mimicked Sara, forcing a smile. Bryan was pretending to do something with his navigation device. Grant stared at them. He could see they were skeptical, but he was still inclined to give it a day or two. It seemed to him that the people at Lastdays were sincere, even if their Christian traditions weren't the same as the straightforward ones his parents and grandparents had handed down to him. He assumed

Dana might be thinking the same thing—but the truth was that she was more attracted to the idea of living and raising her family in a peaceful, pleasant small town like this one.

Within a few minutes, Grant's team had been escorted to their accommodations and introduced to their respective roommates. Lissa would be sharing a room with Emilia Flores, a twenty-three-year-old student slated to graduate that spring. Bryan noticed Emilia the minute she emerged from her door, and she didn't fail to notice Bryan, who had suddenly switched his attention from his navigator to her.

Bryan was assigned to a room with Dayton Smith, a nineteen-year-old student in his first year at Lastdays University. Tadd was assigned a room with Lenny Morris, an athletic 18-year-old who had come here from Ohio, and within minutes they were out on the lawn passing a football. Owen was delighted to be in a room with an older student, Bill Gallagher, who happened to be supervisor of the campus vehicle maintenance department.

There were no kitchens in the dormitory, so everyone convened in the dining hall three times a day for communal meals. Prophet Nordwyn had ordered that the Cochrin party be provided food and accommodations free for several days, which to Grant seemed quite generous.

Additionally, Nordwyn had invited the Cochrin party to audit classes. Religion classes were conducted by Nordwyn, with no clear-cut syllabus. Sometimes he would quote Scripture, other times he would talk off the top of his head. He never appeared to bring his Bible with him—the one in which he claimed to have found coded messages. Even so, Grant in particular was enthralled with the idea that they could actually sit in a classroom and hear someone openly discuss the Bible and Christianity.

Sara looked forward to the classes, but for different reasons. She couldn't help but have an academic interest in Prophet Nordwyn. Based on the few pre-Federation sources of Christian history she had discovered in the New Harvard library (part of what got her landed in the Minot Work Camp), and the descriptions she had read about cults, big red flags were waving in the breeze over Nordwyn and his happiest-place-on-earth campus. The biggest one was his secret Bible code. She had read about such things—and the idea didn't make much sense to her. Embedded in an English translation? It seemed to her that if a coded message had actually come from God, it would appear in the original Greek or Hebrew text. It was highly unlikely that Nordwyn was in possession of those.

The second red flag was his end-times fixation. He was setting dates for Christ's return, and according to Art, the entrepreneur of Jamestown, Nordwyn had set many such dates. Again, Sara knew that the Christian history she had studied was rife with end-times predictions that shared one thing in common: they had all been wrong.

The third red flag was Prophet Nordwyn's exclusivism. He and his followers seemed to believe that they were the only ones in possession of the "truth," that they would be the only human beings protected during the coming Tribulation, and that they would be given special responsibilities in the world to come after Jesus' return. This just didn't ring true to Sara.

In any case, as a scientist, Sara looked forward to examining an apocalyptic cult first-hand. She didn't want to say much to the others yet, especially Grant and Dana. She hoped after a few days of listening to Nordwyn and talking with his followers, Grant and Dana would come to the same conclusion.

Meanwhile, Bryan was talking with students, auditing classes, watching, listening and drawing his own conclusions. He spent most of his time with Emilia who had by no means lived a sheltered life.

Emilia had come to Lastdays from the Safe Zone of Salt Lake City, in the ethnically diverse Westside of town. Her parents had been migrant farm workers, displaced by the war and ecological disasters in California. Her father abandoned them, and her mother died of a heroin overdose when Emilia was age fourteen. To survive, she took all sorts of odd jobs, working in restaurants and bars, and finally becoming a waitress in an establishment frequented by promiscuous wealthy men who wished to remain anonymous. Over a couple of years she managed to squirrel away some money. When her boyfriend ran afoul of the law, they decided to escape to the Wilderness. Making their way to Cheyenne, Wyoming, they struggled in vain to make ends meet. Her boyfriend ran off and she began taking Methaqualone to help her overcome her anxiety and sleep. Soon she was addicted.

Out on the road, she hitched a ride from a trucker, who turned out to be Christian. He took her to his home in Rapid City where he and his wife helped her kick the habit. For the first time in her life, Emilia was experiencing structure, order and peace. The trucker and his wife were followers of a preacher who ran a college in Fargo. They thought this would be the perfect place for Emilia, and that's how she had come to Lastdays. When Prophet Nordwyn learned that she had worked in a kitchen and as a waitress, he gave her a job in his home, serving guests at his frequent dinner parties.

For the next three years, Emilia was on cloud nine. Prophet Nordwyn and his followers had rescued her from a life of horror and chaos. She became a true believer, and was certain that Prophet Nordwyn always spoke on behalf of God. As is often the case, religious rules and regulations seem to be a safe haven for those whose lives have spun out of control.

Then Emilia began to discover disconcerting things about Nordwyn and the organization. At first she was in denial, but as time went on the evidence became harder to deny. She was just at the point of disillusionment, when the Cochrins came to town.

4.

A week after their arrival at the Lastdays campus, it looked to Sara like the team was no longer seeing Nordwyn clearly—not even Grant and Dana. Sara had experienced just about enough of Lastdays. Her friends each seemed to be enchanted by some aspect of Nordwyn, his followers or his campus. Owen had been swallowed up by the campus auto shop. Tadd was out on the football field. Lissa had met some girls her age and was hanging with them, comparing the most recent Safe Zone boy bands (officially banned on campus). Grant and Dana were engaged in classes and endless discussions with students. Even Bryan, who had initially shared Sara's skepticism, spent most of his time strolling the grounds with Emilia, when he wasn't in class or in the dining hall with her.

Sara was shocked at the speed with which Grant and Dana had let down their guard, likely because they desperately wanted this to be their destination. They seemed to be losing their critical thinking and slipping into gullibility.

Sara knew she needed to act quickly, or risk getting stuck here. In the dining hall, she pulled Bryan into an alcove and whispered, "Do you see what's happening here? The team's getting sucked into this cult—except you and me. And now I'm worried about you."

Bryan stared at the floor. "Relax. I'm not buying it. Emilia's been struggling with Nordwyn's ideas too, and Nordwyn's lifestyle."

"Lifestyle?"

"Yeah. Emelia's had a rough life, but she's a smart woman—not just academically, she's got street smarts too. She was orphaned as a kid in Salt Lake City. Had to fend for herself. Eventually she met up with this Christian trucker—a fan of Nordwyn. The trucker brought her here to Lastdays. When the Prophet learned that she'd worked in a kitchen and as a waitress, he gave her a job in his home, serving guests at his dinner parties. Turns out he throws some of the most lavish dinners you can imagine. Back in Boston my family has money coming out of their noses and they don't throw parties half as spendy as what Emilia describes."

"Who does he have these parties for?" Sara asked.

"Anyone who has any kind of power in the area. He flies 'em in on his plane."

"Plane? He's got a plane?"

"Yup. Keeps it at the old airport just north of here. He brings in all kinds of shady characters, including leaders of local raptor gangs. He scratches their backs, and they scratch his. That's why the campus hasn't been overrun by raptors."

"That seems to be the way business is done out here," conceded Sara.

"I think it goes beyond that. I think he's the one pulling the strings. The thing is, he doesn't pay any of his employees with money. He doesn't pay for anything with money, even the food and wine on his table or fuel for his plane. He trades goods and services."

"What goods and services?"

"Goods and services he gets in return for providing protection. Nordwyn is a darn persuasive guy. He's negotiated the raptors around here into a sort of confederation where they all have their own secure territory. If anybody steps out of line, their protection vanishes. Everybody watches everybody else—sort of an accountability racket. He's even got some of these little chieftains believing he's a man of God. Bottom line—the raptor gangs provide him with whatever he needs to run his little Lastdays utopia. At the lowest level, it's extorted from the regular farmers, merchants and craftspersons who are trying to make an honest living."

"My gosh. He's like some mob kingpin from the twentieth century. Or a monarch with divine rights under the feudal system. I've been concerned that his teaching was in error, and I suspected he was a con man. But I didn't think it was that bad."

"The only reason I know is that Emilia works at Nordwyn's house. And my roomie Dayton says there are several students and staff who don't like the whole thing, but they don't know what else to do or where else to go. In spite of the problems, they feel safe here, so they stay."

"I suppose that's one way to look at it, and I'm sure there's a lot of innocent folks who are trying to be Christ-followers here," said Sara. "But I'm not ready to spend the rest of my life in a cult. We've got to take action. We need a plan."

"I'm sure Nordwyn will make us an offer tomorrow to stay—and Grant and Dana will think it's just peachy." Bryan shook his head. "That'll be awkward. How do we wake up Grant and Dana without freaking them out, or alerting Nordwyn? Personally, I'd like to be able to walk out of this place."

5.

Grant and Dana had immersed themselves over the previous four days in Lastdays culture. The people were cheerful, open and sincere. The campus was beautiful and orderly. There was a sense of purpose and belonging in the air. They both began to relax and let down their guard. They felt warmly accepted, as though they had finally come home. Their children would at last have freedom in a Christian environment. A little more each day, Grant and Dana laid aside any skepticism or critical thinking, because they really wanted this to be the end of their journey.

As on the previous four days, they were auditing Nordwyn's class in the university's Assembly Hall. Nordwyn's subject that day was the coming resurgence of Russia and China, described, according to Nordwyn, as *Gog and Magog* in Ezekiel 38, and how they will break the Federation, followed by Christ's return.

"I know for certain that some of you are doubting," cautioned Nordwyn, "but there's absolutely no doubt in my mind that in five short years Christ's government will have replaced the Federation. The code in the pages of my Bible is clear. And through it all, we who live on this campus will be protected."

The one-hundred and fifty students in the assembly hall gasped, exchanged glances and burst into enthusiastic applause. It didn't matter that Prophet Nordwyn had issued similar announcements many times before. It was as if his followers were afflicted with short-term amnesia. Every new eschatological iteration was stunning.

After class, Grant and Dana exited the Assembly Hall filled with positive energy. In spite of Grant's lingering compunctions, they both wanted to believe Nordwyn, and were being drawn into a state of groupthink.

"I know the teaching is strange, but by their fruits you shall know them," said Grant. "If that doesn't apply here, where does it apply? I mean, just look at all these decent, honest, hard-working people. It seems to me that God is blessing Prophet Nordwyn's work." Dana nodded her head in agreement. "I talked to the dean of faculty this morning."

Dana stopped in her tracks and gasped. "Really?" she squealed like a schoolgirl. "And?"

"He said there is a strong possibility they might hire me to teach science and geology."

"Oh how exciting! That would be wonderful!" exclaimed Dana, "and listen to what I found out. You know those beautiful old homes right next to the campus? Prophet Nordwyn personally assigns them to key staff and faculty. If you landed a faculty position here at Lastdays, we could be living in one of those places in a matter of days!"

"Here's another thing," said Grant. "I talked to the headmaster of the school. Lissa and Tadd will almost certainly be accepted for the next year."

Dana was teary-eyed. "What a blessing! They've already made friends here, and they love the place."

"It looks like God has brought this all together," said Grant, feeling vindicated. "I just hope Sara, Bryan and Owen are thinking the same way."

Not twenty five yards from the Assembly Hall, they heard a voice behind them and turned to see Nordwyn, accompanied by an assistant carrying his briefcase. At the same time Sara, Bryan and Owen were approaching behind Nordwyn.

"Well, well!" shouted Nordwyn. "Just the folks I've been wanting to speak to! Tell me—have you enjoyed your stay here on campus? I hope the experience has been wonderful and that you've learned something. I hear good reports about you."

"That's good to know," said Grant, extending a hand to Nordwyn, who grabbed it with both of his.

"They tell me you know something about geology and science in general. We could use someone on the faculty with your knowledge and abilities. Would you consider staying here and working for us?"

Just as Grant was about to answer, Bryan, Owen and Sara joined them. "Well, well!" said Nordwyn, "The gang's all here, except for the kids. I'll bet they're off somewhere with their new friends. Bryan, I understand you have the expertise to compute circles around anyone else we have here on campus." Nordwyn got closer to Bryan's ear and lowered his voice. "And, I understand you've taken a shine to one of our charming and brilliant coeds." Bryan nodded his head and smiled politely, as Nordwyn chuckled.

"And Owen!" continued Nordwyn, "Bill Gallagher tells me you know your way around most any kind of engine, from internal combustion to photon plasma, although we don't have any of those here—yet! Sara, you mentioned New Harvard University—but I didn't know until this morning that you used to be a professor there! I want you to know there's a place for each of you here. God has big plans for you in his Work, and in the world to come!"

Again, Grant opened his mouth, intending to express effusive gratitude—but he was cut off, this time by Sara. "We appreciate the offer and the kind words, Prophet Nordwyn, but we have just a few questions we hope you would answer for us."

Grant and Dana frowned at Sara. Grant stammered, "We don't actually...I'm not sure that Sara speaks for..."

Owen's big hands grasped Grant and Dana's shoulders from behind and gave a slight squeeze. "Why don't we just listen for a minute and find out what Sara has to say?" he said in a low voice. Then he redirected his attention to Nordwyn, with a pleasant smile, "And I'm sure the Prophet will illuminate us with a sage answer."

Grant and Dana said nothing. Nordwyn smiled back at Owen.

Sara continued, "The Bible you have in your possession—is it an English translation?"

"Why, yes it is. It's a New Living Translation, printed in 2059."

"I've never seen one, of course. I once read an article about English Bible translations, and I seem to recall that the New Living Translation one was a thought-for-thought translation. But wouldn't the coded messages be embedded in the text of the original Greek and Hebrew?"

Nordwyn studied Sara and nodded. "Well, you know, God can embed messages anywhere he wants to. They can appear in an English translation just as well as in the Hebrew and Greek."

"I have no doubt that he can," said Bryan. "So then do you have Hebrew and Greek texts to compare with the messages you find in the New Living Translation?"

"Well, no, but I—um—what exactly is your question anyway, young man?"

"I was just interested in the methodology you use to decipher these messages. I did a little research myself back when I had the resources. Seems there was this guy at Hebrew University back in the 1990s named Eliyahu Rips. He searched for equidistant letter sequences in the original Hebrew text. Used a primitive computer, selected an interval (like every four thousandth character) and then he searched forward and backward in the text and came up with a word or a name, although his results were kind of a stretch. Is that how you do it?"

"Well, it's a bit more…"

"And then you have to decide what it means, don't you? I mean it all seems sort of arbitrary, but I'm sure you take that into consideration."

"Young man, given your background I can see how you might think it should be all cut-and-dried, digitized and algorithmic. But you need to realize that I'm a Prophet. God shows me things in his Word that simply no one else can see. And I don't need a computer for that."

"Oh," said Sara. "I see how that works. I have another question."

"Ask away," said Nordwyn, smiling confidently.

"This might be sensitive," said Sara, watching Dana and Bryan, who were both staring at her with narrowed eyes, "but we understand that you've repeatedly set dates for Christ's return."

"Oh—*ahem*—now that's just a misunderstanding. I have always emphasized over the years the imminence of Jesus' return, but nothing was ever set in stone, *per se*. God showed me that certain dates in the future were significant, and I might have mentioned those dates as a possibility, but they turned out to be significant in other ways. If some people thought I said Christ was coming at such and such a time, then they misheard, or they took the statement out of context. Or perhaps some of the faculty or one of our ministers got a little carried away. And you know how rumors get started. Gossip is such a terrible thing."

"Yes it is, sir," said Bryan, "a terrible thing."

"Just one more query," said Sara. "I seem to hear you saying that Lastdays University (which is also sort of a church) is the only group of believers God is working with in what you call 'these end times'—and you are his only Prophet. Is that accurate?"

"Well, Sara, I've searched and I haven't seen any other believers who understand what I see revealed in the pages of my Bible. Oh, you'll find other sincere groups that claim to be Christian, especially to the south and east of here. But they haven't been given the revelation I have."

"I understand you regularly share the message with community leaders in the area," said Bryan.

Nordwyn paused for a moment. "Community leaders…yes! Community leaders. I confer with them often, and always make an effort to share the truth with them. They are guests in my home regularly. Of course that's why God has provided me with such a fine home. Personally, I could take it or leave it, but fine things impress upon community leaders the importance and prestige of God's work." A tiny bit of perspiration appeared on Nordwyn's brow.

"Very well put," said Bryan, with a straight face.

"Mmm-hmm. Thank you," said Nordwyn, frowning a bit at Bryan. "In any case, my offer still stands. I hope I'll hear from you with an answer this afternoon. Give it some thought and prayer. I know you'll make the right decision." Nordwyn and his assistant waved goodbye and continued briskly down the sidewalk.

"Wow," said Sara. "He's one slick con man. He weaseled his way out of every question without so much as a flinch."

Grant's face was flushed, and the veins in his neck were bulging. He moved toward Bryan and Sara.

"What the heck was that all about?" Grant shouted. Students working on the grounds turned to look with astonished faces. Dana was upset too, but her husband's sudden outburst made her move away from him.

Aware that he was attracting attention, Grant lowered his voice again. "You question the Prophet's Christianity, theology and honesty, and you jeopardize our collective future—all in one swell foop!"

Sara, Bryan and Owen began laughing uncontrollably. Dana was not amused. Grant was angrier. "Stop it right now! You know damn well what I mean! I'm just so angry I can't keep my words straight."

Owen stopped laughing and put his hand on Grant's shoulder again. "Grant! Chill, man! You know some questions needed to be asked, and I don't think you and Dana have been askin' 'em. I think maybe we all checked some of our brains at the door when we walked in here. Fact is, it's a nice place on the surface, with a lot of good people. But behind all the happy faces and neatly trimmed shrubbery there are some big problems."

"Of course there are. There are problems everywhere," said Dana. "But we have to focus on the positive things. And this sure beats a work camp."

"Does it—really?" asked Sara. "I think if you take off your rose-colored glasses, you'll see that the problems here are poisoning the good stuff. Lastdays is toxic. Nordwyn keeps his followers addicted to his predictions, which never come to pass. His Bible code doesn't stand up to scrutiny, as you heard. He claims to be the only one who speaks for God, and to have the only group who's truly Christian. And we found out that for all practical purposes he's the local mob kingpin. In essence, this is just as much a prison as any work camp."

"What? That's not only ridiculous but irreverent," said Grant. "After God miraculously brought us out of

the work camp, and inspired my leadership and protected us on the road—you want to throw it all away?"

"We're not saying he didn't protect us, or that he
didn't inspire you," said Owen. "Of course he did—but
that doesn't mean he wants us to give up and stop here.
We gotta use our heads."

"Exactly," said Bryan. "And if I may say so—and if
I remember the story correctly—it sounds like we've got
a little bit of an Exodus metaphor going on here. You're
not Moses, and neither is Nordwyn. There's no cloud
by day and pillar of fire by night. There's no mountain
and no tablets of stone."

No one said anything for a few minutes. They all
stood there, watching Nordwyn disappear down the
walkway with his assistant, wondering if Nordwyn had
heard the commotion.

Dana broke the silence. "I just can't believe this is
all that bad. Just look at this place and the people. It's
a place where we can use our talents and abilities to
make a difference. Even if things don't happen exactly the way he predicts, when the end does come we'll
be protected. Our kids will be protected."

Bryan and Sara exchanged glances. "Wow," said
Bryan.

Dana stared at Bryan. "What!? What exactly is it
you've found out about Prophet Nordwyn that's so horrible?"

Bryan filled Grant and Dana in on what he had
heard from Emilia—and confirmed with his roommate
Dayton.

"Okay—How do you know that's not just gossip?"
demanded Grant.

"Well, for one thing," said Bryan, "it might explain
how a place like this can exist in the middle of the
Wilderness. It's a lot of smoke and mirrors here in Far-

go. Nordwyn's a man who knows what he wants and how to get it."

Bryan let that soak in a moment before he added his last punch, the one he thought might finally tip Grant. "Frankly, I'd like to see if his legendary Bible even exists."

6.

That afternoon, Dana and Grant took some time for soul-searching, prayer and discussion. Yes, the people were charming and sincere. Yes, they wanted this to work. Yes, Nordwyn was persuasive and seemed to be a man of God. But they had been here only less than a week, and in the absence of a Bible, it was hard to evaluate Nordwyn or any other group for that matter. And now their friends—their *trusted* friends—who had suffered huge losses for the sake of Christ, had grave concerns.

As much as Dana and Grant didn't want to think about the questions, they couldn't ignore them. Late in the day, they decided Grant would speak with Nordwyn privately. He had a few of his own questions for the Prophet.

If he was being honest with himself, he wanted Nordwyn to lay his fears to rest. He wasn't ready to leave this place yet. Dana, he and their kids were happy here. This could be their home—the end of their journey.

Grant had to consider the reason he set out on this perilous journey in the first place—to find a community of folks who share similar beliefs, and ultimately, to read the Bible and learn more about Christ.

In the Administration Building, Grant rode the elevator to the fourth floor offices of the Prophet. He was ushered into Nordwyn's office immediately. Nordwyn rose from his desk, shook Grant's hand and offered him a seat.

"Grant, it's good to see you. I trust you have some good news for me."

"If you don't mind," began Grant, "I've got a couple of things I'd like to discuss."

"Why sure," answered Nordwyn, settling back into his big leather desk chair. "What's on your mind?"

Grant leaned forward in his chair. "I've been thinking about the idea that this is the only genuine Christian group in the world. You know, I think back to my parents and my grandparents and the things that they taught me. Does this mean I have to write them all off as unchristian? Then I think about other people I've known over the years, including our little group. Were they not Christ-followers until they met you?"

Nordwyn stared at Grant. "Well, I never said that exactly. There used to be a lot of true Christians in the world. But now most of the people who call themselves Christian are corrupt in one way or another. And now all God has is this remnant here at Lastdays University and our friends who follow us through our media efforts—and he has chosen me to lead them. So when people like yourselves wander in from the confusion out there, they have a decision to make. Will they follow me, or not? If they don't, then it's pretty clear that God just isn't calling them."

Grant thought for a while. "So that's a yes?"

"Yes what?"

"Yes to my question. The only real Christians in the world are your followers."

"No question about it."

"Okay," said Grant. "You know, I've heard the Bible quoted, I've committed parts of it to memory, and I have part of a Bible page. But I've never actually seen the whole thing—I'd truly love to see one. Is there any chance I could take a look at that Bible of yours?"

Nordwyn looked at his desk and shuffled papers uncomfortably. "Grant, I'd love to show you my copy of the Holy Scripture. But if I did that I'd have to show it to everyone. Then they'd want to flip through it and read it. And you know, the Bible is a dangerous book in the wrong hands. They'd read things in there that they wouldn't understand and they'd take those things out of context and we'd have all kinds of confusion. And I think Scripture says somewhere that God is not the author of confusion. So you understand why I can't do that, don't you, Grant?"

"Mmm-hmmm. Yes, I think I understand," said Grant, as he was thinking, *Why wouldn't he want everyone to read the Bible?*

"We have printing presses here you know. I could have thousands of copies of my Bible printed up any time I wanted to. But that might bring the Federation around. And it's just better if the few copies of the Bible that are left are limited to those of us who truly understand it. Which right now is me."

Nordwyn's answers were confirming exactly what Grant's friends had told him. He didn't want to admit it, but it was clear. He and Dana had been wrong.

Nordwyn's work was focused on Nordwyn, not Jesus. If that was the case, the foundation was wrong. If the foundation was wrong, everything built on it would eventually collapse. This is not what Grant had been seeking for his family. He knew what he had to do.

"Okay then," said Grant, leaning forward on his seat and clapping his hands on his legs. "I don't think we'll be taking you up on your offer."

"Excuse me?" said Nordwyn, his eyebrows raised.

"I guess you could just say that God is not calling us," said Grant, leaning back in his chair. "We are truly grateful for your hospitality. But we won't be staying here at Lastdays."

Nordwyn reacted, but not in the way Grant expected. He smiled, a bit condescendingly. "It's okay, Grant. I already knew you were going to say that."

"Let me guess," said Grant, "a coded message in your Bible?"

"Why yes, of course! Grant, please excuse me just a moment!" Nordwyn got up, ducked out the door for fifteen or twenty seconds, and returned. "Everything is in order. Security will see to it." Nordwyn motioned toward the door without saying another word.

When Grant emerged into the lobby, one of the hulking security guards from the building entrance was waiting. This time he was sporting an assault rifle. "This way, sir," said the guard without a smile. Nordwyn's executive assistant continued working without even looking up. Grant got the distinct feeling that he was being removed from the Administration Hall as quickly as possible, in stark contrast to the warm reception they had experienced a few days earlier.

At the front of the building, they waited for five or ten minutes, the security guard holding his assault rifle with his finger on the trigger. People came and went from the building, glancing nervously toward Grant and the security guard but avoiding eye contact. Grant wondered what was going to happen next.

"What are we doing here?" asked Grant.

"Sir, I'll have to ask you not to talk," said the security guard, staring straight ahead.

"Okay."

"Sir! I'll say it again. Don't talk. Don't move. Just stand there until I tell you otherwise."

Grant did as he was told.

After about twenty long minutes a black van driven by another security guard swung into the driveway. Everyone in the team was seated inside—plus two others, whom Grant quickly recognized as Emilia and Dayton.

"Grant—what's going on?" called Dana from the van. "They just came and got us, ordered us to pack up and brought us here. The kids are pretty upset."

"Please stop talking," interrupted the first guard. "We're going to drive you down to I-94. If you're headed west we'll drop you off west of town. If you're headed east we'll take you across the river to Moorhead. And no talking in the van on the way."

The short ride was silent with a mixed bag of emotions. Lissa was crying, mumbling something about a boy she had met. Tadd was wistfully fingering the lacing on a football his friend had given him. Sara was relieved. Owen had enjoyed his time in the auto shop, but had entertained doubts about Nordwyn from the time he met him. Dayton was a little antsy, but more than ready to leave Nordwyn's "work." Dana and Grant sat emotionless, eyes straight ahead.

Emilia and Bryan were happy to be moving on. As Bryan stared out the window of the SUV, he noticed two crows flying in the same direction as them. He thought of the freedom the crows enjoyed. No worries about raptors, religious fanatics or Federation drones. What a life! After half a mile or so he looked again. The crows were still overhead. They continued until they arrived at the I-94. Bryan bit his lip.

The guards dropped the team off on the east side of Fargo, in what used to be Moorhead, Minnesota. They crossed a dilapidated bridge over the Red River and pulled to the shoulder. The group bailed out.

Finally, the guard handed Bryan his weapons. "Sir," ordered the guard, "don't even think of using these on the eyes of the Prophet, or you will quickly find yourselves dead."

The door slammed shut, and the black SUV roared off, making a U-turn across the divider and heading back toward Fargo. They all stared at the retreating van, trying to make sense out of what had happened.

Dana turned to her husband. "I take it your meeting with Nordwyn didn't go well."

"I suppose you could say that," said Grant, and filled the team in on his interview with the Prophet.

Emilia laughed—she was giddy. She had been wondering if she'd ever find a way out from under Nordwyn's thumb. "We've been *disfellowshipped*. They remove troublemakers (*scoffers*, that's what they call them) from the campus as quietly and quickly as possible, so they don't have a chance to 'infect' anyone else."

Dayton spoke up. "I had heard some scuttlebutt about this, but this confirms it. They say the Prophet's 'eyes' are whichever raptor gang controls this stretch of I-94—one of the many gangs that has an agreement with Nordwyn. They'll come by any minute now, you betcha. We'll have to get at least a hundred miles down the road before we're free of Nordwyn's influence. And the down side of that is that the gangs who *don't* answer to Nordwyn are probably more dangerous."

"How come he's gotta have 'eyes' if all he has to do is check out his Bible code?" snarked Bryan.

"Good question. Looks like you'll be able to ask these guys personally," said Dayton, pointing eastward at a small cloud of rapidly approaching dust.

"Oh, no!" said Dana, pulling her children to her sides.

The dust cloud was produced by three motorcycles. One sported a sidecar carrying a large, grinning, heavily tattooed woman. Much to the relief of the group, they didn't stop. They only slowed enough to shout "Scoffers!" and throw rotten vegetables and some other nondescript organic material. Again, the band of pilgrims was in a state of shock as they wiped the slime from their clothing.

"So we have to put up with this all the way to wherever we're going?" asked Dana.

"Hard to say," said Dayton.

Grant was in a daze. Less than four hours ago, he had been sitting in a comfortable classroom with his wife, dreaming about how wonderful it would be to live and work on that idyllic campus. Now, suddenly, he was on a dusty roadside being pelted with garbage. But at least he had his friends and family—and the truth.

In the past he would have been confident of God's protection, but now he was beginning to wonder. He had no idea how to answer his wife's question. He was not the leader he thought he was.

Emilia provided an answer. "I hear there's a group of Christians south of the ruins of Minneapolis in the town of La Crosse, along the Mississippi River. It's a long way, but it's something."

Grant gazed eastward, where the Interstate disappeared into the prairie. "I guess we don't have any choice do we?"

The team began trudging along the highway's shoulder. Another group of bikers appeared in the distance. Over the motorcycle engines, Bryan could hear distinct bursts of fully automatic weapon fire. "Hit the ground," he screamed. Everyone dropped.

The raptors roared by, but the only thing to hit the team was rotten fruit, lewd gestures, and more shouts of "scoffers!" They got up and dusted themselves off. "Looks like they were strafing the side of the road just to terrorize us," said Bryan. "I imagine they are under orders not to kill any 'scoffers,' unless the scoffers try to kill them first."

The miles went by and the pattern continued. Grant consoled himself with the fact that, although the experience was terrifying, no one was hurt so far. But sunset was nearing, and Grant had no idea what tack the raptors might take if they came across the team encamped at night.

He imagined Bryan on sentry duty with his weapon. What if he had to use it against the bikers? The guards had warned them. It seemed like a no-win situation. Grant began scanning the surrounding prairie for possible secluded campsites. They wouldn't be able to build a fire, as that would attract the attention of raptors.

As the sun was hitting the horizon, the sound of a distant truck engine came out of the west, increasing in volume. They turned to look. As it neared, they could see a large, dirty-white van, over twenty feet long. The cab was covered with steel plates, leaving only thin slits for the windows. Judging from the smoke and the sound of the engine, Owen guessed it was running bio-diesel. As it closed in on the band, it downshifted and began to slow.

There was no time for the team to dive over the shoulder. They could only stand, wordlessly, and brace themselves for whatever was about to happen.

The van slowed to a halt on the gravel shoulder, raising a huge cloud of dust that blew across the four lanes of the highway. Nothing happened. The team stared and waited. Bryan reached for his weapon and held it with this finger on the trigger in clear sight of the driver. Still nothing happened.

Then the driver's door slowly opened, and out stepped a thin man in a weathered trench coat, hands raised. Grant sensed something familiar about him, but he couldn't recall what.

The man spoke. "Even with that scary lookin' weapon, you folks shouldn't be out here at night."

It was Bob Kroener.

"Jesus does not give recipes that show the way to God as other teachers of religion do. He Himself is the way."
—Karl Barth

PART IV: LA CROSSE

1.

World Federation President Mehdi Kazdaghli sits at his desk in the Presidential Palace, gazing out of his enormous windows. It is a hazy, warm day. The Presidential Palace, the Capital Building, the Forum and the surrounding governmental buildings had been built in the Cite Yassmina, just southwest of Carthage. Mehdi's desk faces northeast, with a view of the ruins of Carthage in the foreground and the Gulf of Tunis beyond. Swivelling his chair around, he enjoys a sweeping southwesterly view of the city of Tunis.

About three thousand years ago, according to legend and history, Phoenicians (called Canaanites in the Bible) had sailed west from Tyre on the coast of Canaan under the leadership of Queen Dido, quite possibly the granddaughter of the biblical Hiram King of Tyre. Dido founded the City of Carthage (from two Phoenician words meaning "new city" or new Tyre). Queen Dido's historicity had been debated by scholars until the discovery, shortly after the Final War, of her palace, complete with a small library of royal records carved in stone tablets. This find was of no small propaganda value to the Federation.

113

The Phoenicians' intermarriage with the African Berbers created a new and powerful people, whom the Romans called *Punici*, or Punics. The Punics of Carthage, with their mighty navy, ruled the Western Mediterranean for centuries. Even more significantly, Carthage, true to its Phoenician roots, dominated international trade and business—until it was destroyed by the Romans in 146 B.C. But the Romans rebuilt Carthage and it remained a great city for centuries, until it was conquered and again destroyed by invading Muslim Arabs in 698 A.D., to be replaced by the city of Tunis. Thanks to the course of events in the Final War, Carthage finally had the last word. It was a fitting resolution to a long history. Mehdi often pondered the history of Carthage as he gazed out his windows.

But there was another way in which Carthage, and the Punic people, had triumphed. Mehdi doubted if anyone outside of a few scholars had considered this irony. St. Augustine was born in northern Africa, of Punic ancestry. He was educated and spent much of his life in Carthage, later becoming Bishop of Hippo (now known as Annaba), some one-hundred-fifty miles west of Carthage. As the Roman Empire begin to disintegrate, Augustine influenced the Roman Church to fill the vacuum of Roman political power. His philosophy and theology reshaped Christianity. True to his Phoenician heritage, his ideas turned the Roman Catholic Church into a multinational business. Thus Augustine, partly Phoenician/Canaanite—an ethnic group earlier oppressed by the Jews and later suppressed by the Romans—became one of the founding fathers of Western civilization.

This idea of the spiritual destiny and heritage of Carthage was always at the forefront of Mehdi's mind. His family's religious heritage had been Muslim prior to the Final War, but he now rejects that as a form of Arabization.

Mehdi laughs to himself. He realized that the historical truth of the development of civilization was infinitely more complex than this little narrative in which he often indulged. However, he also knew that such a simple thread could be quite useful in persuading others, and he planned to use it in the very near future.

Mehdi's secretary's voice on the intercom interrupts his thoughts. "Excellency, just reminding you of the Foremost Council's emergency meeting in fifteen minutes." The Foremost Council (not to be confused with the main legislative body, the Grand Council) was the executive governing body of the World Federation. Not only was it responsible for electing the president, but for executive political and administrative decisions.

"Thank you, Farah. We'll leave here in five."

Riots had erupted in parts of the Northern Indian Autonomous Region, and were threatening to spread through the whole subcontinent. The president and the Foremost Council needed to decide on a course of action today.

Before Mehdi had lapsed into contemplation (as he did more and more recently), he had viewed drone images of the riots. The technology was similar to that of the common iCap, but much more sophisticated. Images from multiple drones—often disguised as insects or birds—were processed, integrated and finally transmitted directly into the optic and auditory nerves of the viewer, who could be half a world away. It was like being there, floating above or among the surging crowds.

No doubt about it, this was a religious issue, in spite of the Federation's best efforts to eliminate such disputes. Radical Muslims were demanding their own autonomous region, free of militant Hindus. In other parts of the world, the radicals of any religion would have been shipped off to work camps long ago. But the work camps in India were bursting at the seams with Hindus and Muslims. Federation drones had strafed neighborhoods in Jaipur and Bhopal, in what was previously India, as well as Dhaka in the former Bangladesh, with thousands dead. It made no difference—the unrest continued.

One option was simply to move the offending populations into the Wilderness. Another option was to bring the Wilderness to the offending populations by removing Safe Zone status from the offending cities (after relocating loyal citizens). But neither of these draconian measures would solve the core problem: human addiction to religion.

Yet in North America, considered Mehdi, there was little if any religious unrest. People were generally less superstitious and more materialistic. They would do whatever was needed to maintain their creature comforts. And buried in their collective subconscious, North Americans were still motivated by the old Protestant work ethic—a meme inherited from the Puritan pilgrims (with their Calvinist theology, ultimately derived from Augustine, by the way). Say what you want about various religions, but one of the striking advantages of Calvinist Protestantism was that it effectively guilted or greeded people into intrinsically motivated obedience and productivity—perhaps more effectively than any other, more authoritarian faith system. The belief in redemption through the sufferings of a merciful and loving God, and the desire to please God in return, seemed, in Mehdi's mind, to drive that work ethic.

Mehdi had realized some time ago that unfortunately, for some cultures, the Federation's Values were not adequately plugging the gaping emotional hole that only religion or some facsimile seems to fill. The Fed-

eration had been a bit hasty in banning all religion out-
right, even if the ban was enforced somewhat selectively.
He was convinced there was a better system—it could
be quite successful with the right spin, the right leadership and the right implementation. Yes, he and members of his staff were hard at work on a long-term solution. Top secret for the time being, but when the time
was right he would present his plan to the Council.

Now his two secretaries and his security detail join
him, walking the causeway leading from the Palace to
the Foremest Council Chamber in the Capitol Building.

It is like removing a bone from the mouth of a dog,
thought Mehdi as he approached the great doors of
the Chamber. *To avoid being bit, one must first offer
the dog something to replace the bone.*

2.

"Bob? Is that you?" Grant squinted. Maybe the sun was
playing tricks with his eyesight. "How is this possible?"

"You *know* this guy?" Dana asked.

Bob paused. "You look familiar, but...hey! Aren't
you the guy who loaned me tools and gave me a sandwich and coffee somewhere north of Dickinson? I'll
be darned. What are you doin' out here?"

"Long story short, we're on an extended vacation
from the Minot Work Camp. We've been on the road
for weeks, except for a few stops along the way. We
thought we might settle down in Fargo, but apparently we're not welcome there anymore. Now we're headed down the road to La Crosse."

"Uh-huh. If I rememer correctly, that first time we
met I mentioned that the folks in Fargo seemed nice—

but kind of strange. Bob paused again and stared at Emilia. "You look a bit familiar, too. Heck! Aren't you the girl my trucker buddy Ed and his wife Chloe took in for a while in Rapid City? They were sorta hooked up with that outfit in Fargo, and they brought you up here as I recall."

"Yeah, that's me," said Emilia. "Nice folks, Ed and Chloe."

"Well I'll be darned," said Bob. "Hey listen, I'm haulin' a shipment generally eastward to Madison. You saved my butt out there in the prairie, and I'd sure like to return the favor. There's room in the back of the truck. It's windowless, but that could be a good thing if you're tryin' to steer clear of those Fargo raptors. It'll take us two or three days, accountin' for the busted up roads and such."

The team breathed a sigh of relief. The truck wasn't the most comfortable thing in the world, but it sure beat walking. A little rearrangement of the cargo and the deployment of sleeping bags made it tolerable. They decided to take turns riding in the front seat with Bob, who was happy to hold forth with a wealth of information and entertaining stories about his life and adventures in the Wilderness. The first shift fell to Grant.

"So," said Bob, "Wanna tell me more about your 'extended vacation'?"

"Um, well, actually, we escaped."

"Escaped? You're tellin' me you and your whole group here escaped from the Minot Camp?"

"All except Emilia and Dayton. They joined us in Fargo."

"Why the heck would you do that? Kinda risky, wasn't it? How'd you pull it off? I mean, it was sort of a prison, but at least you had a job and a safe place to live."

Grant buried his face in his hands. "Look, in the

last few hours I've asked myself a hundred times what we're doing out here. After I talked to you, I got all excited about the possibility of Christians out here—about joining with them, being with them, learning from them. It seemed like it would be worth any risk. So I uprooted my family and friends and risked all our lives. I really thought God was with us—but now I don't know. If we had the money, I'd be tempted to have you cart us back to Minot and we'd turn ourselves in."

"Well that ain't much of an option no longer, is it?" said Bob.

"What do you mean?" asked Grant.

"So you don't know?"

"Know what?"

"About the Minot Camp. Come to think of it, you wouldn't know, would you?"

"I don't know anything. What are you talking about?"

"It happened yesterday. I talked to another trucker who knew a farmer out there who said there was some kind of vapor buildup in one of those big crude oil storage tanks. Faulty venting system or somethin'. Anyway, one of 'em blew up and it was kind of a domino thing with the other tanks. One big fireball after another. 'Course there was a train full of tanker cars on the siding and all those went up too. Boom! Boom! Boom! Took out most of the camp. Half the inmates and staff are gone, including the warden. Looks like you and your crew got out o' there just in time. If that ain't somebody upstairs lookin' out for you, I don't know what is."

Grant felt his body weaken and a cold sweat break out. His stomach suddenly clenched. His old friends and coworkers. Warden Grimhaus. The camp had been his home from the day he was born. He thought he had adjusted to the fact that he'd never return to the camp again, but now he was deeply disturbed that the camp and the people he knew were gone. Suddenly, part of him felt like he needed to go back to help pick up the pieces and rebuild. But another part said "you need to move on."

Grant took a deep breath before ducking through the small, homemade door of the cab into the truck's cargo area. The team reacted to the news with shock and grief. Dana felt like she'd been hit by a truck. She had dragged her feet about leaving, yet if they had remained in the camp, her family might have been incinerated. But if God had protected them by allowing them to escape, couldn't he have protected them in the camp as well? It was a pointless question. All she could do was thank God they were alive now and hope that things would be better in the near future.

Things weren't. Bryan took Grant's place in the front seat with Bob. About 50 miles down the road, Bob exclaimed "Uff da!"

"Uff da?" queried Bryan.

"Got a bunch o' biker headlights comin' up fast behind us. Generally not a good sign out here."

Bryan picked up his Vikhr and clicked off the safety. The thunder of motors was growing steadily. Grant poked his head through the cab door. "What's going on?"

"Looks like the 'eyes of the prophet' ain't gonna give up easy," said Bob. You better keep everyone low, just in case some rounds fly."

"I thought Dayton said they were under orders not to shoot," yelled Dana.

"Maybe he was wrong," said Bryan, poking the muzzle of his weapon through the slit in the armor-covered passenger door. Bob had the pedal to the floor. The truck was nearing 80 mph, and he didn't know how bad the road ahead was—or if there was a road. Choppers pulled up on both sides of the cab.

Bob could see the rider on his right motioning for him to pull over. "Be damned if I'm gonna let these guys tell me what to do!" He stomped the gas pedal harder. He noticed that there were two raptors on the cycle—and the one on the back was aiming an assault rifle at him. The gunner fired a burst at the roof of the cab, but the armor held. In the less-armored back of the truck, a line of holes suddenly appeared in the wall, and the screaming passengers lay flat on the floor.

"Do your thing, Bryan!" shouted Bob, leaning forward. Bryan jerked his Vikhr out of the passenger's window and swung it behind Bob, poking it through the three-inch armor slit. He squeezed the trigger and for a second the cab was filled with a deafening 22-hertz hum. Both raptors flew from the chopper, which went careening into the median. Bob glanced in his side mirror and saw the bike's gyrating headlight beam flash on a spray of red liquid. Bryan swung back to his window and fired a quick burst at the raptors only two feet away. They disappeared from view. Suddenly the roar of cycle engines was gone, replaced by a distant sound of screams and exploding metal as the back most raptors collided with the wreckage of their ill-fated pointmen.

"All clear!" shouted Bob. "Is everyone back there okay?"

"Near as I can tell we're all intact," answered Owen, "but it sounds like we just put out a few 'eyes of the Prophet.'" No one said anything for a while.

Grant sat in silence, his face in his hands. Thank God everyone was alright. He really didn't want to know the details of what just happened out there, and that bothered him more than the event itself. There was his pacifist mindset, but then there was reality. He had sold everyone here into joining him on this quest, but he found himself unprepared to deal with the violence and volatility of the Wilderness. And if he couldn't do that heavy lifting, he couldn't be the leader that his family and friends needed right now. He rose to his feet and poked his head into the front cab.

Bryan sat grimly with this weapon in his lap, the barrel still smoking. He turned to see Grant, who laid a firm hand on his shoulder.

"Good job, Bryan. I hate that you had to do that, but you saved our lives. I guess you can keep that thing."

"Thanks," said Bryan, nodding his head and staring at the highway.

"Guess I'll have to take a different route back," said Bob. "They'll be lookin' for this truck."

They drove on into the night, putting about a hundred miles between them and Fargo, finally stopping for the night at the town of Alexandria, Minnesota. Bob had an old friend there who cooked bio-diesel. The governance of the town was halfway stable and the team felt relatively safe again.

The next day they continued following the old I-94 south, circumventing the wasteland of Minneapolis, generally uninhabited since it had been vaporized in the Final War.

With Tadd in the passenger's seat and Lissa plugged into her iCap, Grant talked about the Nordwyn experience with the team in the back of the truck. "When we started this journey I thought I would know what we were looking for when I saw it. Now I don't know what to think. I can't believe we were taken in by that guy."

"We weren't *all* taken in," laughed Sara. "I don't want to seem like a know-it-all or come across as being self-important, but I spent time at New Harvard studying twentieth and twenty-first century 'end-times' groups. Once I got beyond the sanctimonious politeness at the Lastdays campus, it hit me in the face. It's all religious manipulation. Dig a little and there's always hypocrisy and corruption. Bryan here studied enough history—or Federation revisionism—to see it, not to mention the finely tuned sense of skepticism he developed with his family."

"Yeah," snorted Bryan, shaking his head. "And of course Dayton and Emilia were living in it."

"Okay," said Grant. "I get the picture."

"Uhh—I don't think you do, exactly," said Bryan. "I wonder if *any* of us do. Our spiritual intuition needs to develop. Call it *cultdar*. These hucksters will appeal to different ones of us for different reasons. That's why we need to look out for each other, even when we don't want to hear it."

"You're right," sighed Grant. "Anyway, maybe the group in La Crosse will be it. If not, maybe we can set 'em straight."

Everyone chuckled—except Dana. She wanted to believe her husband was kidding. And she would give him the benefit of the doubt.

They camped in the ghost town of Hampton, Minnesota and continued south on US 52, joining the I-90, toward their destination of La Crosse, Wisconsin.

Bryan, riding in the passenger seat, and checking his watch-map, wanted to know why Bob hadn't followed the Mississippi from the Minneapolis wasteland down to La Crosse.

"From what I hear it's hard to find any roads at all along that stretch of the river," answered Bob. "When they blew up Minneapolis, they say it sent a wall of water down the river, wiping out dams, locks, bridges and towns for over a hundred miles. The dam and lock just north of La Crosse was no exception. Used to be a huge lake there. I think they called it Onalaska or something like that. No more. Wiped out the bridge on the I-90 too."

Bob headed his truck down US 61 and crossed the Mississippi on the barely intact interstate bridge at La Crosse. It was Grant's turn to sit in the passenger seat as they entered town.

"Do you know where you're going here?" asked Bob. "Because I think I have some idea about where you might want to be headed."

"All I know is that Emilia and Dayton said they had heard of a group here in La Crosse. They didn't know where and I don't either."

Bob continued through the deteriorating city on Cass Street and into the forested hills on the east of town. After a couple more miles, he pulled his truck into a gravel driveway. On their left was a huge wooden lodge, surrounded by cabins and several other rustic outbuildings.

"Where are we?" asked Grant.

"A friend of mine showed me this place once. We're at an old camp east of town. It used to be some kind of retreat for the Franciscan Sisters of Perpetual Adoration back at Viterbo University."

"Looks rustic. But why are we here?

"Well, I don't know if this is what you want because I haven't figured out what you're lookin' for. All I know is there's a Christian group that lives here—headed up by Sister something-or-other. Might be your cuppa tea, or not. You and your crew will have to figure it out from here."

Grant nodded. "Thanks, Bob. You've done the best you can, and I can't tell you how much we appreciate it. If it hadn't been for you, we'd still be trudging along the I-94, getting pelted by rotten fruit and vegetables, or a lot worse."

Dana's head poked through the door from the back of the truck, "Hey! What's going on? Can we get out?" Bob hopped out of the cab, ran around to the back and unlocked the doors. The crew piled out, squinting and scanning their surroundings.

"Wow!" exclaimed Sara. "The middle of the woods."

"Bob tells me that a Christian group is operating out of here. Emilia? Dayton? Do you know anything more than what you told us?"

"Nothing more than what I told you. Except that they specialize in health and healing."

"Dad," said Tadd, pointing at three figures who had just emerged from the door of the lodge, "I think we're about to find out more."

A man and two women were headed down the path. All three sported friendly grins, white uniforms and headdresses that Sara and Bryan recognized from their historical studies as early twentieth century nurses' caps. The woman in the middle appeared to be of African ethnicity, in her late fifties and clearly in charge. She held out her hand and Grant stepped forward to take it.

"Welcome to our place of healing," said the woman. "I'm Sister Aretha Tervis, and these are my assistants, Edwin and Audrey. How may we help you today?"

Grant was momentarily at a loss for words. The team, including Bob, stopped unloading and stared at Sister Aretha and her assistants in their sparkling white uniforms. Owen, transfixed, dropped the backpack he had been holding, with a loud crunch. Sister Aretha regarded him with a wry smile. "My, my! I hope there was nothing valuable in there, Mr...."

"Uh...Fenbert," stammered Owen. "My name is Fenbert. I mean that's my last name, but you can call me Owen. That's my first name."

Sister Aretha seemed to be struggling to hold back laughter. "Oh, a first name! Well, Owen, I'm very pleased to meet you."

Grant cleared his throat. "Thank you, Sister Aretha. To answer your question, we've come a long way, and we heard that there was a group of Christians here in La Crosse. Would that be you?"

"You heard right. We are, indeed, Christ-followers."

"Then we would love to visit with you for a few days, and maybe we can share our stories. We're more than willing to work for our food and a place to sleep."

"We'd be happy to work something out," answered Sister Aretha. "There's always plenty of work to be done here. Edwin, can you see about accommodations for our guests? Audrey, please let Brother Enrique know we'll have ten more pairs of hands to help us with our work."

"Nine," corrected Bob, standing by his truck. "I'm just droppin' 'em off. Gotta be in Madison by tomorrow."

"That's just a few hours away," said Sister Aretha. "Surely you can share dinner, spend the night with us, and have a good, wholesome breakfast in the morning."

"You twisted my arm," Bob answered with a smile. Had Bob known what was on the menu, he might have chosen to continue down the road.

3.

A musty odor permeated the old building. It had sat unused for some thirty years from the time of the Final War until Sister Aretha and her followers moved into it. Brother Enrique and his dedicated maintenance crew had cleaned and repaired portions of the lodge, including the same dining room and kitchen that had been used by the nuns who held their retreats there.

The residents all wore white linen uniforms, sat

on benches at long tables and ate family style. Other followers occasionally came up from town and joined them for the evening meal, conspicuous by their normal clothing. At a separate table, dressed in blue hospital gowns, sat patients who had come to Sister Aretha for healing.

There was no lack of food, but it was like nothing any of the pilgrims had seen before: large bowls of boiled kale, roasted parsnips and Khorasan wheat groats, with a sort of amaranth pudding for dessert, sweetened with raw, unfiltered sorghum juice. They washed this all down with a tea made from Northern Oak Fern—apparently an acquired taste.

Lissa and Tadd were distressed, as might be expected. At least the food they had at the work camp was edible. Dana had tried to feed her family relatively nutritious food, but as far as the kids were concerned, this was torture.

Sitting at the table with Grant's team (and next to a delighted Owen), Sister Aretha explained, "Among the reasons we settled here years ago were the wonderful old medical libraries back in town at the old Viterbo Campus. We've moved them out here. I believe that God wants us all to be in good health. There's a Scripture that my grandmother taught me, 'Beloved, I wish above all things that you may prosper and be in health.' What could be clearer? Our health and prosperity are absolutely the most important things to God."

Grant heard Sara choke, and looked down the table at her. She was visibly struggling with the implications of Aretha's comment. Aretha seemed not to notice.

"For years," continued Aretha, "my followers and I carefully studied these medical manuals. We learned many things, but we finally came to a fundamental conclusion."

"And what was that?" inquired Dana.

"We discovered that the texts were simply wrong about the causes of disease. Simply wrong! Disease is not caused by germs or by genetic predispositions. All disease is caused by *spirits of perversity* which we invite in by consuming the wrong foods."

"Perversity?" asked Grant.

"Indeed," said Sister Aretha. "When perverse spirits enter into a body, they bring with them the bacteria, viruses, other microorganisms and cancers that ravage and plunder our good health."

"Why do they do that?" asked Emilia.

"Because they feed on the energies of the body and mind. Once they have dissipated a body, they move on to the next one. They are metaphysical predators, bleeding people dry of their spiritual and physical energy. People come to us here with gunshot wounds and other violent injuries—clearly the work of perverse spirits, traceable back to bad food."

"That's fascinating," said Sara. "It reminds me of the old 21st Century movies with vampires and zombies."

"Pretty much," said Bryan. "And it's also an apt metaphor for something else I can't quite put my finger on right now. Another kind of spiritual and physical predator."

"I think I know what you mean," said Emilia, winking. "By the way, Sister Aretha, how do you finance your operation?"

"Simple," answered Aretha. "We teach that if you wish to remain injury free and disease free, you must contribute a seventh of your assets to us every year. Not only will you be healthy, but God owes you and will pay you back with interest. If that doesn't happen, of course it means that you're disobeying one or more of his health laws. Or that you have a wrong attitude."

"That's a brilliant business plan," said Bryan. "Too bad I didn't think of that myself."

Sister Aretha regarded Bryan, Emilia and Sara quizzically. Grant clenched his jaw. His resident skeptics were at it again, doing what they had done with Nordwyn only a few days ago. And now Emilia had joined them. True, they had been right about Nordwyn. And sure, Sister Aretha's curious explanation of disease was hard for a scientist such as himself to accept. Nor did it seem to him to be a sound application of Scripture, or what little he knew of it. But he wished the inquisitors would keep a lid on their judgment for a little while longer. After all, they'd only been here for a couple of hours. And they were in the midst of eating a free meal.

Grant turned to Aretha, looking to soothe any concerns she might have about their group. "Sister, this is remarkable. Where did you discover all this knowledge?"

"Most of it came from a wonderful book we found in the library by an early twenty-first century Christian health teacher named Tyler Belknap—titled *The Eleven Principles of Wellness*. He taught about foods and nutrition, and he developed and produced amazing herbal supplements and nutritious foods. He quoted a scripture that promises us one hundred and twenty years of healthy, energetic life, if we follow the rules that God revealed."

"I'd like to see a copy of that book," said Grant.

"Certainly," said Aretha. "I have a copy I can loan you in my office."

Bryan, Emilia and Sara said nothing, and poked at their amaranth-sorghum pudding. Owen, who was hanging on Sister Aretha's every word, wanted to know more. "Wow. What happened to this Belknap guy?"

"We don't know for sure. A traveler once told us that Belknap's granddaughter still carries on his work in South

America somewhere. But in any case we've done additional study and have gone far beyond his teaching."

After dinner was cleared away, the team was put up in the small cabins surrounding the lodge. They slept— a less troubled sleep than they did when they were camping on the road, but not as soundly as they would have if they had been more certain of their destination, and they were pretty sure this wasn't it.

4.

At precisely 6:00 a.m. the next morning, everyone in the compound woke up to the sound of the customary gong, firmly beaten by Brother Enrique. He handed out work assignments to everyone in the group, Lissa and Tadd included. Everyone, that is, except Bob Kroener, who was ready to get on the road. The team said their goodbyes to him over a harsh breakfast of unhulled buckwheat groats and carob bark tea, as coffee was strictly forbidden.

Outside, Grant shook Bob's hand. "We'll never forget you, Bob. You helped get us started on this journey and you probably saved us from the horrible disaster at the camp. And yesterday you saved us again."

Bob gave a sheepish grin. "All in a day's work. Maybe we'll meet again somewhere. In the meantime, keep your wits about ya. Keep your team together. The way I see it, you kinda need each other to keep from bein' bamboozled. There's lots of bamboozleers out here. Don't let anyone bamboozle ya."

With that, he was into his truck and down the road.

For the rest of the day (except for a brief break for a rather slimy lunch of kombucha scoby salad) the team cleaned, scrubbed and painted. The lodge was immense and in need of more restoration than Brother Enrique's current workforce could handle. Sister Aretha, however, remained fully confident that God would provide more workers as her movement grew. Nearly every day someone stumbled in with anything from minor aches and pains to devastating illnesses. Sister Aretha was always ready with a recommendation—but not necessarily one that actually worked.

Two days after the arrival of the Cochrin team, Aretha's assistants Edwin and Audrey were growing concerned about the amount of time Sister Aretha was spending with Owen. Owen and Aretha strolled through the forest paths for hours. Owen shared his life story and his long history at the Minot Work Camp. She shared her story and her ideas about health, longevity, spirituality and the state of the world. It wouldn't have mattered much to Owen what she said, as long as it was she who was saying it.

He was smitten, and Sister Aretha was enjoying the kind of attention she hadn't received in a long, long time. But Sister Aretha tended to micromanage, and issues that needed her attention were beginning to pile up on the desks of Edwin and Audrey.

Bryan and Dayton were repairing the decrepit wiring on the second floor when they smelled smoke. They immediately dropped what they were doing and headed down the hall toward the source of the smoke— a room at the end of the hall with a loud commotion inside. They quietly approached the doorway and peeked around the corner.

Inside, Sister Aretha and several uniformed attendants clustered around the bed of an apparently unconscious, loudly snoring man. One attendant walked around the room muttering something and waving a sheaf of smoking leaves. Others seemed to be praying. Sister Aretha herself was shouting a series of foreign-sounding words that neither Bryan nor Dayton recognized—although apparently they were names.

"Hamazi, Rimush, Shudurul! I name you, spirits of perversity! I name you and command you to depart from our brother and never return! Damiq-Ilishu, Ku-Baba and Ishme-Dagan! Spirits, six in number, who have made your foul home in this mind and body! Leave it now! Leave it, all of you! Leave it sane and whole, as you found it before you entered in and polluted it!"

"Well, this is creepy," whispered Dayton. "What are they doing? Some kind of exorcism?"

"I have no idea," said Bryan. "But I can't stop watching."

The man in bed shook and gave a long groan. Sister Aretha and the praying women grabbed the gold amulets that hung around their necks and waved them in the air. "I command you in the names of St. Gabriel, the man Jesus, Lord Gautama and Lord Dhanvantari! Leave this house!"

"Leave this house! Leave this house! Leave this house!" chanted the women. They waved their amulets high and low and began to dance around the bed. Sister Aretha produced a horn-shaped container from beneath her robe, removed the lid and threw the contents on the man. "I anoint you! I anoint you! I anoint you in the name of St. Raphael the Archangel!" shouted Aretha. The woman with the burning leaves waved them in the man's face. Suddenly the man began coughing and sat up.

"What the heck is goin' on?" said the man. "Why are you pokin' that stinky thing in my face? What's all the noise, and why am I covered with all this oily stuff? I'm tryin' to get some sleep, for cryin' out loud!"

Sister Aretha and the women began to shout and cheer. "He's healed! He's healed! The spirits of perversity are gone!" They high-fived each other. Aretha gave instructions for the man to be served parsnip broth.

Bryan and Dayton didn't wait to see the man's reaction. They scooted down the hall as quickly as they could without making noise. After they finished their electrical repairs, they went downstairs to the dining room for lunch. They weren't that hungry, partly because of what was on the menu (stewed fern sprouts) and partly because of what they had witnessed.

They wasted no time in locating Grant, and gave him a full report on the exorcism, or whatever it was.

Grant was still hoping to find a place to settle down as a group; he was getting tired of traveling and searching. "I know things are little different around here, but..."

"Different than what?" Bryan challenged.

"Different than what I expected Christians to be, based on what my parents and grandparents tried to pass on to me. And what our *remnant* of the Bible says. And the verses we've committed to memory."

"Ain't that the truth," responded Bryan.

"But invoking old pagan gods to drive evil spirits or whatever out of some guy? It's just hard to believe," said Grant.

Dana had joined the group, and was listening intently.

"I had trouble believing it myself. But here's the thing," said Bryan. "We've come a long way. We can't go back and we don't know how much longer we'll have to go. The advantage of staying in a place like this is that we're safer here then we are on the road. The disadvantage is that if this group is clearly not something we're going to buy into, then the sooner we get out of here, the sooner we'll find something compatible."

"Okay," said Grant, "You're saying that we're wasting our time. That might be true, if we had nothing to contribute."

Dana spoke. "Contribute?"

"I think we can bring some balance to these people. Maybe we can help them to look to Jesus instead of all this strange health stuff and spirits of perversity and whatnot. As long as we're here we might as well try to make a difference."

"Like the difference we made in Fargo?" Dana retorted.

"You know what I mean. We can set a right example and maybe they'll follow."

Now Sara had joined the group. "If you're saying what I think you are, I've got a great quote from Julius Caesar: 'Men willingly believe what they wish.' These folks aren't going to change because of us."

"Yeah," said Bryan. "Look, I get it. You're feeling uncertain about where we're headed, so you're looking for some reason to avoid endlessly wandering through the Wilderness. But this isn't the place for us."

Grant leaned over the table, massaging between his eyebrows with his forefinger. "Okay! I hear you. We need to get back on the road sooner rather than later."

"Maybe," said Dana. "But we may have a more pressing problem. Owen and Sister Aretha. When we hit the road again, Owen might not be joining us."

"I'll have a little talk with him," said Grant. "He'll have to make his own decision. Where are the kids, by the way?"

"Tadd's helping out in the kitchen, peeling rutabagas or something. Lissa's not feeling well. She's lying down in her room upstairs. Says she has an earache."

Dayton spoke up, getting back to the original subject. "Since we don't have a complete Bible, how do we know that Sister Aretha's healing methods aren't biblical? I mean, Prophet Nordwyn never talked about healing, but that doesn't mean anything."

"That's a good question, isn't it?" asked Grant. "We have no written standard to guide us, other than our Scripture *remnant* and passages we've memorized. Speaking for myself, I have to rely on intuition, what my parents taught me, and pray that God will give us some guidance."

A few yellow jackets had flown into the dining room, and were hovering about four feet over the table. Bryan had been watching them. Maybe they were interested in the sorghum juice dispensers that sat on the tables from breakfast. Or maybe they weren't yellow jackets at all. He slowly pulled a glove out of his back pocket and began to stand up, intending to swat at the insects. The yellow jackets immediately circled and exited a nearby window. No one else seemed to notice. Bryan put the glove back into his pocket and sat down, contemplating the open window with narrow eyes.

5.

That night was not a good one for Lissa and her parents. Hour by hour her earache escalated. Dana went down to the kitchen, boiled water, poured it on towels, carried them back upstairs and applied them to Lissa's ear. The process only lessened the pain temporarily. The aspirin they carried in their backpacks did little good. Sunrise found Lissa sleepless and moaning. Dana went downstairs and found Sister Aretha having breakfast with Owen.

"I hate to bother you," said Dana, "but our daughter seems to have a serious ear infection. She was up all night and she's in terrific pain. Is there anything you can do for her?"

"Lissa," said Aretha, closing her eyes and pressing her right index finger against her left thumb. "Yes. She is in great pain, and I can feel the cause," answered Aretha. She noticed Dana's look of surprise. "Oh, this? Applied telepathic kinesiology. I can diagnose people thousands of miles away. We'll assemble the PS right now and be up to see her in just a few minutes."

"Assemble the PS?" inquired Dana.

"Yes. The Prayer Stormtroopers—the healing team! But first of all, let me just ask, exactly what kind of bad food has Lissa been eating?"

"Bad food? None, as far as I know. Just whatever you've served here in the dining hall for the past couple of days. And before that, well, they had pretty decent food at Lastdays University. Then we were on the road a couple of days, with a stop in Alexandria. We had some kind of cheeseburgers there and I think bacon and eggs for breakfast. But nothing too horrible."

Aretha winced. "Oh, that right there is enough to let one in."

"One what?" asked Dana.

"One spirit of perversity, of course," said Aretha, looking at Dana as if everyone should know the dire metaphysical consequences of cheeseburgers. "When you start a better diet, they don't like it one bit. So they pull a stunt like this—kind of a *pain tantrum*. But don't worry. We are going to take care of it."

"Well, I'm sure whatever you do will be helpful," said Dana, hesitantly. "We'll be upstairs."

Lissa was laying on her back with a warm, moist towel held up to her ear, when Sister Aretha marched into the room, followed by five Prayer Stormtroopers and finally Edwin and Audrey. Grant and Tadd were there. Bryan, Dayton, Emilia, Sara and Dayton stood in the hall.

Sister Aretha was all business. She pressed her right

index finger and left thumb together again. Her eyes darted around the room, and finally froze on Lissa's backpack, tossed in a corner. "What's *this*?" Aretha demanded, pointing, as if she were reprimanding a dog who had just had an accident on the carpet.

Half poking out of the backpack was an open bag of Sneetos (a wildly popular snack food from the safe zones) made from synthesized starch and genetically modified animal protein.

"We don't allow that kind of thing here," said Aretha. "Take it away!" Audrey snatched up the backpack, pulled out the Sneetos bag and rifled through the pack to see if anything else was hiding there. She found two packs of Sugarslugs and a box of Chockozips. Audrey made a gagging noise and rushed out the door to properly dispose of the offending items in the incinerator.

The female Stormtrooper who seemed to be the herb specialist, lit a leather cone of herbs, waved them over the backpack and over Lissa.

Lissa coughed violently. "What…what are you doing? Can you fix my ear?"

"Just be patient," said Aretha. "We are calling upon God to heal your ear, but first we need to get rid of that nasty spirit of perversity you have. You *know* how it got in there, don't you?"

"Huh?" said Lissa, staring at Sister Aretha and the Prayer Stormtroopers, who were already beginning to mumble, chant and wave their amulets.

Aretha continued, "It got in there because you secretly ate unwholesome junk food! That's how it got in there. Now we have to get it out!"

Bryan and Sara rolled their eyes from the doorway. By contrast, Owen was watching Aretha like a high school boy with his first crush.

"Spirit of perversity?" asked Grant. "Really? Our daughter? I just don't think..."

"Mr. Cochrin, please," interrupted Aretha. "Just give us time to perform the ritual." She turned to Lissa. "I name you, Kurigalzu! I name you, Gandash! I call you by name and I command you in the name of Lord Dhanvantari and Lord Yeshua! Leave this house!"

Sara's mouth dropped open. From her studies and from conversations with Hindus at the Minot Work Camp, she recognized Dhanvantari as a Hindu deity—a four-armed avatar of Vishnu and the god of Ayurvedic medicine.

Dana and Grant were perplexed. They weren't sure who or what Dhanvantari was, but it didn't sound right.

"Leave this house! Leave this house! Leave this house!" chanted the Prayer Stormtroopers.

Lissa's eyes bulged in alarm. She tried to speak but no sound came out.

They began to dance and wave their amulets high and low. One of them pulled out a tambourine-like instrument and started shaking and thumping it with increasingly complex counterrhythms. The herb lady lit another batch of leaves and acrid smoke filled the room.

Dana wondered what was in the herbs, as her head was beginning to feel a bit funny. "How much longer will this take?" she yelled over the commotion, but Aretha ignored her, producing her horn-shaped container of oil and flinging the contents at Lissa.

"Hey! What's going on?" said Lissa. Aretha and the Stormtroopers continued their frenetic commanding, chanting and dancing with no change in Lissa's pain level. Amidst the cacophony, no one except Emilia noticed that Bryan had disappeared down the hall some time ago.

Finally, Aretha produced a small wooden box, decorated with jewels. She turned to Dana and Grant. "I've dealt with these two spirits before," she said. "They can be particularly stubborn. So it's time to deploy the one thing that strikes terror into their hearts."

"And what's that?" asked Grant.

Aretha untied a small thread that was holding the jeweled box together. Inside was a bug about three quarters of an inch long, with striking metallic green forewings. It was obviously alive, as its antennae were wiggling. "Behold," said Aretha dramatically, "the Holy Ghost cockroach!"

"Cool!" said Tadd, grinning.

Dana, Grant and Lissa reacted with horror. "What am I supposed to do with that?" asked Lissa.

"I will place it in your ear, and it will drive out the spirits of perversity."

"No! You're not sticking that thing in my ear!" screamed Lissa. "I'd rather have the pain!"

Grant stood up. "Okay. I'm sorry, Sister. I've got to draw the line here—should have drawn it a while ago. No bugs in my daughter's ear! And what's with Lord Dhanvantari? Why is he even in the same sentence with Jesus? Frankly, nothing you're doing here makes any sense to me. In light of what little bits of Scripture I know, and from what I know of science, it all seems like a bunch of superstition!"

Watching from the hallway, Sara mumbled, "Finally! Now you're talkin', bro!'"

Aretha turned to Grant. "Well, it's clear that…"

"We've tried to be open minded, but I'm sorry, I just can't buy into this stuff, and I…"

"Excuse me? You interrupted. I was saying it's clear that…"

Bryan burst into the room, pushing his way past the Stormtroopers, who stopped chanting. "This should do the trick," said Bryan. He offered Lissa a glass of water and two small, white pills.

"What's this?" Dana wanted to know.

"Thank God, I commandeered someone's motor scooter. There's sort of a pharmacy we passed on the way out here. Not like the ones in Boston or even at the work camp—but good enough, " Bryan explained. "I got some medications freshly smuggled from the Safe Zones—an antibiotic specifically for ear infections—and some decent pain killer for the discomfort. The infection should be over in about two hours."

"Anything except a cockroach," Dana said in relief.

"Thank you, Bryan," said Lissa, popping the pills in her mouth and gulping down the water.

Sister Aretha turned to Bryan, some ten inches from his face. "How dare you! Obstructing this holy ritual with drugs and doubt. It's clear to me that …"

"Please!" said Bryan. "Just shut up! Clear out and let the girl get some rest."

Sister Aretha and her entourage wordlessly turned and rushed out the door, their white uniforms rustling and a trail of smoke behind them. Owen stepped forward, towering over Bryan, who stepped back until he was against the wall. Owen grabbed Bryan's shirt, despite the Vikhr assault weapon hanging from his back. "You can't talk to her like that!"

Grant inserted his hands between the two men and pried them apart. "Guys, knock it off. I think we all agree this isn't the place for us. Except maybe Owen. We'll stay the night and be out of here in the morning."

Sister Aretha appeared in the doorway. "You'll do no such thing. As I tried to say several times, it's clear to me, as my mother used to quote from the book of Two Corinthians, that 'The person without the Spirit does not accept the things that come from the Spirit of

God but considers them foolishness, and cannot understand them because they are discerned only through the
Spirit.' You think this is foolishness because you're all
possessed by spirits of perversity! I can't allow you to
stay here any longer, lest you contaminate all of us with
your lack of faith and sedition. You have an hour to pack
up your things and leave this house!"

Owen looked at Aretha as if his heart had been
ripped apart.

"Owen, I'm so very sorry," said Aretha, "but you
must decide between your friends and God."

"But, Aretha..." said Owen. Aretha was hurrying
down the hall, in tears.

Bryan noticed, with increasing concern, that she
was followed by what looked like two small wasps.

6.

In a darkened room in Carthage, several figures sit in
comfortable chairs. On the other end of the room is a
control console staffed by three technicians. Several
live holographic images hover in front of them, as they
choose the best ones to transmit directly into the visual cortexes of the small audience. The images show the
room in La Crosse where the dramatic confrontation
has just taken place between the Cochrin party and
Sister Aretha. Technicians zoom in on Owen and then
pan over to follow Sister Aretha down the hall, with full
audio. For the audience, it is as if they are there, floating above the action.

"This is impressive," says a deep voice from one of
the seated figures. "Such a cacophony of religious confusion in the Wilderness—even within Christendom!"

"To be expected, Excellency," says another voice.
"There is no standard, no authority."

"How true," says the first voice. "Yet this little group is learning how to navigate their way through the foolishness."

"Indeed, Excellency," says yet another voice. "I haven't seen anything quite so dramatic since that Palestinian Senator skunked the Israeli Senator at a game of five-card ziti."

All the men in the chairs laugh. The second voice comments, "For sheer drama, I would say this scene rivals the close call with the truck and the raptors."

"True," says the first voice. "You know, Sara and Bryan know something of religious history and history in general—even beyond the party line. They are good critical thinkers. They are pragmatic and they take charge. Grant and Dana, however, are somewhat on the idealistic, naïve side."

"Mmmhmm. Like lambs at a hyena convention."

More laughter.

"And yet," says the first voice, "I have a certain confidence in them—perhaps *because* they are idealistic. Their faith leads them—compels them—in their quest. I believe we will see them blossom into capable leaders as the days and weeks go by. Until tomorrow then. Let my secretaries know of any significant developments. And as usual, not a word of this to anyone."

"The kingdom of God never comes by watching for it. Men cannot say, 'Look, here it is,' or 'there it is,' for the kingdom of God is inside you."
—*Jesus Christ (Luke 17:20-21, J.B. Phillips New Testament)*

PART V: THE RIVER

1.

The team beat a hasty exit out the front door of the old lodge with no goodbyes whatsoever. Sister Aretha watched them from her second-story window as they trudged down the gravel driveway. In spite of what Owen's friends thought, she had hoped he would decide to stay and work alongside her. Actually, they both hoped for that, but when push came to shove, they couldn't compromise their beliefs, Owen included.

Following Bryan's watch-map, they headed back into LaCrosse and turned south until they were following Route 35 with the Mississippi to their right. Nordwyn had said there were more Christian groups in that direction, so that seemed like the best bet.

Grant was at a low point. After two failed possibilities, the team had no clear destination. No one else would say it, but they were as disoriented and discouraged as Grant—and he was feeling those vibes. His confidence in his own leadership was rapidly evaporating. Maybe he never wanted to be a leader anyway. Maybe he just wanted his family and friends to join him on his quest. And maybe he was discovering that they needed something under these conditions he couldn't quite provide. It seemed to him that effective leaders have something driving them, something they employ to motivate others.

In Grant's case, that something was his faith. And now he was wondering if God had anything specific in mind for them, or if they were just on their own. Yes, this was a crisis of faith.

On the other hand, thought Grant, *what we're looking for could be just around the bend. We're free. We're walking down the road. All we have to do is find what God has for us and recognize it when it appears. It doesn't sound so hard when you say it like that.*

The day was oppressively hot and humid, and the team decided to take a break under the cover of a grove of trees. Bryan and Emilia sat on a rock a few yards away from the others and shared a lunch of amaranth bread and a raw parsnip—provisions that Sister Aretha had authorized in spite of that morning's terrible scene. The nutritional content was indisputable, but the flavor was something else entirely. As Bryan and Emilia choked down their lunch, they noticed a couple of wasps buzzing around them.

"Wasps everywhere," whispered Bryan.

"So?" said Emilia. "It's early summer. That's to be expected."

"Not like these," said Bryan. "Haven't you noticed how they follow us, hover and circle? No—I think they're something else."

"Aren't you getting a little paranoid? They're wasps. Just wasps."

"Watch, you'll see."

He picked up a dead branch laying on the ground, slowly raised it to his lap and waited for the wasps to fly closer. He swung and connected. One wasp fell to the ground, twitched and was still.

He picked up the mangled insect and held it in the palm of his hand. "Uh-huh. Take a closer look." The abdomen of the insect was split to reveal a miniature maze of wire and metal, with tiny flashing lights.

Emilia gasped. "Oh my gosh! What does it mean?"

"It means someone is watching us now, and I suspect has been for a while," said Bryan. "This is a drone—exactly the kind of thing my family's company was working on when they booted me out of the picture. If I had a magnifier, we could read 'Hantwick Industries' right across the thorax. I think I can see it with my naked eye there between the wings."

The other wasp was still hovering. Bryan addressed it in a low voice, and the wasp moved in about a foot from his face. "Hi, guys. Hope you've enjoyed the show these past few—however long you've been watching. Excellent technology, even if I do say so myself. I'm assuming you're Feds, unless somebody else out here has this stuff, which is unlikely."

The insect continued to hover in front of Bryan, as Emilia gawked in amazement.

"Anyway," continued Bryan, "I don't know what your game is, but I tell you what. Emilia and I won't breathe a word of this to our friends. So you can just keep watching. If you were going to zapp us, you would have done it by now. Frankly, I feel safer with you watching us than I do with raptors or the religious nuts we've visited so far. That's all I've got to say."

The wasp hovered for about 15 more seconds, then turned and flew over to the rest of the group.

2.

In a darkened room in Carthage, the technicians and

145

observers sat in stunned silence. Finally a voice asked, "*Now* what do we do?"

"Take him at his word," another answered. "Bryan is brilliant—probably a genius. It is a shame he ended up in a work camp. We knew he would notice the drones sooner or later anyway. But this is good. He's telling us he's not going to blow our cover, as it were. We just keep watching. I think his Excellency will agree."

3.

The team continued down the east bank of the Mississippi the next day. This part of the shore seemed sparsely settled. They passed two motorcycle gangs that looked like raptors headed north. One gang paid no attention. The other stopped and asked where the group was headed.

"We're looking for a community of Christ-followers where we can settle down," answered Grant, forthrightly. "Have you heard of anything like that?"

The apparent leader of the gang, sporting a massive beard, three two-foot pigtails and wearing a long, fringed buckskin jacket, snorted, "Christ-followers? Dunno for sure, but I hear there's some really psycho groups further to the south, if that's your thing. All kinds of other people too. You'll probably run into some kind of Buddhists or Muslims or somethin'. We try to avoid such religious folk, as you can well understand."

"Why?" asked Tadd.

"Tadd!" scolded Dana in a strong whisper. "Don't talk to him!"

"It's okay, lady. The kid asks a good question. Some o' them Christians and religious people in general can be damn vengeful if you cross 'em—no pun intended. Other gangs like us tend to be a tad more violent than us, and I guess we all get stuffed into the same bowl. So we just try to ride clear o' them traditional God-fearin' dudes and mind our own business."

"Oh," said Tadd.

"By the way," said the leader, "We got an extra can o' ham here that we recently acquired as part of a business transaction, if you can use it. Hell, even if you *can't* use it. Heads up!" The leader volleyed a large can toward Tadd, who caught it, taking two steps backward to keep his balance. "We'll leave you to it. Take care, and keep your finger on the trigger of that weapon there, y'hear?" said the leader, grinning at Bryan. The gang roared off to the north.

"Thank you! God bless!" shouted Grant, although the gang was well down the road. When they finally camped that night, the team ate with gusto, in contrast to the healthful but challenging fare Aretha had provided.

Circumstances had not changed but Grant was feeling better, and so was most of the rest of the group. Unexpectedly friendly treatment from a raptor gang? An unexpected gift of tasty food? Little things could be a great encouragement, but Grant wondered what was next, and if his team was ready to respond to the challenge. And if *he* was ready to respond to the challenge.

Owen sat alone on a log, staring out at the river, clearly hurting from their sudden departure and the loss of Aretha. Grant walked over, sat down and handed him a cup of thinly brewed coffee. "Owen, I'm sorry it didn't work out. I'll spare you the 'it'll be fine and you'll get over it' line."

"It's okay," said Owen, holding his cup but not drinking. "I shoulda kept my head. She just seemed so...well, doesn't matter now. I'll be ready to keep goin' in the morning. You did the right thing back there and you're doin' the best you can."

Grant spent a while staring at the river with Owen, then went back to the camp and slept.

The next morning, as they followed the river, they noticed a vessel that Owen identified as a motorized deck barge anchored in an inlet. It was a small barge, not much more than a hundred and fifty feet long, with the bridge located in the stern. The front deck was scattered with cargo containers of all sizes and shapes.

Grant considered: Supplies were running low. Walking on the roads was dangerous. Which way was the barge traveling? Could they hitch a ride? More to the point—who was running the barge and could they be trusted?

Grant stood on the shore with Owen, Bryan and Dayton. Tadd was busy trying to stab fish with a stick. The women stayed back several paces—swimming through muddy water didn't seem to be something they were interested in at this point in time.

"Well, I can swim out there with no problem," said Owen, "but why don't we just try the obvious first?"

Owen began to jump and shout. The others joined in. Almost immediately a figure appeared on the bridge. He was wearing the traditional Afghan headgear that Sara and Bryan recognized as a *pakol*. "I'll come to you!" he shouted. In a few minutes a small dingy was on its way across the water, with two men wearing pakols. The first man stepped out on the marshy shore, with a broad grin on his face, briefly stopping to disentangle himself from a rope that had attached itself to his foot. "Dang ropes," he mumbled.

"Here, Captain," said the other man in the boat. "Let me help you with that."

"A moment, please," said the grinning captain, finally becoming free of the rope. "I'm Muhammad Lanning, Captain of that old tub. Her name is the *Baraq*, which means 'blessed.' We're anchored here to make some minor repairs, as we do frequently. She's held together with duct tape and bailing wire, but she gets us where we're going. What can I do for you?"

"We're headed south and we wondered if we could hitch a ride," said Grant. "We have work camp scrip— and we also have a great mechanic and an expert in electronics."

"How far south are you going?" asked Captain Lanning.

"We're not sure. We're Christ-followers looking for a community where we can settle down. We've come a long way."

"Christians? Uh…I don't know. We're mostly Muslims, except for a couple of Buddhists—and we don't want any trouble."

"I agree," said Grant. "No trouble at all. Wait. What do you mean?"

"Well…Christians are a bit strange and some are downright disagreeable. They get all upset and nervous when we pray. Try to tell us we shouldn't pray that way. Want to argue about the Trinity or some such. And you should see how they try to pick fights with the Buddhists. I guess mainly they just don't like people who don't believe like they do. And sometimes they're just odd—they talk funny—it just freaks me out."

"That's awful," said Grant. "I apologize. I don't understand why some of us who call ourselves followers of Christ do those kinds of things. But I think you'll find our team is different. If you'll take us on, you have my word we'll pitch in with any work you need. And we certainly don't have a problem with you praying."

Captain Lanning stared at Grant for a moment. "Okay. Okay. I guess we'll try it. As far as Clinton, Iowa. That's just about a day away, unless we have other problems. And if it works out, then maybe all the way to Hannibal, Missouri, Allah willing. That's where we turn around and head back upstream. So, all the way to Hannibal for…mmm, you got nine people, 2,400 a piece, that's 21,600 dinar, in addition to a few chores, for the lot of you. Payable at the end of the trip."

"We can do that," answered Grant, and they shook on it.

It took three dinghy trips to ferry the team and their backpacks over to the Baraq. Accommodations in the cabin were taken up by the crew, so the team had to make do between the cargo containers stacked and tied down on the deck. They got busy creating shelters from a few spare tarps and ropes.

It wasn't long before Owen was in the engine room and Bryan and Dayton were on the bridge. Owen found the ship's engineer and his assistant reinstalling an alternator on which they had replaced a part. "I think we're just about ready to roll," said the engineer. "Let's start 'er up and see what happens."

He flipped a couple of toggle switches and pressed a large, greasy red button. A starter motor wailed painfully, the diesel turned over a few times and clattered into action. The engineer glanced at the gauges. "Ha! We did it again!" He pressed another small, greasy button on the intercom. "We're good to go, Captain."

On the bridge, the captain pulled down a microphone from the ceiling. He fought with the cord for a few seconds, which had become entangled around his hand. "Dang wires," he mumbled. Finally, he gave the order through a scratchy speaker to haul anchor. A man wearing a pakol near the bow of the boat pushed yet another well-worn button that started a winch. After a couple of minutes the anchor clanked into position. Captain Lanning engaged the screws and pushed the throttle. The Baraq began to creep forward.

None of the Cochrin team, save three, had ever experienced anything like this. Owen had worked on construction barges on Fort Peck Lake. Bryan had been on a couple of cruises, including the Nile River, and Sara had been on a small craft on Boston's Charles River. But a commercial barge on the Mississippi in the Wilderness—this was the real deal.

Sara was excited at the prospect of living in an Islamic culture for a few days. Sure, there had been a few Muslims at the camp, but they mostly kept to themselves. Other than that, Sara had taught about Islam, but had never really had a chance to talk and live with devout Muslims like these.

Tadd and Lissa were way beyond excited. It even seemed to Dana that Lissa was shedding some of her annoying teen obstinacy and regressing to the wonder and curiosity of late childhood. Lissa had even stowed her iCap and was happily hanging out with her brother on the prow of the barge.

As the old vessel moved out into the center of the river and approached its running speed of about 9 mph, Captain Lanning explained his challenges to Bryan and Dayton.

"Upstream this far, the river isn't dredged regularly, and the channel markers aren't maintained very well. The people who use the river sorta have to do it themselves. That means you can't have too much of a draft, or you'll get stuck for sure. South of St. Louis, of course, the river is kept in tip-top condition, with all the best navigation aids. Big barges goin' up and down the river all the time haulin' grain and coal and ore."

"Let's see," said Bryan, "would that be because it's in a safe corridor?"

"You got it," said the captain. "They got these big red warning lights on the river as you near St. Louis. Then if you go beyond that without authorization, they got a gauntlet of mega zappers that'll shoot you full of holes like Swiss cheese gone bad. And we're not authorized. Some say they got these huge, hovering machines that'll pick whatever's left of your ship right out of the river and use it for scrap metal."

"So I've heard," said Bryan. "With no one in charge, how do you guys decide about navigation protocols and how much it should cost you to dock at a port and so forth?"

"It's like anything else out here," said the captain, repeatedly poking a button on the navigation system that didn't want to respond, "Power in numbers. The ships that sail the river are members of the Shipping Guild. You pay your dues, you get to sail. You don't, something happens to your boat—or you. The ports are controlled by whatever gang or politicos are running the towns. Let's just say the Shipping Guild sends their boys in occasionally to make sure everyone cooperates, if you know what I mean. It might be a corrupt system, but it's better than none at all."

"Mmm-hmm," said Bryan. "I think I know what you mean. And I see you have an adequate navigation system—GPS, radar, echosounder and lasers. Screen imaging but no holographs."

"Oh yeah. It's a few years old but it gets us where we're going. At least we know where we are, and we can usually dodge the sandbars and all the junk in the river."

"Does that mean you run at night?" asked Dayton.

"Sure does. The quicker we turn this cargo around

the quicker we get paid, and..." Suddenly an alarm went off. The captain glanced at his clock. "Oops! Time to pray. Wanna take the helm for a few minutes?"

"Well, actually I..." stammered Bryan.

But it was too late. The first mate and the captain had deployed some ancient-looking rugs and were flat on the floor chanting something in what seemed to Bryan to be bad Arabic. Bryan held the wheel and squinted intently at the river while Dayton monitored the sonar. "I totally have no idea what I'm doing," said Bryan.

"I...I think the river is getting shallower here," said Dayton, peering at the navigation screen. "It's hard to tell with the way these colors are configured—but I think it's a *lot* shallower!"

The captain's and first mate's chanting continued.

"Great!" said Bryan. "Just tell me which way to turn."

"I don't know. Right, I think."

Bryan spun the wheel abruptly clockwise and the bow began to swing starboard.

"Shouldn't we reverse the engine or something?" asked Dayton.

Bryan pulled the throttle back and the tone of the engine dropped.

"What's going on up there?" Grant called from the deck. "The crew down here seems to have taken a sudden prayer break."

"It's all under control!" shouted Bryan.

"Alrighty then!" interrupted Captain Muhammad, hopping up from his prayer rug and grabbing the helm and throttle, "I'll take 'er from here. This little bend in the river gets kinda dicey."

"What do you do when there's no one on the bridge to take the helm?" asked Dayton, perspiring.

"Oh, usually one of the Buddhists takes over. Or if they're busy we just let 'er drift a bit," said the captain. "Usually turns out okay. Allah looks out for us if we say our prayers on time. Allah, the exalted, tells us, 'Woe unto the worshippers who are heedless of their prayers.'"

"Can't you make up for prayers later or say them earlier?" asked Dayton.

"I suppose some Muslims do," said Captain Lanning, "but Allah, blessed be his name, doesn't like it. No sir. Doesn't like it one bit. No excuse, no emergency too big. Allah makes the sun rise and set on time every day. The least we can do is pray on schedule. Five prayers a day at the exact time, facing the Ka'aba in Mecca. That's what we do here, with the exception of those two guys." Captain Lanning pointed toward the deck, where two figures sat cross-legged atop a cargo container.

"Who are they?" asked Bryan.

"Karl and Bart, our two Buddhist crew members. They do that thing a couple of times every day—mindfulness meditation they call it. Kinda like prayer, but not really, as far as I'm concerned. But whatever, they're good men. Hard workers and honest. So we all live together in peace."

4.

For a day the team enjoyed the relative security of floating downstream. No worries about raptors. No worn out shoes. Just the peace of flowing water and passing trees, with an occasional small settlement on the shore or overgrown ruins of an abandoned town. But that evening, about twilight, they were jolted by a sudden, jarring turn of the ship. Three containers on the deck near the bow shifted, scattering the team's belongings. The Baraq was listing slightly to port, with the bow noticeably elevated. The team looked up to see a commotion on the bridge. Bryan and Dayton ran up the stairs. "What's the problem?" asked Bryan.

"Our navigation system crashed," said the captain, "and we've run aground on a sandbar. To make matters worse, when the ship lurched onto the sandbar, I tripped over the navigation system cable and I think it snapped. Bart and Karl are going under the ship to see how bad the situation is. If they can get the screws and rudders free, we can back 'er off, with a bit of fancy bow and stern thruster work. But right now the current is working against us—pushing us into the bar."

"Isn't it dangerous to go under the ship in these conditions?" asked Bryan.

"Says the guy who carries a Vikhr," snarked the captain. "Of course it's dangerous. But it's part of the deal out here. Bart and Karl do this kind of stuff all the time."

"In the meantime, Dayton and I will tackle the navigation system," said Bryan. In a few minutes Emilia joined them on the bridge to offer assistance (but mainly to be near Bryan).

Karl and Bart were experienced divers. It was their job to handle anything below the waterline, including repairs to the screws, rudders and hull from frequent scrapes and collisions with river debris—all in a day's work for them. They emerged from their quarters in full gear: wetsuits, aqualungs, toolbelts and masks equipped with lights, although visibility would be limited in the muddy water. With tethers attached, they jumped off the transom and splashed into the dark water.

The team tried to stay out of the crew's way, but that didn't stop them from hanging over the transom. Grant and Owen were intently interested, as Owen once had similar duties working on the oil rigs on Fort Peck Lake. For a few minutes, only bubbles and a glow of flashlights emanated from under the craft. Then Karl broke the surface.

"It's bad, but not impossible. The screws and rudders are buried in sand and they're tangled in some kind of cable and metal debris. It'll take us a little while to dig 'em out." The crew quickly set up floodlights on the transom and deployed a small dredge pump, dropping a four-inch duct into the water.

Twenty minutes went by. The pump whirred and the duct pulsated with sand and water that gushed out of another hose on the port side of the ship. The sky was growing darker by the minute, and Captain Lanning prayed to Allah that any traffic coming downstream behind them had functional navigation and night imaging.

Tadd noticed that the tethers, which had been relatively slack, were pulled tighter than a sumo wrestler's cord. Across the deck, Lissa had been watching the sand gush out of the other end of the dredge pump duct. Suddenly she noticed that murky water had replaced the flow of sand.

She ran across the deck to her brother. "Tadd! I thought mud and sand were supposed to be coming out the other duct, but it's just water."

Tadd thought for a second and grabbed the Captain's sleeve. "Captain!"

"Kid, can't you see we're working? Why don't you…"

"Your dredge pump isn't working right, and look—the tethers are pulled tight. Something's wrong down there!"

"Huh? I didn't see that!"

At that moment one of the tethers went slack again. A crew member yanked on it. There was no resistance, and the end popped out of the water, revealing a clean slice. The crew stared. They also noticed approaching lights about a half mile upstream. Some vessel, at least their size or larger, was bearing down on the disabled Baraq.

An alarm sounded, and a crew member called out, "Maghrib prayer time!" Without a word, a crewman produced rugs from a nearby cabinet and the captain and entire crew fell to the deck and began chanting in Arabic.

The Cochrin team was aghast. Meanwhile, Karl and Bart were clearly in some unknown predicament. Grant and Owen looked at each other for a second, stripped off their shirts, and jumped into the river, but not before Owen instinctively grabbed a coil of rope and secured one end to an eyelet on the transom.

Under the stern of the Baraq, Owen tried to assess the situation through murky water. Karl and Bart were nowhere to be seen. They had successfully dredged away much of the sand from both screws and rudders, and apparently had been trying to move some sharp metal debris which had left a long scrape on the hull. One tether was tangled around the metal and stretched away toward the bow, where there was a glow of flash-lights.

Owen worked his way along the tether, and found Karl desperately holding on to Bart with one hand. He had been pushed by the current along the keel about ten feet toward the bow, and was up to his chest in what was apparently quicksand.

Meanwhile, Grant was holding the rope with one hand to keep the current from sweeping him under the ship, while trying to unwrap Karl's still-intact tether from the metal debris. With a breath limit of about 30 seconds, Grant couldn't get much done. He had to pull himself back up the rope and surface. Owen, who could hold his breath for a good two minutes, tied his rope around Bart. He hoped it would keep Bart from being sucked further into the sand. He motioned to borrow a breath or two from Karl's aqualung, and Karl complied.

Up on the deck, Dana, Sara, Tadd and Lissa watched anxiously over the transom. They had seen Grant surface for a few seconds to gulp air and go back under. The ship heading downstream was only about fifty yards behind them now and looked like it was going to pass them narrowly—if at all.

On the bridge, Bryan, Dayton and Emilia were feverishly trying to reboot the navigation system.

Yet the crew continued with their prayers, oblivious to what was happening around them.

"This is insane," said Sara to Dana. "Is there nothing we can do?"

"I guess we could pray ourselves," said Dana.

The big barge that had been coming up behind them was now slipping by their port side—so close that Dana and Sara could see the faces of the crew illuminated by the displays in the darkened bridge. Sara even thought she saw their mouths drop open as they saw the crew of the Baraq laying prostrate on their prayer rugs.

Then the wake of the passing vessel hit the Baraq. The port side rose and then fell. As it fell, the vessel slid to port some five feet, and everyone felt the ship begin a slow clockwise spin, as the current caught the stern.

The captain and crew got up quickly from their prayers. "Get those men aboard!" shouted the captain. "We've got to get control of this tub!"

"Hold on!" said Sara. "They're in trouble down there. We can't move now."

"Lady, we're movin' whether we like it or not! Abdul! Kareem! Haul that line!"

Two burley crew members grabbed Owen's rope and pulled like their lives depended on it.

Under the ship, things were chaotic. The hull had risen, fallen and shifted above them. Now Karl's tether had been severed by the debris. Bart had disappeared entirely into the sand, yet Owen's rope was securely tied around him. In fact, now the only salvation of all four men was Owen's rope. Suddenly they felt the rope tug from above, and took courage. Someone was hauling them in.

Above, Sara, Dana and the kids, not knowing what else to do, fell in behind Abdul and Kareem, pulling the rope. Below, Owen looked over his shoulder to see Bart's head emerge from the sand. The rope was rubbing against the sharp metal debris, and Grant, still wearing shoes, tried to push against the twisted metal with his feet while holding the rope away with his hands. But again, he needed air. He surfaced, gasping, and shouted, "Keep pulling! We've got Bart stuck in quicksand!"

Captain Lanning was on the bridge, and had already engaged the stern thrusters to slow the ship's pivot to port, but they were little match for the river's current. The second the men were out of the water he would engage the screws full astern.

Now Bart was free of the quicksand, but there was another problem. The ship's sideways drift had caused the rope to drag heavily over the metal debris, despite Grant's efforts.

Bits of fiber and strands of rope were being scraped off. Would the rope hold? The men were pulled into the metal shards, as they desperately pushed away with their feet. Finally they were clear.

When the men surfaced below the transom, a cheer went up.

"Alhamdulillah!" shouted the crew. "Praise Jesus!" shouted the Cochrin team. "Dharmakaya!" shouted Karl and Bart.

Captain Lanning pulled the throttle into full reverse and the engine roared. He gave three sharp blasts of the ship's horn to indicate that the Baraq was moving astern. At the same time he engaged the starboard bow thruster.

The ship slowly responded, moving backward with the bow turning to port. Everyone heard a scraping noise as the ship moved over the debris, and off the sandbar—then they felt the ship rock and level out. The Baraq was back in the channel again.

Bryan, Dayton and Emilia had tried to boot the navigation system twice without success. They finally determined that a bad connection had caused the software problem. They were frantically trying to correct the software, while the ship's electrician soldered the bad connection and repaired the cable the Captain had tripped over.

Right now, the Baraq was navigating blind, except for a few unreliable navigation lights on the shore and the distant lights of the ship that had just passed them. In the meantime, Captain Lanning ordered soundings to be taken the millennia-old way—by lead and line, with one man port and the other starboard. Ironically, they informed the Captain of each sounding using tiny communicator implants near their ears.

Finally, the navigation screen flashed back into life. Bryan, Dayton and Emilia had not only had succeeded, but also removed a couple of ongoing glitches. Bryan had tweaked an algorithm to enhance the colors and show greater definition of depth. Captain Lanning was delighted. The river and all its underwater features appeared on the screen. The ship was back in business.

5.

The next morning, it was evident that the crew had lost any skepticism they had about the Cochrin team. Karl and Bart brought a tray full of breakfast goodies out on the deck to share with the team. They took Owen and Grant aside.

"What you did was way above and beyond the call of duty," said Bart.

"Yeah," said Karl. "When you're down there you never know when things are going to go wrong. You think it's all good and then it happens real quick. The currents in those sand bars are unpredictable to begin with and then under the ship—it's anyone's guess."

"Well," said Grant, "I guess we couldn't do much else, since the rest of the crew was busy."

"Yeah, that scheduled prayer thing takes a little getting used to," said Bart. "Listen, we've got something we want you to have. We came by it in Clinton. We were in this bar and..."

"We don't drink," interrupted Karl. "Well, maybe a little sometimes, but the bar was kind of the center of town where people meet to do business, you know? So we were just hangin' out there."

"There were these two guys," continued Bart, "sitting at a table, and they had these two old books they were showing each other. Both books were pretty tattered, but it looked like one of the guys really wanted this—King Jacob's Virgin, I think he called it."

"King James Version," corrected Karl.

Grant's head jerked back and his eyes opened wide. Owen whispered, "Wow!"

161

"Whatever," continued Bart. "Anyway they were negotiating and finally arrived at a price."

"How much?" asked Grant.

"Oh, I think they settled on about three hundred thousand dinar."

"Incredible!" whispered Owen.

"Anyway," continued Bart, "after their transaction was complete, I heard the guy who bought the King James Version say something like, 'At last! The original Bible used by the apostles—the only one authorized by King James—one of the Three Kings who visited Jesus in the manger!'" Then he kinda waved his old Bible around and said, 'This one is fulla errors. Piece o' junk. Might as well throw it away. Does anyone here want an old NIV Bible?'"

"We looked at each other," said Karl, "and we were thinkin' the same thing. If we find the right buyer down the road somewhere, we can clean up. So we spoke up, he handed it to us, and we've had it ever since. But we haven't run into anyone who wants to pay the price."

"Well," said Grant, clearing his throat, "we're definitely interested, but I'm afraid we don't have the financial…"

"No, that's not what we're saying," said Karl. "You already paid the price when you risked your lives to save us. We want you guys to have it." Bart produced a small package wrapped in plastic and tied up with twine. He held it out to Grant and Owen, who were stunned.

"I don't think we can do that," said Grant. "We just did what we did—didn't give it any thought."

"No, no, no, no! You did it because of who you *are*. You love your fellow human beings," said Bart. "And that comes from some higher source. We may differ as to the nature of that source, but we must acknowledge it.

And the way we have chosen to acknowledge it is to give you this, your sacred text."

"I...I don't know what to say," said Grant, taking the package. Hyperventilating a little, he sat down on a crate and carefully untied the twine. Sara had noticed something happening and was approaching. Grant handed the package to Owen, who carefully lifted the plastic wrap, and then an inner wrapping of thick white paper. Inside was a thick book bound in tattered black leather. Owen gently opened it, and it fell to the copyright page. Grant's eyes fell on the line: *Text: New International Version, Copyright 2059, International Bible Society.*

By now Sara was looking over Grant's shoulder. Dana was headed across the deck, as were Dayton, Bryan and Emilia.

"This is simply unbelievable," said Sara. "Just three years before the Final War."

Grant looked at Bart quizzically. "You say that the buyer of the King James Version thought this was worthless? I don't understand."

"Fascinating," said Sara. "I believe I can shed some light on his statement. As I recall, there was a belief among certain fundamentalist groups that the King James translation of 1611 was somehow more accurate or 'holy' than the newer translations, such as the NIV. In fact the opposite is true, as the more recent translations incorporated ancient manuscripts, discoveries in archaeology and advances in linguistics. Many of these fundamentalist groups, sadly, were anti-intellectual, and feared the newer translations (especially the NIV) were part of a liberal conspiracy. Apparently that idea is still extant out here."

"Okay. If you say so. I guess that explains the buyer's actions," said Grant.

Owen slowly turned the pages. They were worn, and portions didn't fit into the binding evenly. On closer inspection, it seemed that chunks of pages had been re-glued into the binding, in fact, all the pages seemed this way. *Who knows what kind of a story is behind this?* thought Grant.

Curious, Grant turned to the gospels. He had some knowledge of the order of Scripture, but this was certainly the first time he had ever turned to a passage in a Bible. There was so much to see. So many books and chapters. Finally he arrived at Matthew 5. He stared. Half the page was missing. It had been torn. The others hadn't recognized what they were looking at, with the exception of Dana, who gasped.

"Can you...?" asked Grant, looking up at Dana with wide, hopeful eyes.

"Yes. I'll be right back," said Dana, already running down an aisle between containers to their makeshift quarters.

"What's going on?" asked Bart, looking back and forth between Dana and the Bible.

"I'm not sure, but I think we may have a surreal coincidence here, or something else."

"Oh my gosh!" said Sara, as the reality dawned on her. Bryan, Dayton and Owen were frowning, trying to figure out what was happening.

Dana came running back, with Lissa, Tadd and the leather pouch containing the *remnant*—the torn half page that his father had given him. He opened the pouch and carefully removed the fragile paper, holding it delicately between his thumb and forefinger. The page was browned at the edges and looked like it might turn to dust in a strong gust of wind.

Slowly, he lined the page up against the torn section in the Bible. Everyone gasped. It was a perfect match. Grant carefully flipped to the title page in the front of the Bible, which he had skipped over a few minutes earlier. There, in faded pencil, was his grandmother's name—*Joyce Cochrin*.

6.

Bryan sat on a barrel on the other side of the ship, away from the others. A wasp hovered in front of his face, and another hovered a few feet away. He addressed the wasp in a voice just above a whisper. "What kind of game are you guys playing here? What just happened is next to impossible—someone set it up, and of course that had to be you, whoever you are. What I want to know is why are you messing with our heads like this? If you're the Feds, why don't you just come swooping in with your big warships and arrest us all, or just kill us? You know we escaped from a work camp. Why do you need to frame us with possession of a Bible? And why *this* Bible?"

There was, of course, no answer from the wasp, which continued to hover several inches from Bryan's face.

"Okay," Bryan sighed. "I suppose you've got a whole lot of time on your hands. And this is how you amuse yourselves. Playing around with people before you bust 'em. Fine. But I don't imagine his excellency would be too happy if he knew how you were wasting your big Fed salaries. Just think about that." He shook his head, as if shaking away the issue. "And don't worry. I won't blow your cover. Not yet anyway."

7.

Far away in a darkened room, His Excellency, President Mehdi Kazdaghli watches Bryan's face fill the holographic field. The room is silent as Bryan finishes his rant. "What exactly is going on here?" Mehdi asks, slowly turning his chair to face his staff. "Which of you did this without my authorization? And why?"

"Excellency," responds Security Director Aymen Jugurtha, "I assure you that none of us here knew anything about this. We are as dumbfounded as you. It is simply incredible, unless some other interest is at work—perhaps one of the gangs who controls the river or the Wilderness…"

"Sir," another voice interrupts, "we surveill those groups regularly and there has been no indication that they are paying any attention to the Cochrin group, much less orchestrating something like this."

"What about this Karl and Bart? What do we know about them?" Mehdi asks.

"We investigated them last night, Excellency. They are who they say they are. Devout Zen Buddhists, good friends, trying to earn enough money to settle down and raise families someday. We checked the captain and the rest of the crew, too. All clean. Except the cook, who was once a raptor assassin. Poisoned his victims. But since he became a Muslim he has been clean."

"Go back to the scene of the Bible," orders Mehdi.

An image of the open Bible hovers in the middle of the room. A hand moves a torn page into the scene, fitting it perfectly to the page in the Bible.

"Stop there!" orders Mehdi. "This is humanly impossible. Someone would have had to steal the torn page they call the *remnant*, find an old NIV Bible of the same edition as the *remnant* page, tear the page in the Bible to match it precisely and reproduce Joyce Cochrin's signature exactly. It would take a team of researchers, technicians, conservationists and specialists to pull this off—and for no discernible reason."

"Yes, Excellency."

Mehdi ponders for a few seconds then says: "I believe it was the English novelist Sir Arthur Conan Doyle who wrote: 'When you have eliminated all which is impossible, then whatever remains, however improbable, must be the truth.'"

"Not entirely airtight from a logician's perspective, Excellency, but a practical rule of thumb in our business."

Mehdi looks at his security director with exasperation. "You are nothing if not pragmatic, Aymen. But my point is, ladies and gentlemen—*if* we have eliminated *both* the impossible and the humanly possible, then the *truth* is—what we have here is a blatant, fantastic *sign*!"

8.

"Allah has been merciful to us," commented Captain Lanning to his first mate, Youssef. The captain scraped his shoe on the floor, trying to shed a piece of duct tape that had become attached to his sole. "Dang tape," he muttered. "It seems like he sent these folks knowing we would need them exactly when we did."

The first mate was watching through binoculars as one of the Christian passengers appeared to be talking to something unseen on the starboard deck. "Of course, if Allah had been paying attention, he could have prevented our navigation system failure in the first place, and then we wouldn't have needed anyone's help."

Captain Lanning cast a jaundiced eye toward Youssef. "You'd best be careful. You're barkin' up the wrong tree if you question how Allah works. We just accept his will. Maybe he brought these passengers here to show us something important—maybe he wants us to see that not all Christians are half-wits. Or maybe he wants *them* to learn something about *us*."

"Well, case in point," said Youssef, still looking through the binoculars. "It appears that one of your Christian friends, Bryan I believe, is having an animated conversation with a flying insect. Which is troubling, considering he's toting an assault rifle."

"What? Let me see," said Captain Lanning, grabbing the binoculars. "Hmm. You're wrong. He's just praying. That's the way these Christians do it, you know—they just talk to God anywhere at any time. They don't know any better. But on the other hand, there's something comforting about that."

"Whatever you say, Captain," said Youssef, "but *you'd* best be careful."

"You heard about that old Bible the Buddhists gave 'em," said Captain Lanning, "how it matched exactly with that torn page Grant inherited from his grandparents. Some might call it a miracle."

"Oh, I don't know. Coincidences happen all the time."

"Whatever you say, Youssef," said the Captain, echoing Youssef's sardonic line. "But I think we'd best afford our guests some respect, or risk disrespecting the works of Allah, blessed be his name. The Koran tells us '…whoever rejects evil and believes in God has grasped the most trustworthy hand-hold that never breaks. And God is all-hearing and all-knowing.'"

"Indeed," said Youssef, continuing to watch Bryan through his binoculars.

On the deck, between chores, the Cochrins and the team were poring over their new acquisition. It held surprises on nearly every page, as they discovered inaccuracies in their memorized passages.

The first verse of the torn *remnant* page had read

...for they will be shown mercy. They had often wondered *who* will be shown mercy. Now Grant and the team saw that the *merciful* will be shown mercy. They saw that instead of metaphorically hiding their lamps under a bowl, Christ-followers should put them on a stand, giving light to everyone.

Likewise the team learned how Jesus condemned capricious divorce, and how God's mercy and generosity extends to both evil and good people, the just and the unjust. The team learned the fifth chapter of Matthew, the source of their *remnant* page, was similar but not identical to a passage in the book of Luke. They wondered why the four gospel books didn't all say exactly the same thing—and why the Gospel of John was so different than the other three.

They wondered why God, in parts of the Old Testament, seemed to be unlike the God described in parts of the New. With every page, they had more answers and even more questions. There was so much to digest. It would take weeks, months, years even to begin to assimilate it.

Sara's head was spinning, as she tried to integrate what she was reading with her earlier studies. Owen took comfort in seeing with his own eyes some of the passages from the Psalms his mother had recited to him.

Dayton and Emilia were discovering a whole different perspective than the one they had been fed from Prophet Nordwyn. Even Tadd and Lissa were enthralled by stories from the Old Testament—as exciting, passionate and sometimes as violent as anything they had seen on holovideo and iCap.

This Bible changed everything. If Grant was having a crisis of faith before, it was gone—replaced by the certainty that they were headed somewhere, even though they didn't know where that was, and that a divine Hand was involved in their journey. And now they had some point of reference by which to evaluate any Christian groups they might meet in the future. Even more to the point, they had a standard by which to evaluate their own understanding of God.

Aside from the miraculous matching of the Bible with the *remnant* page, Grant thought it was strange that this had come to them the way it did, through Buddhists working for Muslims. Was God teaching them something? Even while being drawn out of deceptive aberrations of Christianity, were they being drawn into appreciative interaction with other faiths?

Grant wanted to reattach the *remnant* to the book from which it had been torn, but he would wait. Maybe down the road he would find a craftsperson who would do it properly, along with other repairs to the Bible. He would hand this book down to his grandchildren as a memento of the long journey. Maybe the world political landscape would change and Christianity, along with other faiths, would once again be accepted.

But right now, this book was a dangerous thing to have.

"Everyone on the boat knows about this," Grant commented to Bryan, "but we've got to keep it quiet when we get ashore. A lot of people would love to get their hands on it—or the money it would bring."

Bryan stared at an odd-looking spider perched on the gunwale. While it was possible that the appearance of the Bible was miraculous, his pragmatism and his awareness of the ongoing drone surveillance made him suspect something else was at work, although he couldn't say for sure how or why.

Bryan commented to Grant, "Ben Franklin said, 'Three may keep a secret, if two of them are dead.' You already know the crew is going to spread the news around town. We're going to have to watch our backs."

The town of Hannibal was only a few hours away, and after that, all their time might be spent walking. At this point, they didn't know exactly which road to take. They hoped someone in Hannibal would have a suggestion.

Smoke from Hannibal's chimneys rose over the trees in the distance. It was time to prepare for a return to land. The team broke down their temporary digs and stowed the gear in their backpacks. The Baraq passed between two islands and rounded a bend in the river. About half a mile ahead was a deteriorating bridge, with hanging pieces of concrete and steel. Just beyond that was Hannibal.

From the bow, Lissa and Tadd gazed at the rickety bridge as they passed underneath. "We don't have to walk across that thing, do we Mom?" asked Lissa.

"I don't know," responded Dana. "Ask your Dad."

"I know about as much as you do," answered Grant. "It all depends on what we find out here and which way we go. It's probably not as bad as it looks. See? The right side still seems to be intact all the way across. And I think I see someone walking up there."

"I'd rather pay someone to ferry us across the river," commented Dana.

As this was the Baraq's southernmost destination, the ship slowly passed the Hannibal dock on her starboard and pivoted in the river, finally docking on her port side. Tough-looking longshoremen secured the vessel to the dock and began the task of unloading cargo. A small, aging crane lifted the containers onto the dock. A row of beat up trucks waited to haul the cargo away.

Captain Lanning was at the gangplank as the Cochrin team disembarked. Grant handed him an envelope with the agreed-upon fare, which he took without opening. "I almost don't feel right taking this after the heroic work you folks did. And you pitched in with the chores just like you said you would. I sure hope there's more Christians around like you."

"Almost makes me wish we'd held on to that book we gave you to see what's in it," said Bart, who was standing nearby. "But I think it's in the right hands now. It rightfully belongs to you."

"May Allah richly bless you in your quest!" said the Captain.

"May God bless you, my friend," said Grant, warmly shaking the captain's hand. "And may he steer your ship around those sandbars and debris!"

As they walked down the gangplank, Grant turned briefly to see the captain trying to extricate his foot from a curly length of poly strapping hanging from a shipping crate. "Dang strapping," Grant heard him mutter.

Grant smiled. He hadn't intended his parting comment to be metaphorical, but he couldn't help but think how wonderful it would be if Captain Lanning and his crew, along with many of the Christians they had met, could be freed from the entanglement of thinking they need to do something to make God happy with them.

9.

The group arrived in front of a large oak door, with one of those little cast iron hinged windows for the resident to peek out and see who's there. The door was framed with ivy that had overtaken half the cottage, which was nestled in a grove of trees.

The team had inquired in town about Christian groups in the area. None of the people they talked to on the street could give them any specifics, but two folks recommended they visit a woman who lived in this house on the edge of town. The team was a little anxious after the events with Sister Aretha's group, and couldn't help but wonder what was next.

Grant knocked on the door. The little iron window creaked opened. "Yes?" It was the voice and eyes of an elderly woman.

"Good morning. Some folks in town mentioned you might be able to help me and my team here," said Grant.

"I'll do what I can. Help you how?"

"I'm Grant Cochrin, and we're Christ-followers in search of a reasonable Christian community where we can settle down."

"*Reasonable*, you say? Let's talk." The door opened to reveal a tall, white-haired lady apparently in her seventies or older, elegant but comfortably dressed. Behind her was a living room lined with shelves overloaded with old books and papers. She had the demeanor of a college professor, and Sara, watching behind Grant, took an instant liking to her.

"Oh my," said the lady. "So many people all at once! Please come in. I think I have enough chairs."

With the exception of Tadd and Lissa, who chose to stay outside, the team filed through the door as the lady shook each person's hand. "I'm Sharon Stevens," she said to each individual, who introduced themselves and sat down on well-worn couches and chairs.

"Wait," said Sara. "Doctor Sharon Stevens?"

"Yes, I was at one time. But I don't suppose it really matters anymore, does it?"

"Of course it matters!" said Sara. "You wrote the textbook for the class I taught on comparative religious history at New Harvard." Sara tilted her head in curiosity. "And then you disappeared."

"I did, didn't I? I got tired of the whole thing and

walked off into the Wilderness, with the help of a few friends. Somehow I ended up here. Far enough west to be away from some of those crazy groups, and yet far enough east to be relatively civilized. Wilderness-wise, anyway. But you must have a similar story if you taught at New Harvard. And now you obviously don't teach there."

Sara related a short version of her history, her interest in Christianity, morphing into an interest in Christ, her discovery of hidden files of the Bible and other religious works in the New Harvard archives, her forced relocation to the Minot Work Camp. She also told of their escape and adventures in the Wilderness to date. As Sara talked, her eyes kept wandering over the shelves stuffed with books. Were these contraband religious works? Were actual Bibles hidden in here somewhere?

"How do you manage to live in this place without any trouble from the locals?" asked Bryan.

"Oh, I have a longstanding arrangement with the—ah—aristocracy who run this neck of the woods. I tutor their kids and they take care of me. It's as simple as that. They're interested in keeping their families in control and they know they need some smarts to do that."

"That brings me to the reason we came here to see you," said Grant. "The people we talked to in town thought you would have some answers for us. They seemed to be aware that you know something about the Christian landscape hereabouts."

"Well," said Sharon, "I've been discreet, but I've never covered up that fact. More than a few people who are interested in Christ have dropped by asking for my thoughts."

"Then I guess we are among those people. What can you tell us? Sara filled you in about where we've been so far. What direction do you recommend we go?"

Sharon smiled. "That's a difficult question to answer, without me asking *you* a question. You're obviously Christians, and you seem pretty level headed compared to some people who call themselves Christians. But you're looking for a group." The team was nodding along as she spoke. "Can I ask why you're looking for a group? What is it you think you can find in a group that you couldn't find if you just settled down somewhere and lived your lives?"

Grant was caught off guard. To him, the answer went without saying. No one they had met in the Wilderness so far had asked that question. After all, the Cochrins and their friends had been isolated in the work camp. They had relied on shreds of tradition, some questionably memorized Scripture passages, a half-page *remnant* of the Bible and whatever inspiration God provided. Their underlying assumption— well, *Grant's* underlying assumption—was that surely they would be able to learn *something* from *some* community of believers out here. So far, that had happened in more or less negative ways, but of course now they had a Bible, and Grant supposed they could probably learn a whole lot by just sitting and reading it without some self-styled prophet infusing it with his or her own special interpretation.

One thing Grant was hoping he would discover in his newly acquired Bible was a simple list of criteria for what constituted an authentic Christian church group— do this, don't do that, case closed. He hadn't yet found it spelled out, but he couldn't for the life of him understand why such a definitive, explicit list wouldn't be there in Scripture.

Grant realized his family, the team and Ms. Stevens were all staring at him, waiting.

He cleared his throat. "We hoped to find, or we hoped God would lead us to a Christian community with an approach to Christianity similar to ours. A place where we could settle down and be comfortable. A place where we could learn and grow. We still hope for that, of course."

"May I speak frankly?" asked Sharon.

"Sure thing," answered Grant.

"Are you sure that what you say you're looking for is what you want? I mean you're searching for a *group*. What's wrong with the one you have now?"

"What do you mean?" stammered Grant.

"I mean you *are* a group. The nine of you. Or is that too small? Did you have an optimal size in mind?"

Sara stifled a laugh, Bryan, Dayton and Emilia smirked. Owen pursed his lips and stared at the ceiling. Dana, however was not merely entertained by Sharon's provocative irony, rather, she was taking Sharon's argument to heart.

Grant managed a lopsided grin. "I think we imagined more of an established community..."

"Oh!" said Sharon. "A non-pluralistic community. Someplace with governance and standards to keep out the nonbelievers—Muslims, Hindus, Buddhists, atheists, agnostics, sinners and the like? Perhaps even Mormons, Catholics, Quakers, Episcopalians..."

"I wouldn't phrase it like that," said Grant.

"Good, because for a minute there it sounded a little like you were looking for an exclusively Christian community. And if that's what you have, then you also have a governance that will of necessity determine who is Christian and who is not. To be honest, groups that identify themselves as Christ-followers are like individuals who identify as Christ-followers. They all belong to Christ, as you do. But they're all dysfunctional to a greater or lesser degree, as we all are. Yet by its very nature, the governance of a group will more often than not presume to define Christianity for its constituents in ways that exceed or run counter to Scripture. Nowadays they probably don't have access to Scripture. But I'm glad you aren't comfortable with that."

"Well, no, I'm not. We're not. What's your point? I'm not clear on what you're driving at here. All we want to know is if you know of any other Christian groups around here. Can you help us or not?"

"Yes but no. Yes, I do know of nominally Christian groups south and east of here. But no, I really don't think you're going to find what you're looking for unless you look inwardly. Find a place and settle down—that could even be here. And then you'll have what you're looking for."

Grant stared out the window for a moment. "I don't know if we're ready for that."

Sharon smiled and laughed a little. "I'm sorry, Grant. I'm being contrarian, falling back into my old professorial habits. Something I used to do to make my students think, and I know you've probably thought this through and debated among yourselves 'til the cows come home."

Dana, true to form, was resonating with Sharon's talk of settling down. "Grant? We need to talk more about this. Dr. Stevens has a point. Maybe we've searched enough. I mean just look at our gifts—technical, academic, scientific, mechanical. What's wrong with our little team? And what's wrong with Hannibal?"

"Nothing, I guess, except, what if the community we're looking for is just a hundred miles down the road? What if God has something waiting for us and we don't know because we didn't look for it?"

Sharon studied Grant. "Yes, we all tend to have

those doubts when we're on the precipice of a major decision—*what if there's something better*? But as I'm sure you know, thinking that way too often can lead to decision paralysis."

"Yes, yes, I know," said Grant. "But back to our original question. What if we give it another chance? What if we look east of here—Illinois or maybe Kentucky? What can you tell us?"

"Okay," said Sharon. "Here's what I've heard. There's a group in Springfield, but you may find them to be a bit exuberant for your tastes. There's another in Lexington. More strait-laced and then I would venture a guess that they have someone they consider as a divinely appointed authority figure to set boundaries for them. There are other groups dotting the landscape as one heads south and east, but I don't know specifics. One can only imagine."

Everyone was silent for a while. Then Bryan spoke up. "I have a suggestion. Why don't we put it to a vote?"

"A vote?" said Grant, a little surprised.

"The way I see it, we have three viable choices."

"Three?" asked Grant.

"Yes. One—trek eastward as you seem to be inclined to do. Two—stay here in or around Hannibal."

"And?" said Grant. "What's the third?"

"Split up," said Bryan. Grant's mouth dropped open, and the rest of the group stared with disbelief at Bryan. "I'm just sayin'. It's a possibility we should consider."

"Okay," said Grant, "but let's make it a secret ballot, so no one judges anyone afterward. If a majority chooses option one or two, that means we stay together—although really, anyone who wants can stay behind."

"Fair enough," agreed Bryan.

Sharon volunteered to act as the vote counter. Agreeing to include the kids in the vote, as they would have to live the rest of their lives with the implications of this decision, they cut nine little pieces of paper. When Sharon tallied the votes, no one wanted to split up. Four voted to stay in Hannibal and five wanted to go on.

Grant surveyed the group. "If we go with these results, it looks like four of us are going to be putting the group ahead of their own preferences," said Grant. "That's a sacrifice. And I know we'll probably face more dangers down the road. But I believe we're better off together. Is everyone okay with that?

Heads nodded.

"We can always come back here, you know."

The team camped in Sharon's wooded yard that night, and in the morning Sharon prepared a hearty southern breakfast of ham, eggs, corn hoecakes and coffee.

As they headed down toward the river, Grant asked Sharon, "I never really asked because I sort of assumed—you are a Christian, aren't you?"

"Good question," said Sharon. "I absolutely believe in Christ, but I don't make a religion out of it."

10.

Back on the dock, Mike Cologne of Michael's Ferry Service explained the team's options to Grant and Bryan. "There are two ways to get across the river here. You can hike across the bridge and take your chances. Many people do, especially if they're not carrying anything much, and they have no fear of heights, and they're good swimmers. It can be very exhilarating. It also helps to have a good heart. Or, you can take my ferry. It's safe, it's comfortable, it's fun. Free drinks for the kids. You get to the other side or your money back."

"How much per person?" asked Grant.

"Fifteen thousand dinar," said Mike, grinning.

"What? That's outrageous!" shouted Grant, loud enough for the rough-looking guards on the shore to take notice.

"Oh, you're right! I'm sorry. I forgot to add luggage. That's an additional two thousand per person," said Mike, still grinning.

"C'mon! For that we can buy a boat, row across and sell it on the other side," said Bryan.

"Oh, I'm afraid there are very strict safety standards around here," said Mike. "Only licensed pilots can operate craft on the river, so even if anyone sold you a boat, you would find yourself under arrest the minute you launched it. And you just don't want to run afoul of the local authorities. And also, I have the only ferry franchise for miles."

Grant and Bryan both shook their heads, turned and walked up the gangplank from the dock.

"Since you're such a nice group, I'll give you a five percent discount!" shouted Mike. They ignored him.

"We're taking the bridge," said Grant to the group waiting on the shore. "That guy is a thief. "

Dana was conflicted. "Grant! I know it's a lot of money, but do you think the bridge is safe?"

"Well, we'll need to be careful, but I saw someone walking across it when we sailed under it yesterday," answered Grant as they walked north along the shore toward the bridge.

"We've braved greater challenges," said Bryan.

A weathered plaque with a stone portrait of the bridge's namesake declared that this was the *Mark Twain Memorial Bridge*. The plaque explained that it had been built in 2000, replacing an earlier bridge built in 1936.

Bryan and Owen surmised that the 2000 bridge

had been slated for replacement before the Final War, but it was never done. It had been a handsome bridge to accommodate traffic on Route 36—four lanes wide and nearly a mile long, with a trussed main span over the channel of about six hundred feet on the western end. Now, some of the trusses were broken, with girders hanging toward the water.

"Mark Twain?" asked Lissa.

"Yeah," said Emilia. I think he wrote books back in the 19th century or something.

"You are correct," said Sara. "He wrote novels about life along the Mississippi. I read somewhere his home was right here in Hannibal.

The chatter continued, belying the increasing anxiety the team was feeling about the bridge. The only one who remotely anticipated the crossing was Tadd. Sure, a sixty-foot drop to the water would be a bit daunting, even dangerous, but possible. You'd just have to stay out of the way of any falling bridge pieces.

Tadd had watched high divers on holovideo at the camp. The world record was over a hundred and twenty feet, and this was only half of that. But none of this self-encouragement made him feel much better, since he wasn't a very good swimmer. Neither was Lissa.

Grant stared across the span. "I think prayer is definitely in order before we cross this thing."

"You got that right," agreed Owen.

After asking for God's protection, they headed out onto the bridge and through the trussed section, staying to the intact right side as much as possible. The remainder of the bridge was open deck. For about a quarter mile or so, all four lanes were intact.

Looking southward, they could see Michael's Ferry, slowly crossing the river with a small crowd of travelers. "We could have paid through the nose to take that guy's ferry and been safely on the other side by now," commented Dayton.

"You mean *he* could have taken *us*," corrected Grant. Dayton laughed.

The pavement narrowed to two lanes, then one, then half a lane. Finally, the railings and abutments had crumbled away, and all that remained was an isthmus of pavement about two feet wide. Everyone hoped that an intact I-beam was supporting the pavement, but there was no way of knowing for sure. In fact, there was a twisted network of metal and rebar protruding from both sides of the pavement, revealing that the deck, including its reinforcing elements, was over three feet thick. Someone had stretched a rope from a protruding piece of steel, over the narrow span, to the intact railing ahead of them, where the pavement widened into the comforting expanse of four lanes.

Grant was first to venture out, followed by his family. The rope wasn't much help, although it would be something to hang from for a while if you slipped off the pavement. But then what? Bits of pavement crumbled away here and there, falling for a few seconds and splashing into the muddy current below.

Lissa tried to focus on her feet and not on the fact that the pavement was only a foot wide in some places, and cracked, and that she was top-heavy, carrying a forty-pound pack and that there was sixty feet of air between the pavement and the river.

"It's only water," said Sara, behind her.

Emilia and Bryan brought up the rear. Emilia was about three quarters of the way across the pavement isthmus when a grinding sound came from under her feet. She stopped for a moment, but the chunk of concrete she was standing on broke loose and began to fall to the right.

With a scream, Emilia dropped with it through a gap in the twisted rebar. Her backpack caught on a broken piece of rebar and she grabbed hold of another, her legs dangling in space. Behind her, Bryan watched, frantically searching for a way to help. There was no way. He yanked his firearm holster off and hurled it toward the group watching from the other side of the pavement isthmus.

"Let go!" he shouted to Emilia. "I'll be right behind you!"

She turned briefly with sheer panic in her eyes, and then let her grip go. Now she was dangling from her backpack. The short piece of rebar bent under the added weight, allowing the backpack to slip off. Emilia dropped for less than two seconds and hit the water.

Bryan stumbled to a place clear of protruding metal and jumped. He hit the river harder than he had imagined he would. But both his and Emilia's backpacks acted as flotation devices, and the two figures drifted downstream. Within a minute, Bryan had reached Emilia and was pulling her toward the heavily wooded shore.

The team watched the two figures from the south railing of the bridge. Grant ran to a point where he could easily jump from the railing, then he scrambled down the bank, followed by the rest of the team. They met the soggy couple as they struggled though fallen branches and mud. "Are you both okay?" asked Grant as he waded into the mire to help them ashore.

"I think so," coughed Emilia. "Water is really hard at 60 feet. I know one thing for sure—Bryan will take care of me!"

Bryan was knocking water out of his ear. "You had me scared to death there, and I...*mmppphh*..." Emilia had grabbed Bryan and was kissing him as they stood ankle deep in mud.

Grant laughed in relief. The team applauded. Tadd groaned, "Eww!"

Back up the bank and onto I-72, they took one last look at the river that had caused them such peril, but had transported them hundreds of miles, saving them nearly a million steps. Now they were back to using up shoe soles. If they couldn't hitch a ride on a bus or truck, they would have a six-day trek ahead of them.

"Tolerance isn't about not having beliefs. It's about how your beliefs lead you to treat people who disagree with you."
—Timothy Keller

PART VI: SPRINGFIELD

1.

They were less than ten miles up the road, past the point where I-172 joins I-72. There was more traffic out here, as the leg of I-72 that led to the bridge was nearly unused for obvious reasons. The team was looking for a place to camp for the night.

Sharon had reported what she called a "nominally Christian" group in Springfield, and another in Lexington, far to the southeast. Grant wondered to himself if this would turn out to be another fool's errand. Bryan had checked his watch for any electronic information or some kind of radio broadcast, but there was nothing. Only an eerie, distant analog audio signal fading in and out that sounded something like a man screaming. Was someone in trouble? Was it some kind of bizarre music? He had no way of knowing, but the Wilderness radio spectrum was punctuated by all sorts of oddities.

As in the past, they heard the rumbling of motorcycle engines in the distance. "Oh, no! Not again!" said Dana.

They turned to see a gang of maybe six or seven raptor cycles fast approaching. The raptors had almost certainly seen the team. Running to hide in the underbrush would be like a squirrel running from a dog.

"Just keep walking like you don't care," said Grant. The cycles were downshifting—not a comforting sound. Bryan pulled his coat back so his hand on the Vikhr was visible. Suddenly the cycles were rolling along beside them at walking speed. Would these be friendly, like the team's last encounter with raptors, or would they be like the ones who strafed Bob Kroener's truck? It was hard to ignore these hefty riders, all grinning, some toothlessly. A woman, equally hefty, rode a motorcycle with a man riding on the back seat. Two had small children in sidecars. Nearly all were wearing heavy rawhide and chains, and everyone sported multiple braids. Leather holsters on gas tanks held assault rifles, nunchuks and other assorted weaponry.

Tadd's eyes were big with adventure. "Cool!" he exclaimed.

"Shut up, you idiot!" whispered his sister, a little too loudly.

"Well, now, girly!" laughed the largest rider, who seemed to be the leader. "Let's not be too hasty to judge your brother, or whoever that is. He's obviously a kid with fine taste! He thinks we're 'cool'! What about the rest of you? Do you think we're 'cool'? What about you, girly? Apparently you don't think we're 'cool.'"

Lissa tried hard to ignore the rider, thinking this was clearly not a gang to interact with.

"Cat got your tongue?" said the rider. "You're kinda cute."

Grant and Dana cringed. Grant looked behind him to see a grim-faced Bryan with his right hand poised at the edge of his coat.

"I think what you need," continued the head raptor, "is a nice ride with me on my conveyance here to show you just exactly how cool we are!" He reached out to grab Lissa's arm, but the woman on the seat behind him slapped him hard on the side of his head.

"Ow, Joplin! Wha'd you do that for? I'm just havin' a little bit o' fun!"

"Don't even joke about it, Garvin. Ain't no girl gonna ride with you except me!" said Joplin.

"Okay, okay! Calm down! I was just thinkin' in terms of business," said Garvin, rubbing his head. "This one would bring us a significant sum on the market in Nashville."

"Oh. Okay. That's different," said Joplin.

Garvin moved his cycle ahead and pulled up beside Owen. "What about grandpa here? He wouldn't be worth much in Nashville, but I'll bet he thinks we're cool. What do you think, grandpa? Are we cool, or not?"

Owen turned and looked Garvin in the eye as he walked. His piercing gaze startled Garvin a bit. "I think," said Owen, "that anyone who rides a 2045 Triumph Rocket XX must have some kinda cool. V4? Two hundred and ten horsepower? Sixteen valve fuel injection and aircraft ignition? That's extremely cool."

Garvin's mouth dropped open. "Hey! You're a gearhead! I'm impressed." Garvin stared at Owen, who kept walking. "But here's the greater question—what are you folks doin' out here on our turf and what should we do about it? Whadda *you* think we should do, little lady?" Garvin pulled up alongside Emilia. Bryan's grip tightened on his weapon.

"Nice to meet you, Garvin," said Emilia, without flinching. Garvin was again slightly unnerved. Usually his victims didn't react quite this way. "We're on our way to Springfield. There's a group of Christians out there we want to check out."

"Oh, a group of Christians. Hmm. I think I know

the um—*institution*—you're talkin' about. I guess you could say they're—unique. Gonna check 'em out are you? Excellent. Checkin' out the Christians."

The bikers all laughed raucously.

"Now," said Garvin, "we don't object to your mission in any way shape or form. But since we're who we are and you're who you are, we have some business to attend to. More specifically, we'll need to inspect all those backpacks, as you may have certain things in them that we might find useful. Money, food, items of value and the like. Since you're Christians I would be shocked if you had any drugs or liquor, but we'll check for 'em just the same. Heck, I could even use a change of underwear, although it appears that none of you are quite my size."

Joplin snorted. "Joplin, please," said Garvin. Joplin glared at the back of his head. "A word of caution," continued Garvin, "you may want to drop those packs on the ground right quick because Newgent here has anger management issues he's still dealing with, and he tends to be…impatient." Garvin motioned to a huge, grinning man with blond, braided beard and hair, who was slipping brass knuckles onto his fingers.

The team stopped walking. Grant was about to say something, when Emilia spoke again. She spoke with the assurance of someone who had faced fear and survived. "Hi there, Newgent." She waved. "Garvin, I'm sorry I forgot to introduce myself. I'm Emilia. And this is my fiancé, Bryan."

Jaws dropped, but none more than Bryan's. He quickly regained his composure as he realized that Emilia was probably saying this for effect and he played along.

"It's funny about Newgent because Bryan has anger issues too," said Emilia. "There's one big difference, though. Want to show 'em honey?"

Before Garvin or any of his group had a chance to react, Bryan was aiming his SR-6M Vikhr at Garvin. The raptors instantly recognized the powerful weapon. They knew that in less than a second Bryan could spray them all with enough 9mm rounds to kill them several times over. Bryan flashed his best insane look.

"Hey, hey, hey!" said Garvin with both hands in the air. "Let's be reasonable! We were just bein' facetious. Never intended any harm, did we Newgent?"

"No, boss, never," said Newgent who had suddenly lost his grin, and was slipping his brass knuckles back off.

"That's good to know," said Grant. "Shall we call a truce then?"

Garvin stuttered, adjusting to the sudden inversion of power. "Well, I..."

"Unless you folks have somewhere else to be," said Grant, "why don't we all just camp here for the night. We can share dinner and swap a few stories. I've even got a few beers in my backpack."

"And there's something wrong with the ignition on that V-Rod over there," said Owen. "We can fix it."

Garvin stared at Owen, then turned to his friends for a brief conference.

"Grant!" whispered Dana. "What are you doing? These people are killers!"

"Yes, they are. So they could leave us alone now, and then come back in the middle of the night. Or we can keep them here and keep an eye on them. Maybe even make an alliance. And nobody's gonna give us any trouble as long as we're with them," whispered Grant. "Beyond that, I think Jesus would take the time to talk with them."

"Alright," said Garvin. "You ladies and gentlemen can crash our squad. We'll camp here. But stop aimin' that piece at me." Bryan lowered the Vikhr, but kept his finger on the trigger. "Aim it at Newgent instead. Ha."

Newgent sneered, and growled a little.

2.

Both groups shared a dinner of chicken jerky (which Sharon had given the travelers), a tasty sausage of uncertain origin (contributed by the raptors) and a large batch of fire-grilled yams and potatoes.

Grant told the story of their journey to date. Garvin and his group listened without much interruption. Afterward, he commented, "You guys are either totally insane, stupid or...sincere!"

"Maybe a little of all three," said Grant.

"But at least you're not brainless, like some of the other Jesus fanboys we've met," commented another raptor, who went by the name of Funky Claude. "We were thinkin' you were low-hangin' fruit, so we didn't even have our weapons out, and you got the drop on us."

"By the way, that guy Mike back there in Hannibal with the ferry?" said a raptor called Henlee. "You were way better off crossing the bridge."

"Why?" asked Dayton.

"He's a real schmuck. He spots people passing through with large backpacks like yours. He not only rips you off on the fare, he gets you out there on the river, gives you a drink or two, slips you a mickie, distracts your kids with fishing or something, and then rifles your packs while you doze. Nothin' you can do about it 'cause he's workin' with the gang that runs the town."

"Isn't that kinda the same thing you do?" asked Tadd.

Garvin flashed a crooked grin. "I suppose—but we prefer not to think of ourselves as schmucks. And we like to think we're more up front about our activities."

"But don't you kill people?" pressed Tadd. Dana and Lissa both looked horrified.

Garvin noticed their reaction. "It's a reasonable question. The answer is yes, on occasion. But only if we need to."

"Need to?" asked Dana.

"You may not have noticed, but the whole world is predatory. Eat or be eaten. The delightful little birdies that cheer us with morning song?" said Garvin, mockingly fluttering his fingers. "All competin' for territory, food and mates. All these trees? Competin' for sunlight and water. Same thing with humans. Everybody's got their hand out, trying to get your money, your belongings and your time. The huge corporations back in the Safe Zones? All out to get your last dinar. Big Federation government? Out to get you and everything you own. Those bizarre church groups that you visited—or any religion for that matter? Same thing. They chew you up and spit out what's left of you. So if you need to dispatch a few people to stay alive—that's just the way things are. Survival of the fittest."

"Sounds like you've been burned somewhere along the line," said Owen.

"Don't even go there. The way I see it, we raptors are just the same as anyone else, once you scrape off that thin, cracked varnish you call civilization. We're just playin' our little part in the vast scheme o' things. Soon as you realize that, you'll start playin' the game too."

"What about the human trafficking?" asked Sara.

"We prefer to think of it as finding new employment for folks," grinned Garvin.

The team was surprised when raptor McGwynn pulled out a small acoustical twelve-string guitar and started singing songs about raptor life, mixed in with popular contemporary songs, and a few as early as the mid-twentieth century. He had a clear tenor voice and a unique picking style, prompting Lissa to pull off her iCap and listen. He didn't seem to fit the part of a dangerous gang member, but his .38 sidearm and the nunchuk hanging from his belt said otherwise.

The two groups bedded down about fifty feet apart. Bryan, Owen, and Dayton rotated watches sitting on a rock with the Vikhr. They could see Newgent and Funky Claude doing the same duty in the raptor camp. It was unclear whether they were merely keeping an eye out for another gang or watching the Cochrin team for an opportunity.

3.

In the morning Owen set to work as promised on raptor Entwhistle's faulty V-Rod ignition. Bryan completed the work with improvements to the software. The twin-cylinder machine had never run better.

Meanwhile, Brenda, Roland's girlfriend, was suffering from an infected cut on her leg. She had the look and mannerisms of a user, including a bit of paranoia. Dana calmly reassured her as she cleaned and dressed the wound, while Lissa gave her some of the antibiotic capsules that Bryan had bought for her back in LaCrosse. Although the antibiotic had been designed to combat ear infections, it also worked on the infected cut, which showed marked improvement within a couple of hours.

Emilia and Dana had both noticed that the raptor kids, Argent and Benitar, both about five years of age, were coughing and sneezing a lot. Apparently, Argent belonged to Joplin and Benitar had been picked up along the way somewhere. With Joplin's permission,

Emilia gave the kids some anti-viral medication she had acquired at Lastdays University. The symptoms disappeared within an hour.

Garvin had been watching all this, between philosophical discussions with Grant and Sara over rather strong coffee.

"Everyone here might not agree," said Garvin, "but I been thinkin'...these roads can be dangerous, what with people like us around. No sense you walkin' when we can get you to Springfield in two or three hours. What do you say?"

"I guess—yeah," said Grant. Reaction from the team was predictable, ranging from Dana's dubious frown to Tadd's ecstatic delight. The two groups broke camp. It took a little planning to squeeze all of the team and their backpacks onto the motorcycles and sidecars. Newgent carried Lissa and Tadd in his sidecar. Owen rode pillion saddle (back seat) on Entwistle's V-Rod. Henlee carried Bryan. Funky Claude squeezed Benitar and Sara on his pillion. Brenda's back seat was taken up by her boyfriend, Roland. McGwynn's Harley trike had the biggest load with Grant and Dana in his sidecar and Emilia riding pillion. Quaiff carried Dayton and young Argent. Of course, Garvin and Joplin were plenty by themselves, even for their V4-powered Triumph.

They thundered eastward along I-72, slowing down only when the road was damaged so badly they had to take dirt-road detours. They passed three gangs of raptors going the other way. Strangely, they all gave a Nazi-style salute to Garvin, who returned the gesture. Grant, Dana and Emilia were thrilled to hear McGwynn break into song as they rumbled along the road. He sang classics from the late 20th century as well as a few new songs.

"You do this all the time?" asked Emilia.

"Oh yeah," yelled McGwynn over the roar of the

engine and wind. "I've played in bands off and on over the decades—spent seven years in one called Bite the Wax Tapeworm. You know, my great, great, great, great grandfather was really big in psychedelic rock in the late twentieth century. Wrote *The Ballad of Easy Rider* to go with that old movie about cycle gangs—with Peter Fonda, Dennis Weaver and Jack Nicholson?"

"I think I saw part of it once," said Emilia. "It's like you guys have picked up on that culture."

"Well, yeah, maybe," said McGwynn. "But I think it never went away. It was always there on the fringes."

When they came to Springfield, Garvin headed straight for the center of town. They stopped in front of an old Lutheran Church with a huge stone steeple and large stained glass windows set in gothic arches. Down the street some three or four blocks to the west stood the old Illinois State Capitol Building, with its partially collapsed dome. On the north side of the street was the Lincoln Presidential Library. The gang shut down their engines and wandered around. A few locals on the sidewalk suddenly made themselves scarce.

"Welcome to Springfield," said Garvin.

"I believe this is in the general vicinity of where you want to be, if you're really serious about hangin' with these folks."

"I think so," said Grant. "If nothing else we'll learn something more about the state of Christianity in the Wilderness. We want to thank you for your kindness and generosity in bringing us here—and of course for not killing us or robbing us or abducting us."

"Well," chuckled Garvin, "to tell you the truth, we've never met up with folks quite like you. Just between me and you, it makes me consider reconsiderin' what I was tellin' you last night. Maybe there are a few people like you who ain't out for themselves. I'll have to think on it. So I guess the thanks goes to you folks for helpin' us out with a few things. We gotta be on our way. Got a couple of people to see here in town."

The Cochrin team said their amicable goodbyes—the third time they had done so in as many days. Garvin and his gang started their engines, and he motioned to Grant. "If anybody gives you any guff, just tell 'em you know Garvin. Better yet, flag down any raptor and give 'em this sign." Garvin held his fingers up in a configuration that resembled ASL (American Sign Language) for the letter G. "They know how to get in touch with me." With that, he roared off down the street in the direction of the capitol building, followed by his gang.

Now it was time to reconnoiter surroundings. Grant and Bryan were absorbed in consulting his watch for local landmarks, unaware that a short, rotund man with a shock of black hair and a Van Dyke beard had emerged from the door of the old church. He had come up behind them and was looking over their shoulders.

"Hello, folks. Just to let you know, we don't want any trouble," said the man. Bryan and Grant jumped a bit and turned to face him.

"Excuse me?" said Grant. "I'm not sure what you mean."

"You just rode up here with those raptors, didn't you? With Mr. Garvin?"

"Yeah, but we just hitched a ride with…wait…*Mr. Garvin?*"

"Mr. Garvin. Don't you know? He controls the entire former state of Illinois, from what's left of Chicago all the way down to Kentucky. Commands hundreds of raptors—maybe thousands."

"But he didn't act like a powerful guy. In fact his whole group seemed pretty rough around the edges."

"Of course not. That's his thing. He'll take you by

surprise. He prefers to stay low key and travel the roads with his family and cronies to keep an eye on things. He can call in scores of riders at a moment's notice. Most people hide when they know he's in town. Just as soon shoot you as look at you—or grab you up and sell you down in Nashville. Oh yeah, there's a lot of people who'd like to get rid of him, but he's got more who would die to keep him in power. It's hard to believe you didn't know that, riding around with his gang and all."

The team was dumbfounded. Grant couldn't help but remember Durward Alder's parting advice: "People out here aren't always what they seem to be."

When Grant recovered from his shock, he enquired, "We understand there's a Christian group here. Know anything about it?

"Why, indeed I do. I'm the steward of this church, Reverend Sigfrid Karg-Elert. And yes, yes, before you ask, my parents named me Sigfrid after the early 20th century German composer. Their surnames were Karg and Elert, respectively. So it just seemed like the natural thing to do. Not much of a musician myself, except I do sneak into the sanctuary late at night on occasion and knock out a hymn or two on the old pipe organ. Always in need of tuning. Never gets used in services."

"Actually, I'm not familiar with that composer..." began Grant.

"My friends call me Sig...Reverend Sig. We meet on Sunday mornings and Wednesday evenings to hear God's man of faith and power, Elder Khenton Lancepod. We'd love to have you join us tomorrow morning. Services start at 10 and Elder Lancepod usually continues for about three hours. It's best to be there a little early, as the Elder likes everyone to be seated when he begins. And he will begin precisely at 10."

"*Three hours?*" whined Lissa.

"I'm sure they have something to keep the teens and kids occupied," said Dana.

"Oh, everyone is definitely occupied during services," said Rev. Sig. "You're welcome to camp in the grassy area east of the church. Just south of us, around the block, is Elder Lancepod's home. He lives in the old Abe Lincoln residence, appropriately enough."

"Appropriately?" asked Sara.

"Why, yes. Because just as Lincoln freed the slaves, Elder Lancepod has set us free."

"Okay..." said Sara.

"You'll see," grinned Rev. Sig.

4.

That night the team camped in a quiet garden in back of the church, a safer and more comfortable choice than the deteriorating, mostly-abandoned buildings in the town, although a few were clearly lived in and kept up. Bryan, Emilia and Sara walked down the street and around the block for a glimpse of the old two-story home where Abe and Mary Lincoln and their children once lived—and where Elder Lancepod currently resided.

It was on a corner, light brown with dark brown trim and dark green shutters. It had been restored and well-maintained, unlike many of the surrounding homes and buildings. As it was twilight, the home was fully lit. Shadows of figures inside moved across the sheer draperies.

"Elder Lancepod certainly can't complain about his living conditions," said Emilia. "It sort of reminds me of Nordwyn's place. Why do some people who claim to be Jesus' servants live way better than Jesus apparently did?"

"It looks like Lancepod either has family or staff," commented Sara. "I wonder how he claims to have set his followers free? I thought that spiritual distinction belonged to Jesus."

"There you go, thinking critically again," said Bryan.

At 9:45 a.m. the team entered the sanctuary of the stately church, its ceiling supported by soaring open wooden beams. Ponderous cylindrical light fixtures hung from the ceiling. The choir was flanked by two towering cases of organ pipes. A central case of pipes stood in the apse with bombarde trumpets on each side. A stained glass window dominated the rear of the church. None of the team, with the exception of Sara and Bryan, had seen anything like this. While the Federation had banned religious observances, many churches, synagogues and mosques had been preserved in the Safe Zones as public meeting places and historical curiosities, mostly cleansed of religious iconography. Here in the Wilderness, however some church buildings were still being used for worship.

The people were exceptionally friendly. Word had already spread that some raptors, or friends of raptors, had decided to come to church. Such a thing was highly unusual, and the team noticed that scores of people were nervously but happily staring at them as they made their way to the center of a pew.

On the way into the church, Dayton had struck up a conversation with an attractive young woman. She sat next to him, filling him in on various details of the edifice.

"What about me and Tadd?" asked Lissa. "Don't they have something for us to do?"

"No one has said anything about that, so let's just see what happens," said Dana.

Suddenly, the congregation was silent. A door opened to the side of the chancel. Two figures walked in. One was Rev. Sig, and the other was a tall, lanky man with a Lincoln-style beard, but a head bereft of hair except for a few strands above his ears. Rev. Sig sat down in a chair in the choir, and the tall man, whom the team assumed was Elder Lancepod, mounted the huge wooden pulpit. He looked down at the congregation with a benign smile. The congregation smiled back. He raised his eyes heavenward and opened his mouth.

Aaaaeeeeeeeiiiiiieeee! A piercing scream filled the sanctuary, echoing off the walls. The team jumped in their seats and looked around for the source. It took them a few seconds to realize that the scream was coming from Elder Lancepod himself—but no one was running to his aid. He didn't appear to be in distress. He was just standing there screaming. The congregation smiled and nodded their heads in agreement as if they were listening to a well-crafted speech. Others closed their eyes as if they were enjoying a fine musical performance.

Aaaaeeeeeeeiiiiiieeee! The screaming continued. The team looked at each other. Dana leaned over to her husband. "What's going on? This is crazy. Don't tell me we have to sit through three hours of this."

"You know as much as I do, honey. Maybe this is just some sort of introduction. I'm sure the sermon will begin soon."

After five more minutes, the team began to realize this *was* the sermon. Dana was getting a splitting headache. Tadd, predictably, with a goofy grin, was deriving great entertainment value from this. Lissa had deployed her iCap and was listening to music that blocked out the screaming with other screaming. Meanwhile Sara, Bryan and Emilia whispered snarky comments to each other. Owen and Grant sat with their characteristic endurance as a half-hour passed, and the screaming continued unabated. Now members of the congregation were getting into the act and a crescendo of hundreds shrieking voices began to rise.

Dayton, however, was mesmerized by the whole experience. Bryan studied him. His eyes were closed and he was wearing a smile. Normally, Dayton would have been careful about getting swept up, but Bryan suspected that his new female friend had something to do with his lack of skepticism.

Bryan turned to Emilia and Sara. "We'll have to keep an eye on Dayton. It looks like he's enjoying this a little too much. In the meantime, I've had all I can stand, personally." He looked down the pew at Dana and Grant, motioning his head toward the side door. Grant and Dana nodded, and the team began to make their way down the pew. Most of the congregation was too preoccupied with the service to even notice they were leaving.

"Coming with us?" Grant asked as he passed Dayton. "No," said Dayton. "I think I'll stay through the service and see how it turns out."

"Okay," said Grant, noticing Dayton's new friend.

They all exited a side door and headed to their campsite at the back of the church.

"Good grief!" exclaimed Dana. "What was that?"

"I'm not entirely sure," said Sara, "but it reminded me of an historical phenomenon I read about that was characteristic of some churches, especially in North America. Congregants would enter an ecstatic state and speak unintelligible gibberish, claiming to be under the inspiration of the Holy Spirit, and citing a scriptural precedent of some kind. Others would laugh uncontrollably. Still others would bark like dogs or fall to the floor as if comatose."

"Yeah," said Dana. "I seem to remember reading something about that years ago, but at the time it seemed so ridiculous that I thought it was just anti-religious Federation propaganda."

"Unfortunately," said Sara, "much of that propaganda was based on fact. Religion—even Christianity—has often been its own worst enemy. Anthopolgists called the phenomenon we're talking about *glossolalia*. It was also practiced—and probably still is—in pagan mediumistic traditions."

Grant was listening intently. "Hmm. I guess it goes without saying that I'm disappointed. But I guess we've done our due diligence here. Springfield is on the way to Lexington anyway—sort of."

By the time the team had broken up their camp, it was about 1:00 p.m.—time for the service to conclude. Not that they needed to watch a clock. They could tell because the screaming had subsided.

Grant decided to make a foray back into the church to see if he could locate Dayton, and maybe converse with a few people to better understand the phenomenon they had just experienced. The rest of the team followed.

They found the sanctuary nearly empty, but following their noses, they discovered a fellowship hall packed with congregants conversing and enjoying coffee and donuts. They each grabbed a donut and a cup of coffee—not quite as good as what they occasionally had at the work camp, but passable.

Grant spotted Rev. Sig and moved toward him through the crowd.

"Brother Grant!" said Rev. Sig. "What did you think of our service?"

"Well, I think one of our number may have resonated with it more than the rest of us," said Grant, trying to be diplomatic.

"That's to be expected. You know, my paternal grandmother, Elsie Karg, had a favorite scripture she liked to quote from the book of "First Collusions": 'The natural man receiveth not the things of the Spirit of God: for they are foolishness unto him.'"

"But it was just screaming," said Emilia.

"Oh, it was much more than screaming," said Rev. Sig. "It was *holy* screaming. My grandmother had another favorite scripture from the book of Ramen: 'The Spirit itself maketh intercession for us with groanings which cannot be uttered.' When Elder Lancepod speaks to us, which he does for three hours every Sunday and three hours every Wednesday night, he is doing just that."

"But if they can't be uttered, then how can we hear them?" asked Tadd, "They sounded way loud to me."

Rev. Sig smiled benignly at the precocious youngster. "Folks, I'm afraid you just don't get it. That's all I can say. Like so many, you rely more on reason and the gray matter in your head than just letting your spirit flow. Think of it as purely abstract, in the way you would think of pure form and color. Or think of it as the wordless music of an instrument."

"That helps a bit, but maybe Elder Lancepod can explain it all to us, if we can meet with him," said Sara, more out of academic curiosity than anything.

"Oh, that's not possible," said Rev. Sig. You see, except for his six hours per week of holy screaming, Elder Lancepod is silent. He says nothing. He writes nothing. His faithful attendants see to all his needs. My staff and I handle all the administration of the church, and arrange for the daily radio broadcasts, which consist of carefully selected excerpts from Elder Lancepod's weekly messages."

"That explains the odd signal I got on my watch after we left Hannibal," said Bryan. "It sounded like screaming—and it was."

Dayton appeared with his new friend and joined

the conversation. "Hi, folks. This is Cashmere O'Nepim. She's been filling me in on some of the local history, and telling me how she came to follow Elder Lancepod. You know," Dayton lowered his voice and spoke closely to Grant's ear, "I don't think we should be too hasty to write these people off. Sure, they've got a few things out of whack without the benefit of Scripture, but I found the service compelling in a way I can't explain. It's more of a feeling."

Bryan and Grant studied Dayton. "Okay," said Grant. Cashmere smiled coyly at Grant and Bryan, and returned her gaze to Dayton. "I think I understand," said Grant.

Grant wondered what Dana and he would *feel* when they found the right group. They had felt good about Nordwyn, but had turned out to be wrong. Now apparently Dayton was experiencing that feeling, colored by the attentions of an attractive young lady. Suddenly, the chatter in the room stopped. Everyone was looking toward the door. There in the doorway stood the towering, bearded figure of Elder Lancepod himself.

"Merciful heavens!" exclaimed Rev. Sig. "The Elder has determined to join us!"

Lancepod smiled and nodded at everyone as he slowly made his way across the room. The crowd parted respectfully to let him through. He touched the arm of a few people, mostly women who grinned giddily. Finally, he arrived in front of Rev. Sig and the team.

"Elder, how wonderful for you to be here," effused Rev. Sig. "And you arrived at an opportune time. These fine folks have come to visit our church."

As Rev. Sig introduced them, Lancepod shook the team's hands, he said nothing, but looked deeply into each person's eyes. Grant and Dana were both struck by the intense, almost hypnotic quality of Lancepod's gaze. They watched as Tadd frowned a little, and as

Lissa almost recoiled. Lancepod stepped back from Owen a bit, as Owen exuded a calm confidence that could be off-putting, meeting his gaze head-on. When Lancepod came to Sara, he winced a little, as if he could read her skepticism. Yet as he paused in front of Bryan and Emilia, he closed his eyes and his smile turned to a tight, grim line.

When Lancepod came to Dayton and Cashmere, he grinned, put his hand on Dayton's shoulder and nodded. Dayton gazed up at him with wide eyes and Cashmere beamed. Lancepod turned to Rev. Sig and stared for about twenty seconds.

"Yes, sir, I understand," said Rev Sig, who turned to Grant. "The Elder hopes that you all will join us for a special communion service tomorrow around noon in the Sanctuary. And—if the Spirit so wills—we will have a cavortation afterward!"

"Um—*cavortation*?" asked Sara.

"Cavortation. Just like old King Davis did as they were carrying the Arch of Coventry. It's another thing you must experience to understand," said Rev. Sig, smiling benignly.

5.

In spite of the fact that something strange was going on with Elder Lancepod, Grant decided to take him up on his offer. They would stay another night. Sara was interested in studying the group first hand. And it looked like Dayton was weighing the merits of Lancepod's community. Yes, they could leave immediately and drag Dayton with them, but neither Grant nor anyone in the team wanted to operate that way.

Early the next morning, Dayton showed up at the team's camp and sat down with Grant. "I know you may not agree," said Dayton, "but I really like it here and I'm considering staying."

Grant was quiet for a while. "Are you sure? We arrived only day before yesterday—and I'd be blind if I didn't notice that you and Cashmere are attracted to each other. That can color your decisions, to put it mildly."

"Yeah, I know," grinned Dayton. "But it's beyond that. Elder Lancepod has awakened something within me that I didn't know was there. Something beyond facts, words and reason."

"Gosh," said Grant. "By its very nature, it's hard to reason with that position. But you're the one who has to decide." Grant thought for a while. "One thing I can see far more clearly than when we started in our search for faith—there's always some element of truth. Every group we've visited has shown us something. With Nordwyn, there was the sense of community and order. With Aretha, there was the compassion to see people healed. With our Muslim friends, there was the desire to please God. Even Garvin's gang was seeking answers. But somehow the truth gets distorted or displaced by other elements."

Dayton nodded in agreement.

"Here, they have a longing to somehow experience God. But it seems to me their search for experience with God has become something else. You have to learn that for yourself, Dayton. Who knows. Maybe you can help them sort it all out."

"Maybe," said Dayton.

"At the risk of sounding like a parent," concluded Grant, "we don't want you to make a decision that you might regret later on. Anyway, there's still a few hours. I'm pretty sure we'll be hitting the road after the communion—and cavortation."

"I'll let you know," said Dayton.

As noon approached, the team again filed into the sanctuary. This time there was no screaming. Rev. Sig and Elder Lancepod stood behind a table in the chancel, on which rested several loaves of bread, along with some large urns.

In the past, the team had followed the communion tradition of wine or grape juice and bread, a tradition passed down from parents and grandparents in Grant's case. Even Prophet Nordwyn had done the same thing. Grant had confirmed the tradition in his newly acquired Bible.

But the urns on the table seemed to have flames below each one, with steam rising from them. *Hot wine for communion!* thought Grant. *Is that the way it's supposed to be done?*

"What in the world is that?" whispered Dana. "Are they serving coffee for the Lord's supper?"

Grant shook his head, unsure. "It certainly looks like they're brewing something."

Bryan leaned over. "Hey. Do you smell that?"

Grant sniffed, "No, I don't think I…" Grant sniffed again. "Oh my gosh! It's cannabis! They're brewing cannabis tea!"

An old man in the pew in front of them turned and smiled. "No, no, no. Many visitors make the same mistake. It's not cannabis at all. It might be a distant relative, but that stuff will put you to sleep. This is way more powerful than cannabis and gives you a whole different outcome. Elder Lancepod's grandfather discovered it, but it's not cannabis. We believe this is the same stuff the apostles used. Oh, sure, some people use wine or grape juice—but they're wrong. It's a mistranslation of the original Latvian text, you see."

Owen stifled a laugh and Sara rolled her eyes.

"Thank you for the explanation," said Sara.

Elder Lancepod had begun dispensing cupfuls of the brew from the urns, while Rev. Sig was breaking dark brown loaves into bite-size pieces. Congregants from the front pew were lining up to receive the elements, such as they were.

"Good, grief," whispered Dana. "We're not going to stay for this, are we?"

"No, I don't think so," said Grant, standing up.

"Hey! I wanna see what happens when they drink that stuff!" said Tadd. Congregants turned and glowered, while the team made their way out of the pew.

Outside, as they gathered their backpacks, Dayton followed them out.

"I've decided to stay here," said Dayton. "It's not easy for me to leave the team. I just want you to know that. But I think I've found what I'm looking for. And I hope you'll send word somehow when you arrive at your destination."

Sara and Bryan tried to dissuade him, but to no avail. Dayton had made up his mind. The team said their goodbyes and headed down Seventh Street, passing the old Lincoln house.

Bryan's watch informed them that after several blocks they would want to turn east on Grand Avenue, connecting with US-29 southeast, in the general direction of Lexington.

They stopped at a small grocer and used some of their dwindling funds to purchase a few staples for the next few days of their journey—dried fruit, cooking oil and a few loaves of rustic bread which looked remarkably similar to those in the communion service back at the church.

The leg ahead of them would be the longest of their journey yet—over three hundred and fifty miles, and a lot of it on smaller rural roads. If they had to walk the whole distance, it could take nearly a month. But Lexington was the next location that Sharon Stevens had mentioned, so this was the direction they would head.

"I hate to see us lose Dayton," said Bryan, "but he seems to think he knows what he's doing."

"God will give him what he needs," said Grant.

They had put a few blocks between them and the church, when they heard a commotion that sounded like some sort of riot or party—they couldn't tell which. Turning around, they saw nothing up the street. The sound seemed to be coming from a side street, and getting louder by the second.

Suddenly two people pranced out onto Seventh Avenue. They were jumping, pirouetting and flailing their arms, all the while shouting and singing unintelligibly, punctuating their singing by the occasional scream. Increasing numbers of people followed, until the street was full of the revelers.

"Sheesh," said Dana. "Is this what I think it is?"

"Yup," said Bryan. "This must be what Sig called a *cavortation*."

It looked now like Lancepod's entire congregation had filled the street—perhaps more. It seemed to Grant that some of these people were just showing up so they could have a justifiable reason to get crazy and have a good time. Grant spotted Rev. Sig among the cavorters.

Suddenly Dana was hit by a cavorter who almost knocked her over. It was Dayton. She grabbed him by the shoulders and looked him squarely in the face. "Dayton!" His glazed, distantly focused eyes gave no hint of recognition, and he broke away, babbling and careening down the street, followed by Cashmere.

The mob was rapidly thickening, threatening to engulf the team. "Mom!" shouted Lissa, caught away by a solid line of cavorters. Bryan elbowed himself into the throng and pulled her out. The team stood with their backs flat against a brick wall as the revelers pressed by.

Amidst the chaos, Emilia happened to look up and see an old sign on the wall. It read: *Walk Right Inn.* "Hey Bryan!" shouted Emilia. "Is this place open?"

Bryan tried the door under the sign. It creaked open. He motioned and shouted for the others to duck in, which they did without hesitation.

It took a while for their eyes to adjust to the low light level. When they did, they saw that they were in an old tavern. Eight or ten customers sat around tables, and a portly bartender polished the bartop with a soiled towel. "Good afternoon, folks. Welcome to *Walk Right Inn.* What can I pour you today?"

"Water for me," said Grant, sitting down at the bar. The kids wanted Joy Juice. Bryan and Emilia ordered the local beer. Sara had a glass of Merlot. Dana had a glass of whiskey to assuage her headache.

"Lemme guess," said the bartender. "You folks popped in here to get out of the way of those loony Christians and the other riff raff they scoop up along with 'em when they do their cavortin' thing."

"Yeah, I guess you could say that," said Dana. "Although we're Christians ourselves. And we try not to do too many loony things."

The barkeep's face suddenly turned grim. "Hey now. We don't want no funny stuff in here. Last time we had Christians in here they tried to get us to shut down on Sundays. Heck, Sunday is a pretty good day for me—mainly because of people tryin' to get away from the cavortin' thing."

"You don't have anything to worry about with us," said Grant. "We're on our way southeast to Lexington."

"Lexington you say, sweetie?" said a female voice

with a southern twang. Grant turned to see a woman smoking a cigarette, wearing a black Stetson cowboy hat and a well-worn blue denim jacket. "I'm Zebby Edwith, livestock trader. Headin' that general direction. There's room for y'all in my stake truck, if you don't mind sharin' the space with a couple pigs, a cow and two goats."

"I suppose we could tolerate that," said Grant, in spite of Dana's look of revulsion. "It'll save weeks on foot, and it'll be a whole lot safer."

"You're taking animals all the way to Lexington?" asked Bryan.

"You bet, honey," said Zebby. "There's a top-drawer herd of Guernseys near Lexington, and I deal in Guernsey cows, so I drive down there on occasion to get 'em bred. The pigs and goats are to finance the trip. You guys will help a bit, of course. There's a few nasty roads between here and there, but some nice flat stretches too. I figure a couple of days, if all goes well. My rig is out back of the tavern—just hop in when you're ready. Best to climb over the stakes so the animals don't get out."

"When you haven't found inner meaning, you will always substitute outer performance."
—Richard Rohr

PART VII: LEXINGTON

1.

In the darkened viewing room in Carthage, the president and his staff laugh out loud. "Go back to the scene where the pig drools all over Lissa!" shouts Security Director Jugurtha.

Lissa is sitting on her backpack, reclining against the rails that enclose the truck bed. Her eyes are closed as she experiences her music videos while the truck bounces along. A curious and friendly pig approaches her, sniffing and slathering her face with its flat nose. Lissa screams and jumps to her feet, her face dripping with brown slime. The insulted pig snorts and ambles away. Lissa screams again and swats at a hovering wasp. Her brother Tadd is rolling around on the truck bed, guffawing uncontrollably.

"Tadd!" says Dana, stifling a giggle. "Have some respect for your sister!"

A grinning Bryan addresses another wasp hovering near him. "Did you get all of that, guys? Almost better than the cavortation parade back there in Springfield, eh?"

"I wish you wouldn't just…talk to them like that," says Emilia. "It makes me uneasy."

President Kazdaghli chuckles at the scene. "I must

211

say, the last few days have been entertaining, to say the least. Our team is coming face to face with the insanity that is the Wilderness—religious chaos. This is a real education for them."

"The group in Lexington will not be quite as insane as the others, Excellency, but they seem rather dysfunctionally strict and flamboyantly ritualistic, in my opinion—based on our surveillance. Yet it is possible that the Cochrin group may choose to stay there," says one of the President's aides.

"Yes," says another, "It is difficult to predict how a given religious culture will appeal to one individual and not another. Dayton for example—otherwise an intelligent and rational man—who could have foreseen his fascination with the screaming elder? He must be driven by some deep-seated need for an ecstatic experience.

"Yet I am inclined to believe that Grant will not be taken in again," says the President. "He has changed. Think back to just a few weeks ago in Fargo. Grant and Dana were naïve enough to be hoodwinked by that 'end-times' huckster. They had to be set straight by their friends. Now, while Grant respects how others may worship, he is rapidly developing specific ideas about what he will personally endorse, and what he will insist on in terms of faith. I don't believe he has encountered anyone in the Wilderness so far who meets these criteria, except maybe Sharon Stevens back in Hannibal. Grant is very persistent and determined. Those with him may not have the same doggedness. But we shall see what happens in the next few days."

2.

Zebby headed her truck in a generally southeasterly direction. Twice, as they lurched through muddy detours, the Guernsey lost her footing and nearly toppled over, almost crushing the team against the rails of the truck. Both times they were able to push her away. Finally they secured the cow to the opposite rail with rope.

Grant took his turn riding shotgun in the cab with Zebby. A couple of times they saw bearded men with black hats driving horse-drawn buggies on the other side of the road.

"What's that all about?" asked Grant.

"You ain't never seen them, sweetie? Them's Amish," said Zebby. "Kind of strict people who don't cotton to new-fangled things."

"I think I remember hearing something about the Amish. I think they're Christian, sort of. I wonder if we should stop and visit them. Maybe they're a group we would want to consider."

"Not likely!" said Zebby. "Since the Final War, they keep to themselves. When the Feds tried to push everyone into the Safe Zones, they stayed put like fence posts set in concrete. Now they don't even talk to anyone else. They've gone back to speakin' a German dialect like their ancestors. So unless you speak *Plautdietsch...*"

They camped that evening near Effingham, where one of Zebby's friends brewed and sold bio-diesel. Zebby also scored some feed for her animals. The next morning they continued southward, eventually arriving at Elberfield, Indiana, where they would cross the Safe Corridor connecting Cincinnati to St. Louis. It roughly followed the old I-64, and was elevated over the prairie and trees, with concrete barriers on either side, punctuated by sensors and beam weaponry.

The team watched the tops of Safe Corridor trucks and trains as they whizzed by. It seemed strange that inside those barriers was a whole other "civilized" world, with people traveling in comfort and safety—

with fine meals, luxurious homes and great entertainment awaiting them at the end of their day. Sara and Bryan were acutely aware of the difference. The others not quite as much.

At this point, Wilderness travelers could pass beneath the massive corridor deck with relative safety, as long as they did not stop, or look like they were considering tampering with the supports or anything related to the Corridor. Cameras and weapons followed them from one side to the other. They passed the grim wreckage of a couple of cars and a few human skeletons, left there as a reminder of what happens to those who linger too long.

From there they headed east by southeast, and crossed the Ohio River into the former state of Kentucky. Here the prairie gradually gave way to forests and rolling hills. They noticed fewer bikers on the roads, but Zebby explained that raptors generally confined themselves to the old interstates, as there were more "customers" there. Grant remembered Garvin's offer of aid if they encountered any kind of trouble, but he wasn't sure if that applied outside of what used to be Illinois. Maybe Garvin had some alliances here, maybe not. Grant hoped they wouldn't have to find out.

They camped the last night with Zebby near the legendary Fort Knox, the site of the United States' gold reserves just after the Final War. Within a matter of minutes after the battle, Federation warships had descended and carried away what was left of the reserves to Tunisia. The Federation had also removed all weaponry and ammunition from the surrounding military base, which stood abandoned and deteriorating.

In the morning they continued their journey, passing well south of the ruins of Louisville—a city that did not fare well in the Final War.

Before the Final War, Lexington had been equestrian country. Not so much anymore. Nearly all the wealthy people had chosen to move to Safe Zones to maintain their business interests and lifestyles—and they took their best horses with them. Small herds of wild horses roamed the countryside, descendants of those culled and left behind.

They were about ten miles out of Lexington. Zebby had taken a small road that paralleled the Interstate to avoid raptors, but there were no guarantees. In her side mirror, Zebby saw a disturbing thing—a tricked-out Harley trike was gaining on them. She found it odd that the rider was alone, but Zebby wasn't taking any chances. She grabbed her handgun and clicked the safety off, hoping that Bryan, in the back of the truck, had seen the trike and was readying his assault rifle. Then in her rearview mirror, she could see Bryan standing against the back rail, along with everyone else!

"What's wrong with your people?" shouted Zebby at Grant, sitting next to her. "Don't they know bullets are 'bout to fly?"

"I don't know *what* they're doing," said Grant, urgently rapping on the window and motioning for the team to lie down.

The team turned briefly and returned to watching the trike, which accelerated and pulled up beside them on the left. Zebby raised her handgun and aimed it at the raptor through her open window. The raptor frantically waved his hand and pulled ahead, his three long braids of hair waving in the breeze.

"Hey!" yelled Grant. "Put your gun down. We know this guy." It was McGwynn, but without his sidecar. "Pull over," said Grant. Zebby flashed a worried look at him but complied at the next turnout. Grant hopped out of the truck and a grinning McGwynn dismounted his trike.

"McGwynn!" shouted Grant. "What on earth are you doing here? Is everything okay?"

"I left the gang," said McGwynn. "Tried to find you, but by the time I got back to that church there in Springfield, you had skedaddled. I talked to Rev. Sig and he said the last he saw of you was in front of some bar on Seventh Street. I figured it was the *Walk Right Inn*. Been there many times. Anyways they said you'd headed off to Lexington with some girl haulin' livestock. I picked the most likely route, assumin' you'd want to stay off the interstates, owin' to the more aggressive raptors down here. Needed to stay on the sideroads myself, since I'm a lone Illinois raptor in Kentucky territory. Flashed our sign to a couple of 'em and it worked."

"But why did you follow us? Is something wrong?" asked Grant.

"I want to join you guys," said McGwynn. "Got to thinkin' about stuff—about what you said and didn't say—but mostly what you *did*. Guess I'd have to say that your picture of the man Jesus makes all kinda sense to me. Totally different than what I've seen from a lot o' folks who like to wave him around like a fork at a sweet potato pie-eatin' contest. I don't care what they may say. I don't care what they may do. Far as I'm concerned, Jesus is just alright! So whadda ya think? Can I tag along?"

"Well of course," said Grant. "But we heard about how Garvin's really the big boss there in Illinois. Won't he send someone to bring you back?"

"Heh heh. I figured you'd be blown away when you found that out," said McGwynn. "No problem. Got his word on it. I'm free to hit the road and do whatever I need to do. And Garvin's been doin' some thinkin' himself. But he's got all kinds of entanglements, you know—although there's a lot of people who would like for him to disappear—for years he's been a boil that won't go away. So one day he just might show up on your doorstep. Assumin' we find a doorstep somewheres."

Grant and Dana were both amazed. Things like this made Grant feel like they were headed in the right direction—like something or Someone was guiding them. But where?

The entire team was happy with this development. They piled back in the truck. Since Tadd was the first one to ask, he got to ride pillion on McGwynn's trike the rest of the way into Lexington. "Cool!" he shouted, as they roared back onto the highway.

3.

Zebby headed for the center of town, based on her recollection of Christ Church Cathedral. It had been an Episcopal church, an impressive Gothic revival structure built in the nineteenth century. Now it had been taken over by a new group, but Zebby had no idea what they were about.

Zebby's truck pulled up in front of the church, followed by McGwynn's rumbling trike.

"Here you are, folks," said Zebby. "I hope this is what you're lookin' for. Not my particular cup o' hooch, but everyone's gotta do his or her thing."

Grant paid her for the trip, out of the team's dwindling funds. If this group didn't pan out, Grant had no idea what to do next. Maybe Sharon had been right. Maybe they should find a piece of land or abandoned town and become their own community. Maybe they should head back to Hannibal. But without any funds, getting back would be an uphill battle.

Now that they were in Lexington, Grant was eager to give this place a chance. He hoped this group and these leaders would be more Christ-centered rather than being preoccupied with peripherals such as strange healing rituals, dangerous prayer regimens, bizarre prophecy interpretations, or freakish charismatic manifestations. What else could there be?

Grant stepped up to the ponderous oak door of the church. An elegant stone scroll above the door identified the building, not as Christ church as Zebby had said, but as St. Alypius. Grant tried the door, which was locked. He knocked and waited. There was no answer.

"I sure hope this isn't gonna be like the last three places we visited," said Lissa. "I just want you to know that I'm totally icked out on churches and stuff like that. Why can't we find a place with at least somewhat normal people who don't do super weird things? I can't believe that God is actually a nut case like some of these guys."

McGwynn flashed a lopsided grin, and several others of the group nodded their assent.

"I couldn't agree more. In fact I was just thinking the same thing. But let's give them a chance. We don't know anything about this group—but first we have to *find* them," Grant responded.

"I understand what you're saying, Lissa," said Dana. "We're trying to find a 'normal' Christian community. But we're still learning about what that looks like, aren't we? Still—maybe this will be it. Try to be patient."

As the team was wondering what to do next, Emilia spotted a sign on an adjacent building that said *Abbott's Residence*. Grant walked over and knocked on the door. A tall, solidly built, balding man with grey hair around his ears, wearing a hooded cloak, opened the door. When he saw the group he grinned heartily.

"My, my, my!" said the man. "What a fine-looking and—I must say—*diverse* group! A resplendent morning to you, friends! I'm Dale McFallow, Abbot of St. Alypius the Stylite. How may I serve you today?"

Grant related the team's sojourn to date, trying unsuccessfully to make it brief. McFallow was mesmerized by the story. The group stood on the porch and on the lawn, recounting their journey. Tadd wanted to toss his football around with McGwynn, but McGwynn was interested in what Abbot McFallow had to say.

Grant finished his story, embellished with comments from the others. The abbot was speechless for a moment. "I'm so sorry! I neglected to invite you in. Come! Sit down! I think I have enough chairs."

Abbot McFallow's quarters were comfortable, but not fancy. On his wall, portraits of saints, including St. Alypius, flanked a large, faded print of Matthias Grünewald's 16th century painting *Resurrection*, in which a smiling, shining yellow Jesus, framed by a bright green halo, floats above an open sarcophagus. His arms are raised in victory, showing the wounds on his hands and side, while Roman guards fall to the ground, overwhelmed. Tadd couldn't take his eyes off the striking image.

"First things first!" declared the abbot, grabbing a firm hold of McGwynn's buckskin clad shoulders and bending to kiss him squarely on the forehead.

"Hey—what the…?" exclaimed McGwynn, backing away, then sheepishly covering his mouth with his hand.

"Oh, please forgive me!" said McFallow. "I didn't explain. I'm greeting each and every one of you with a holy kiss. It's an ancient and biblical custom in our order."

"Ew," said Lissa, under her breath, so that only her mother heard. "This is *normal*?" Dana opened her hand in a "calm down" gesture.

The abbot systematically kissed and welcomed the entire team. Afterward he opened a cabinet and produced a small, ornately decorated bottle, which he vigorously waved in each person's face. Lilac scented drops flew out, splashing in eyes, hair and mouths.

"This is Water of Righteousness. We sprinkle it on honored guests. Now then—how about nice cups of hot tea all around?" asked the abbot.

"That sounds wonderful, thank you," said Grant, wiping his face with a napkin.

"Um, what kind of tea?" asked Dana.

"Black tea," said McFallow. "The finest orange pekoe. We bought it from a traveling merchant just yesterday. Is that okay?"

"Yes, that'll be fine," said Dana, relieved.

Abbot McFallow turned to a curtained doorway. "Mother Shirley! Come meet our guests and prepare some tea, please." The sounds of running water and a teapot being set on a stove immediately came from the doorway, followed by the sound of an igniting gas flame. A smiling, matronly lady appeared in the doorway, wearing a hooded cloak matching that of Abbot McFallow. "This is my wonderful help-mate, Shirley. She shoulders fully half the load of my ministry here at St. Alypius." Shirley nodded, waved to everyone and went back through the doorway.

"Shirley has taken a vow of silence," explained McFallow. She hasn't uttered a word for some twenty years. Our community often takes similar vows, you see. We believe that such things are important spiritual disciplines, to demonstrate one's level of devotion to God."

A smiling Shirley emerged again with a tray holding cups, a pitcher of milk and a bowl of sugar.

"Wow!" said Tadd. "I betcha *a lot* of husbands wish their wives would take a vow of silence!"

"Tadd!" shouted Dana. "You're coming outside with me this instant!"

With the exception of Grant and Dana, the team tried very hard to stifle their laughter. Owen and McGwynn turned their faces to the wall. Even Shirley set down the tray and covered her mouth with her hand.

"Friends, friends, it's okay!" laughed McFallow. "Your son is quite the comedian, and will doubtless have an entertainment gig waiting for him someday. But Mother Shirley and I are not married. We live together as brother and sister."

Sara and Emilia both happened to be watching Shirley. They saw a slight blush cross her cheeks.

"Listen, my friends," continued McFallow, "after tea, and after you settle into your accommodations, perhaps we can share a meal. And then perhaps we can show you our wonderful sanctuary."

"Uh...accommodations?" asked Grant.

"Well, how should I put this? You have a certain... *aroma* about you. As if you had been in close quarters with farm animals of some kind. And additionally you all *look* like you could use a shower. Our volunteers have renovated a couple of the neighboring buildings here for the homeless and for weary travelers like yourselves. Our rooms are sparsely furnished, but much better and safer than sleeping outside with no restrooms."

"I can't tell you how much we appreciate this," said Grant. "It's been a few days since we slept in beds."

4.

The rooms of the dormitory were simple, each with with a cot or two, a chair and a table—apparently this had been office space prior to the Final War. Restrooms were down the hall. At least the plumbing, water and sewer systems were functional, owing to the efforts of McFallow's volunteers. Members of his order staffed the buildings, keeping the peace and guarding against thievery.

After giving the team a few minutes to settle in, McFallow directed them to a kitchen adjacent to the church where he and Shirley served them a simple but delicious meal of lamb stew and crusty bread. "We have some five hundred people in our group," explained McFallow. "Most of them are regular members who live here in Lexington. Some struggle to survive. Some farm or hunt. Some have businesses. But most of them faithfully give a tenth of their income or harvest to support the work of St. Alypius, which is done by the talented and capable members of our order."

"What's the difference between regular church members and members of the order?" asked Sara.

"Members of the order take a vow of celibacy and poverty, that they may devote themselves to prayer, work, study, hospitality and renewal."

"Oh," said Sara. "And what do they study?"

"Well, of course the Bibles are all gone, as are many other religious texts and writings, so to fill the void I have written on a wealth of subjects over the years, including the rule for our order."

Everyone cast a sidelong glance at Grant, who stared at the carpet and said nothing. Something inside him wanted to pull his Bible from his backpack and go through it page by page with McFallow, showing him that there was nothing there in the New Testament commanding celibacy, holy orders, veneration of saints, lofty church edifices or tithing. On the other hand, there was nothing that he had read so far specifically prohibiting such things, or other spiritual disciplines, so long as they didn't create a "yoke of bondage." In any case, the better part of wisdom told him to keep his Bible under wraps for the time being.

After lunch, they headed toward the sanctuary. Inside, Abbot McFallow gave them a tour of the various features of the old church, explaining how his order and other volunteers had repaired and remodeled much of the structure.

No one in the team had any point of reference as to how a church building was supposed to look on the inside (or the outside, for that matter). Owen vaguely remembered the Baptist church that his family attended before the Final War. Back in the Safe Zones, Sara and Bryan had been in several old church buildings—now scrubbed of their religious iconography and converted to public meeting halls. The chapels where Prophet Nordwyn and Sister Aretha conducted services were quite plain, except their lecterns were placed center stage. Elder Lancepod's church was a bit more elaborate, but not anything like the embellishment here at St. Alypius.

The most striking feature was a fifteen-foot Ionic column in front of the altar, topped by an emaciated, white-bearded man emanating bright, undulating flames. Bryan recognized it as a holographic image. The whole unit was slowly and silently rotating. On the steps in front of it stood a large open censer with smoke rising and glowing as it interacted with the light of the holograph. Two robed figures knelt at the altar rail.

It was hard for the team not to keep staring at the altarpiece while Abbot McFallow talked. But he had saved the altar for last. "And this, my friends, is the namesake of our church and order, St. Alypius the Stylite. Members of our order are here day and night, offering prayers to him and attending to the incense, which is always kept burning. Other brothers insure that the generators powering the holographic projector never run out of fuel—so it never ceases. We have some highly creative technicians and artisans here, as you will discover as you look around—and especially when you attend our Sunday mass."

"I regret to say that most of us here are not all that familiar with St. Alypius," said Grant. "Maybe you can tell us more about him."

"Yeah, like why he's up there on that pole," blurted Tadd.

"Tadd!" exclaimed Dana.

McFallow smiled, although this time a bit forced. "St. Alypius lived sixteen centuries ago. He took a vow of poverty, built a church, started an order of monks and nuns, and lived atop a pillar for most of his lifetime—which turned out to be one hundred and eighteen years."

"That's amazing. Where did you learn about this?" asked Bryan.

"My grandfather passed it down to me. He was an admirer of St. Alypius," said McFallow. "He taught me many, many other things as well, much of which I have tried to include in my writings, so they will not be lost."

"But why did Alypius live on top of a pillar?" asked Tadd.

"To participate in the sufferings of Christ," answered McFallow.

"I have a question," said Sara. "You pray to St. Alypius. Why don't you just pray to God directly?"

"That's a fine question," said McFallow. "I will answer it *with* a question. I assume you pray. Do you pray for each other? And when you have needs, do you also ask your friends to pray and intercede for you?"

"Well, yes, we do."

"Then why not ask your friends in heaven to pray for you?"

"Hmm," said Sara. "I guess I never thought of it from that perspective."

5.

That afternoon, the team was free to explore the church and the surrounding buildings that were being used by the order. McFallow encouraged them to talk with anyone, ask any questions and pitch in and help with the work if they felt like it. They did. Bryan spent time with the techies who developed the Alypius hologram. They had created many other features and systems to enhance the old church building, which the Cochrin team would see on Sunday, they emphasized.

Owen and McGwynn took some time to explore Lexington on the Harley. They happened to spot a small trailer for sale and bought it for a few dinar, taking a couple of hours afterward to adapt McGwynn's hitch to the trailer. If they decided to settle here, McGwynn and Owen could make some money hauling stuff around town. If they decided to move on, they were ready to transport the team.

In the warm evening air, sitting around in the open courtyard of their dormitory, the team began to compare notes.

"There are some things about the group here that I'm not that excited about, but beyond that, they seem to be sincere people who are interested in serving their community and serving God," began Grant.

"From what I understand about traditional Roman Catholicism, this seems to bear a striking resemblance," said Sara. "You know—the church with the pope. But of course there is no more pope. So instead they have an abbot."

"Yes, he and Shirley seem to be humble and dedicated," said Dana. "Pretty decent people, compared to the three other places we've been—Nordwyn using people's fear of the future to line his pockets and expand his power, Aretha and her bizarre rituals, Lancepod and his screaming and cavorting."

"Don't be too tough on Sister Aretha," said Owen, wistfully. "Her heart was in the right place."

"Don't forget the Muslims and Buddhists," commented Bryan. "They were good folks, if not stuck in a sandbar of rules and regulations."

"What's your point?" Grant asked.

"Well, a lot of people can be decent and humble, but I thought we were searching for a community of Christ-followers," Bryan responded.

"And don't these folks here in Lexington seem to be Christ-followers?" prodded Grant.

"Yeah," said Bryan, "except for the preoccupation with St. What's-his-face. I mean, sure, it's a cool hologram, but it occupies the most prominent position on the chancel, obscuring the altar and cross behind it. I'm not sure how that's supposed to work, but just off hand it seems to be symbolic of misplaced priorities, to me. I'm just sayin'."

"It's interesting," added Sara, "that the great historical cathedrals and churches were filled with liturgical art and sculpture, in keeping with the best technologies of the day. In the late Renaissance and early Baroque, churches were filled with music and art, including magnificent ceiling paintings and frescoes with scenes of heaven, deliberately intended to draw worshippers' eyes upward, inducing feelings of awe and wonder—creating a sort of ecstatic religious experience. Of course St. Peter's and Notre Dame were victims of the Final War and there are no such places in the Safe Zones anymore, unless they've been turned in to museums. But out here we might expect that the Abbot and his associates would use their best available technology. I think the operative question is—is it to illustrate and proclaim the freedom of the gospel or is it merely to wow people and keep them firmly entranced by the religious institution?"

For the next few days the team continued to keep their eyes and ears open. They were more open than before, in many ways, and yet, also more critical. If this was to be the place they landed, they wanted to be certain it was right for all of them. They were still smarting from the loss of Dayton. Grant, Dana and a few of the others were beginning to think that if they could put up with a few quirky practices, this might be a good place to settle down.

6.

Sunday morning the team cleaned themselves up and headed to St. Alypius' sanctuary. Regular members from the community were filing in. "The Abbot and his order will arrive shortly," explained one of the congregants. The team found seats and waited. The congregation here was quiet. *No screaming or cavorting...yet,* thought Grant. Just the steady turning of St. Alypius' pillar, and the wafting of incense.

Suddenly a voice rang through the church. "This is the day that St. Alypius hath made! Let us be glad and rejoice in it!" A capella choral music filled the sanctuary in a language Sara recognized as Latin. The congregation stood and joined in the singing, but the Cochrin team didn't know the words. Dana tried to join in, pretending she knew the lyrics as well as the music. Grant, Lissa and Tadd stared at her.

"What?" she asked. "I'm harmonizing."

Soon the whole family was grinning and singing in mock Latin, trying to follow the music as much as possible. A young acolyte holding high a gilded processional cross marched down the aisle, followed by a long line of men and women two by two in white robes—and helmets.

Owen nudged his neighbor. "What are those things on their heads?"

"Oh, those are the Helmets of Salvation," said the man. "The Abbot says they are mentioned in Scripture. Years ago, he discovered these helmets down at the old University of Kentucky. They used to be blue with a big UK on them."

The acolyte reached the altar rail and turned to face the congregation as the white-robed, helmeted procession split, women left and men right, ascending to the chancel and standing in the choir pews flanking the altar.

Another acolyte marched down the aisle swinging a silver censer. After him came three more acolytes, one carrying a large, leather-bound tome, another carrying a tall bottle, presumably wine, and another carrying a wide basket of bread.

Grant asked his neighbor, "I'm guessing those must be elements of the communion—but what is that book? Surely it's not a Bible?"

"Oh, no," said the woman. "Those are the writings of Abbot McFallow."

Finally, the singing finished, a signal for the congregation to face the back door. The lights in the church dimmed and the air seemed to take on a purplish glow. The old pipe organ, a three-manual Holtkamp, remarkably in tune, began the driving rhythmic F-sharp minor of a tempestuous piece that Sara recognized from her music appreciation courses.

It was *Tu Es Petrus*, by the early twentieth century French composer Henri Mulet. As she recalled, it was based on what she had just recently discovered were Jesus' words to Peter in Matthew 16:18 ...*thou art Peter, and upon this rock I will build my church; and the gates of hell shall not prevail against it.*

As the dramatic, rising bass line rumbled through the church, two stately figures emerged from the door, but they were barely recognizable as the humble Abbot McFallow and Mother Shirley that the team had come to know in recent days. The abbot was sporting a robe of gold filigree, his head crowned with a huge carved oaken mitre with spun gold lappets hanging from the back. He held a heavy golden crozier with a tiny image of Alypius on a pillar in the center.

Mother Shirley was wearing similar vestments, except her oaken headdress was in the shape of a nun's cornette. It looked even more uncomfortable than Abbot McFallow's mitre, but probably less heavy.

They moved slowly down the aisle, their robes trailing behind them, their faces raised beatifically toward the image of St. Alypius, which had stopped rotating but was flaming more intensely. Bryan noticed that they moved smoothly, as if they weren't taking steps but *floating*. He looked closer. There was space between their robes and the floor, with no feet visible. They *were* floating!

Bryan's mouth dropped open, not because such a thing was impossible, but because he knew the graviton plasma technology to accomplish it was strictly classified and reserved only for Federation warships and weaponry. Where had these people acquired it? They certainly couldn't have developed it on their own. Yet here it was! This was just exactly the kind of thing that the Federation had violently nipped in the bud in times past. Sure, now it was just a special effect, but it was only a matter of time before some aspiring warlord started building a floating army, then vehicles, then warships. Bryan scanned the aisle behind Mother

Shirley. There! Just as he expected, two wasps hovering a couple of feet above the carpeted floor. If the Feds hadn't known about this before, they did now.

As the music increased in intensity, the abbot and the mother floated up the steps. The abbot ascended the pulpit, and the mother took a seat behind him. Now the organist added the edgy 32-foot *posaune* stops, coupled with the 16-foot festival trumpets, thundering out the final measures of *Tu Es Petrus*. As the light in the sanctuary dimmed further, McFallow stood in the pulpit and gazed out at the congregation. A concluding, triumphant F-sharp major chord shook the floor, and the abbot and mother appeared transfigured as bright yellow flames billowed out from their faces.

The congregation was in a state of awe and bliss, even though, presumably, they experienced this every week. They were prepared to accept whatever the good abbot had to say. Then the purple haze, flames and sound dissipated and the house lights slowly came back up. The abbot and the mother reassumed human form. He began to speak.

"My friends, you see illustrated the power and the light of our Lord that shines through St. Alypius. We who are of this church have a calling. We are called to build this church and to build this community. We work hard, but my friends, we must redouble our efforts. Each and every week we see growing numbers of sojourners among us. They witness our dazzling radiance and they look to us for an example. We must show them, through the rule of St. Alypius, how authentic Christianity shines forth when it is lived.

"Those of our order follow the rule of St. Alypius in all they do, say and think. But as I look out on the laity, I see there are many here who fall short of the radiant splenor of St. Alypius. I see those failing to practice their daily disciplines and devotions. I see those who do not daily recite aloud the rule for the laity. I see those who do not tithe fully, instead squandering what belongs to God on the transitory things of this world, such as food, clothing and shelter, about which we need take no thought, knowing full well that God will provide. I see time wasted on vacuous sports and entertainment, which do not serve to edify the spirit, but rather to inflame the passions. I hear gossip and contempt against those whom the Lord has chosen to drive his flock. More egregious yet, I see women wearing immodest raiment, provoking the lust of men, and leading to what is called in the vernacular, *hanky panky*!

"Listen my friends, do you imagine that our Lord turns a blind eye to these things? I think not, my friends, I think not! Anyone who sins against the rule of St. Alypius, whether by omission or commission, let not that person think that he shall receive anything from the Lord—save the ever-burning fire which shall ever consume, yet *never* consume, soul and body for all eternity, with sizzling of fat and charring of sinew, as a chicken leg that drops from the turning spit upon the white-hot coals. Come! Confess your sin. Accept your penance. Feel your pain. Be cleansed of your wickedness and let your hand return to the plow in the field wherein the Lord has called you to cultivate! Twas ever thus and thus it shall ever be! World without end! Amen!"

Abbot McFallow floated back from the pulpit and over to the altar, where he prepared the Eucharist, offering prayers as an acolyte held the big leather tome open for him to read.

"As you partake of this blood and body of Christ, the fierce wrath of God against you is appeased—for now," intoned the abbot.

Members of the order filed down from the chancel and the congregation filed up to receive the wafers from abbot and mother, and to drink wine from a golden chalice. They returned to their seats, stood for the Abbot's benediction and sang a recessional hymn—a shortened version of the ancient *Dies Irae*—as the helmeted order filed down the center aisle, followed by the floating Abbot McFallow and Mother Shirley.

The team headed outside and visited with a few congregants. Bryan, however, headed to an upstairs room in the rear of the sanctuary that housed the technicians and their equipment. They welcomed him with smiles.

"Bryan! What did you think of our service?" asked Brother Simon, a member of the order and the chief technician.

"Well of course it was outstanding," said Bryan. "But where did you get the graviton plasma technology?"

"Graviton…what are you talking about?" asked Simon.

"Abbot McFallow and Mother Shirley. I saw them. They floated. No one has that technology except the Feds. When they find out you have it, you and the whole town are potentially toast."

Simon laughed a bit nervously. "They *do* seem to float, don't they? But it's certainly not anything we're doing. What did you call that—*graviton plasma*? We have no idea what that even is, do we brothers?"

The technicians all shook their heads.

Bryan stared at Simon. Telling the truth was part of the rule of St. Alypius. But perhaps these brothers were bending the rule. Then his eyes fell on a small black box among the racks of equipment adjacent to Simon's control panel. Clearly visible was the Hantwick Industries logo. It was a device that Bryan had been involved with before his incarceration—a graviton plasma router—an interface for the generator, which was probably located somewhere under the altar. It had somehow been stolen from the company or the Fed military and found its way out here.

"Good point, Simon," said Bryan. "Things happen that can't be explained. Anyway, you guys do an amazing job here. Very impressive. And very inspiring."

Bryan hurried down the stairs and out the door, where Emilia was waiting. "What's wrong?" she asked.

"We're in danger. I'll explain when we find Grant," said Bryan.

They found the team and pulled Grant aside. "We need to leave this place as soon as possible. They have top secret, classified technology, and the Feds know it. It's only a matter of time before they fry 'em."

"What?" said Grant. "What is it? How do you know the Feds know?"

"Don't ask because I can't tell you. But you know how the Feds deal with military technology leaks—they nip them in the bud. They don't care about collateral damage. They destroy everything and everyone that might know about it. It's how they keep the Wilderness subdued. And I know what you're thinking—we should warn the Abbott. But that won't do any good. Once the Feds know, there's no escape and it's only a matter of time. Maybe minutes."

Dana had joined the conversation. "These people have a few funny rituals and some heavy-handed requirements, but they also have spiritual disciplines and humility," said Dana, "and I think we should give it more time…"

"No, no, no," said Bryan, shaking his head. "We can have this debate later. Right now, we have to leave. *Right now!*"

"But I..." Dana protested.

"Honey," said Grant. "I think we need to respect Bryan's judgment. Round up the team. Then back to the dorm to get our stuff and we're out of here."

As the others headed for the dorm, a wasp hovered in front of Bryan and Emilia. Bryan addressed the insect, "Please don't do this," said Bryan. "These are good people. Maybe a little strange, like everything else out here. And I know you don't believe in a Higher Power. But c'mon. There's got to be a more civilized way."

7.

"Excellency, I don't know how we didn't detect this breach in our earlier surveillance, but we can't allow it to continue," says Security Director Jugurtha.

The president sits at his desk, with his face in his hands. "I know it's a problem. But I was hoping, considering the great transformation in the works, that we could employ less drastic methods in dealing with such things, even in the Wilderness."

"I understand, Excellency, but a firm hand at this point will save great bloodshed in the future."

"A firm hand?" laughs the president, sardonically. "Our standard operating procedure in such instances is well beyond a firm hand, and you know it, Aymen."

No one says anything for two or three minutes. Then the president speaks: "Send in our special operatives from the Richmond base. Have them perform an extraction of the abbot and his technicians, and remove the contraband technology. I have to go now—I have a meeting in five minutes with the senator from central Africa."

"As you wish, Excellency," says Security Director Jugurtha. "Operatives will be on site within the hour, pending further surveillance. I just hope this covers the entire breach."

8.

Rolling past the eastern suburbs of Lexington, six members of the Cochrin team had crammed themselves into the little trailer and two had squeezed onto the pillion of McGwynn's trike. He headed eastward on I-64 as fast as he dared, considering the trailer. He was trying to put as much distance as possible between them and the doom that Bryan insisted was coming to the town.

"I hope we're doing the right thing," said Grant over the roar of the trike, "because right now, we have no clear destination, hardly any supplies, and from what they said in town, this is dangerous territory."

Bryan said nothing. But in a few minutes, as he had predicted, a circular silver craft rose over the trees ahead of them. McGwynn slowed to a stop and everyone stared as the craft quietly slipped westward over the treetops. Then, in plain sight, it vanished.

Interesting, thought Bryan. *Why would they engage their cloaking to destroy a city?* Cloaking—the light-bending technology to render equipment and personnel invisible, was another classified military secret jealously guarded by the Feds. *But in a case like this,* thought Bryan, *wouldn't the Feds want folks to see their warship—to know who was punishing them?*

The team expected to see flashes and hear rumbling, but there was none of that. They continued on their way, looking nervously over their shoulders.

9.

Back in downtown Lexington, the abbott and his flock

wondered where the Cochrin group had gone. Regardless, they were enjoying a Sunday afternoon picnic in an open, grassy area near the church. Above them the sky seemed clear, blue and empty—except for a faint whirring noise, causing Brother Simon to look around for the source of the sound. Suddenly, Abbot McFallow, Mother Shirley, Brother Simon and his four assistant technicians felt an upward tug. Congregants and members of the order gasped in disbelief as they watched the seven surprised figures rise into the sky and disappear. Later, witnesses would affirm that the group had been raptured, whisked off to heaven for reasons known only to the Lord and St. Alypius.

Meanwhile, Federation operatives descended on the other side of the church building, locating and removing the technology in question. The operatives and the equipment were all lifted up to the cloaked airship, just as the abbot and his friends had been.

After a few minutes' flight to Richmond, the abbot and his party were questioned as to where they acquired the graviton plasma technology. A trucker, a security guard and a Hantwick Industries employee were identified and dealt with. The abbot and his party were transported the same day to a special facility in Tunisia. With appropriate reeducation, they might be useful to the Federation in the near future.

"I have held many things in my hands, and I have lost them all; but whatever I have placed in God's hands, that I still possess."
—Martin Luther

PART VIII: POINTS EAST

1.

Bouncing down the road behind McGwynn's trike, the team had traveled less than fifty miles when they saw the silver warship pass overhead again, this time headed eastward. They concluded it had done its grim work, leaving downtown Lexington a smoldering wasteland littered with corpses of people that the team had been talking with only a couple of hours ago. No one spoke for a long time.

"I wish we could go back and help," said Dana.

"I know," said Grant, "But we would be risking our lives to do that. We don't know what the situation is there. They may have left troops."

Bryan knew full well that Federation drones were watching the team leave, and that they could be subject at any time to the same fate as the people in Lexington. He hoped his plea for mercy hadn't fallen on deaf ears. But he didn't want to tell the team what was going on because it wouldn't change anything, and would just create more anxiety.

The team had seen a couple of bikers on the way. Maybe they were raptors, maybe not. No one bothered them. McGwynn still looked the part, and Bryan, Vikhr in hand, sat on McGwynn's pillion beside Owen. Maybe it looked like they were transporting a load of captives somewhere, although they certainly weren't headed toward Nashville.

That night they camped near the half-abandoned city of Charleston, the former capitol of what had been West Virginia. A couple of locals affirmed that there were no Christian groups there, save a small cadre of snake handlers. Over the campfire and roasted rabbit, Grant tossed out some thoughts. "You know, in retrospect, I'm thinking Sharon had the right idea. Instead of looking for a group to join, maybe it's time to pick a place and settle down."

"Now you figure that out," said Dana, exasperated.

Grant continued, "They say there's hundreds of little 'hollers' around here, many of them uninhabited—and even more as we get into the Appalachian foothills. Tomorrow we hit a crossroads. Bryan tells me that we can head northeast on I-79 or southwest along I-64. Either route will take us into the Appalachians. Southeast, we'll come up against the Richmond Corridor and Safe Zone, and the big Fed military base there. Northeast will eventually take us toward the ruins of some of the big cities—Pittsburgh, Baltimore, Washington. I'm thinking we take the road less traveled, I-79—and keep our eyes open for someplace to build our own community."

"I'm ready for that," said Bryan. "Ready to start a new life with Emilia here. Maybe do a little farming and hunting." Emilia flashed a contented smile.

"Anyone else agree?" asked Grant. The group all nodded their heads, especially Dana and the kids.

Their journey had taken them nearly fourteen hundred miles and some two months. Grant had come to realize that this experience had been far more valuable than the immediate fulfillment of their quest. They had learned so much from the various permutations of Christianity they had encountered, as well as other religions. They had learned from the people they met—sincere believers, victims, opportunists, manipulators and thieves alike.

Grant and the rest of the team could now see that there were no perfect Christian institutions or communities, anymore than there are perfect Christians, and that searching for one was a fool's errand. They had seen first-hand how people who were mostly well-intentioned could pool their efforts to get something done in the name of Christ.

Grant was considering the fact that "church" is most of all the inner life of Jesus which he lives in those who follow him. So Grant concluded that "church" is who we are in Christ far more than a place to go or an institution to join. The danger was always one of exchanging a direct relationship with God for a relationship with an institution or a leader, whether a hierarchy or an anarchy. Grant was realizing that an institution always takes on a life of its own and begins to assert its power, often in authoritarian ways. And then it always produces toxic side effects. Or does it?

Out of all this, Grant wanted a place to settle where they could discuss Jesus and the Bible openly, valuing critical thought—with faith leading them.

Likewise, Dana, in the course of their journey, had gone from skepticism about her husband's quest to confidence, or at least hope, that they would find some community they could be comfortable with—that they could find or even create their own open, encouraging community, following the scriptural Jesus and without excluding any person or or any faith.

"You know," said Grant, "if we do this, the big question will be—what will we look like in ten or twenty years? Will we develop all kinds of of odd traditions, rules and requirements like the groups we've encountered or not?"

"Maybe this is what God wanted us to see all along," said Owen. "Maybe that's the reason for our journey."

"I think you may be right," said Sara. "The thing is, religion in the general sense of the word is about external, visible things—buildings, practices, art, music, convocations, food, ceremonies, observances, relics, texts and so on. Those make it easy for the Federation to identify a religious person. If they can see it, they can nail you for it. But I don't believe that's what the Jesus way is all about. It's about the internal, the invisible, such as faith and connection with God. Visible things will ultimately emerge from from invisible faith, things like concern and service for your fellow human beings. But why should the Feds have a problem with those things? They make for a healthy civilization."

"If there's anything I've learned on this trip," said Grant, "I'd have to say that the most important is that Christianity functions poorly as a religion. It's most healthy when it's an active trust in Christ—a friendship in which he leads, obviously, since he's our Shepherd. I suppose that's true for everyone—they just haven't acknowledged it yet. Or maybe they're in the process but they have baggage and issues and ambitions and obsessions and addictions that they have to work through. Or that God must work out in them."

"Sounds to me like maybe that's what we're supposed to share with the folks in our little part of the world," said McGwynn. "*To everything there is a season,* y'know. I heard that in a an old song somewhere."

Even though they were still on the road and in unfamiliar territory, the group slept better that night than they had in two months.

2.

They were about twenty miles northeast of Charleston on I-79. A light mist was draped over the forest and hills, and the team was huddled in their rattling trailer with rain gear on. This time Owen was in the trailer and Grant was with Bryan on the back of McGwynn's trike. With the help of Bryan's map-watch, they were already scanning the territory for abandoned towns that might make good candidates for settlement.

They were also keeping sharp eyes out for raptors lurking in the trees. But the sharpest eyes can only see so far into a forest. In his rearview mirror, McGwynn spotted a rider, then two, then three. Suddenly a half dozen or so more came pouring out of the woods.

"They're after us," shouted McGwynn. "We're not gonna outrun 'em, and we won't win a firefight on the road, especially with the trailer in the middle. We'd best stop while we're ahead and let the group run for cover in the woods, while we hold the raptors off."

They skidded to a stop on the shoulder. Owen helped the others jump out of the trailer and rushed them to cover in the woods. Grant and McGwynn ducked behind the trike, and watched with surprise as Bryan ran behind Owen into the woods.

"I think he has a plan," McGwynn whispered, as he pulled out his Chinese T-110 5.56 mm assault rifle. At fifteen rounds per second, it was not not as formidable as Bryan's 22 rps 9 mm Vikhr, but it was still a respectable weapon by Wilderness standards.

Grant, of course, was unarmed. "Don't use that thing. I'll talk."

"I don't think you..." started McGwynn, but hung his weapon just out of sight on a hook on his gas tank.

The raptor bikes were downshifting, and the two

men could clearly see that the pillion riders were holding weapons. They stopped, surrounding Grant and McGwynn in a semi-circle, and took aim. Grant and McGwynn stood, hands raised. Grant looked the man squarely in the eye who seemed to be the head raptor and spoke calmly, "We're almost out of money and almost out of food, but how can we serve you?"

McGwynn winced. "Ha! Let me count the ways!" responded the head raptor. "You can start by callin' for your folks who just ran up into the woods to come back out so's we can see 'em!"

"Lower your guns first and I'll do that," said Grant. "You can see we're not holding weapons, but you *don't* know that about our friends in the woods. No reason anyone should get hurt."

"Suit yourself," snarked the head raptor. "We lower our weapons, you holler for your friends and I'll count to ten. If they're not back here by then, both of *you* get it in the face, and then we'll go round 'em up. For all I know you two were cartin' 'em off to sell 'em and they just now escaped."

"Owen!" shouted Grant. "Bring everybody back here immediately!" Owen emerged from the trees about twenty feet behind Grant and McGwynn. Sara stepped out behind Owen, when a sudden burst of gunfire came from the woods behind the raptors. Three raptors fell, and the others swiveled toward the source returning a hail of fire. With their attention diverted, McGwynn grabbed his weapon and fired at the head raptor, missing and hitting his front tire instead, which deflated. The head raptor, armed with a Glock 9 mm automatic handgun, squeezed off a round and hit McGwynn in the right shoulder. McGwynn's weapon dropped to the ground.

"Good choice, brother," yelled the head raptor. "Too

bad your buddy up there in the woods didn't get the message."

McGwynn and Grant turned and watched in horror as Bryan, covered with blood, emerged from the bushes and fell to the gravel on the road's shoulder.

"Charlie! Ralph! Sammy!" ordered the head raptor. Get your butts up there and grab those runners! Try not to hurt 'em too much. We're takin' 'em to Nashville! And we get a trailer and a Harley trike to boot!"

A raptor cuffed Grant and McGwynn, as they both stared at Bryan, rapidly bleeding out. Grant tried to struggle against the cuffs. He wanted to reach Bryan.

"Please—my friend is dying," begged Grant.

"What about *my* friends?" sneered the head raptor, pointing at the three men Bryan had gunned down, in defense of the team. "Those who live by the sword die by the sword!"

Grant looked back over his shoulder at the crumpled figure of Bryan. How could it end this way? He felt a wave of guilt and sadness at having brought his friends and family out here. And Bryan—his brave, confident buddy who had saved the team's lives more than once.

3.

In a matter of minutes, Charlie, Ralph and Sammy were herding their six cuffed captives out from the bushes. Emilia spotted her fiancé and ran to kneel beside him. "Bryan! No!"

Sammy followed and gave her a kick with his jackboot. "Forget it, woman. He's just about done for. But don't worry. You're gonna have someone new *real* soon..."

Sammy's cruel comment trailed off as he realized that a huge, silver, disc-like warship had suddenly materialized in the road less than fifty feet away! Three bright orange orbs flashed from an aperture on the ship's bow and hovered over the group, radiating heat.

A strong female voice filled the air, seeming to come from nowhere: "Drop your weapons and release your captives *immediately*!"

The raptors glanced at their boss, "Do it!" he commanded—the last thing he would ever say in this life. They dropped their weapons, moved back from the captives, and they all fell lifelessly to the pavement. The team stared in disbelief as the orange orbs flashed back to the craft.

Then a door opened in the ship, and five Federation troops marched out, carrying particle beam weapons, followed by two medics carrying a gurney. The group was still in shock, but Grant expected to feel the searing heat of the troops' weapons any second. Instead, the medics attended Bryan, and the troops used some kind of metal disintegrators to remove the cuffs from the captives. A petite blonde woman who appeared to be their commander had emerged from the craft.

"Mr. Cochrin," she said, extending her hand, "I'm Federation Special Forces Commander Teri Reed. We deeply regret Mr. Hantwick's injuries. But please be assured we will do all we can to save him."

Grant and the team stared with mouths gaping. Was this some hallucination? Emilia was sobbing, following the medics as they carried Bryan into the ship.

"Now, we must get you and your belongings out of here," said Commander Reed. "Don't worry. You're safe."

Everyone looked at Grant. He mumbled, "I don't think we have a choice, do we?" The team headed toward the craft while troops shouldered their backpacks from the trailer.

The commander noticed that McGwynn was

removing belongings, including his guitar, from his trike, as blood spread across his right sleeve. "I think you'll need to leave that here, Mr. McGwynn. Someone will get your belongings for you, and another crew member will be here in a few minutes to remove your motorcycle and place it in storage. And we'll take care of your weapon. Let's get you in the ship and have the medics look at that shoulder."

McGwynn looked confused. "I'm way more worried about Bryan than my shoulder or my trike or my guitar. I don't understand what's going on here, but you're the gal with the particle beam weapons, so whatever you say."

Aboard the ship, the troops strapped themselves into seats and attendants strapped in the Cochrin team, while medics frantically worked on Bryan in a bay packed with complex equipment. Another medic treated the wound on McGwynn's shoulder, which turned out to be a graze.

Grant's family was terrified. Dana and Lissa were pale with fear. This was one of the few times Grant had seen his son terrified beyond words. Grant tried to reassure his family. "Thank God you're alive and safe. We just need to pray that Bryan pulls through. This is one time I was glad to see a Federation warship."

As the craft lifted off, the wall beside Tadd and Lissa's seats turned from opaque grey to transparent. They instinctively pulled back, as there seemed to be nothing between them and the ground. Then they watched, amazed, as the road with the trike, trailer and blood on the gravel became smaller below them. Then they were in the clouds. Then above the clouds.

"Are we under arrest?" asked Grant as an attendant brought everyone bottles of water, and a medic checked them for abrasions and bruises.

"No," said Commander Reed, "you're in custody."

"Where are you taking us? asked Dana.

"My orders are to deliver you to Cincinnati for transfer to another, more comfortable ship," said the commander. "They didn't tell me anything beyond that. Of course our priority now is to do all we can to save Mr. Hantwick. Our flight should take only a few minutes."

As Commander Reed had promised, the ship settled down on the tarmac at Cincinnati airport. This was not a major military base, but a section was secured for government operations. Before the transparent walls winked out, they caught a glimpse of their next ship. It was larger, sleeker and looked like it might indeed be "more comfortable."

Commander Reed motioned for the team to stay seated and stepped over to the medical station. Grant felt a wave of disappointment and grief as he saw a medic shake his head. The commander returned, looking genuinely distressed. "I'm terribly sorry. We were unable to save Mr. Hantwick."

Emilia broke into uncontrollable weeping. "Why? Why? I thought I'd found someone—we found each other. And now he's gone. No—he *can't* be gone. Just a few minutes ago we were together..."

Sara held Emilia against her shoulder and Owen reached and patted her arm with his strong hand. There were no words.

Commander Reed lowered her voice and spoke to Grant. "If you all could board the other ship, our medics will prepare Mr. Hantwick's remains for the journey. The troops will transfer your belongings."

Grant spoke to the team, and they exited the warcraft. He quickly noticed that entry to the other ship was guarded not by troops but by men and women in black suits.

"Good morning, Mr. Cochrin," said a man in a black suit. "Our condolences on the loss of your friend. Please take care on the escalator." As Grant rode up the steps to the aircraft, he heard each individual on the team addressed by name, even Tadd and Lissa. What was happening? It was understandable that the Feds would know who they were, since most of the team were considered fugitives. But why were they being treated as if they were guests instead of captives? And where were they headed? To Boston for arraignment before some high court? And then back to a work camp—or worse? If Bryan were still alive, he would have definite ideas about what was going on here.

Grant felt another deep stab of grief and pain. He was in shock about Bryan nearly as much as Emilia was. He had relied on him for navigation, for technical expertise and for his often contrarian and skeptical opinions. And, beyond that, for protection through the journey, even when Grant felt conflicted. Aside from Dana, Bryan was his best friend. Grant wished Bryan had relied more on God and less on his gun for security.

Just the previous day Grant had read the same words the head raptor had cited from the book of Matthew, where Jesus was talking to Peter: "'Put your sword back in its place,' Jesus said to him, 'for all who draw the sword will die by the sword.'" Grant wished now he had brought that to Bryan's attention. Maybe he would be alive now. On the other hand, Bryan had sacrificed his life protecting his friends. What could be more like Jesus than that?

Grant stopped short in the doorway of the aircraft. The luxury of its interior was astounding. Of course Grant had never been in any kind of aircraft before, except for the warship the team had just exited. But this didn't seem anything like the stories he had heard of public airliners. The interior seemed more like a living room—far nicer than Prophet Nordwyn's office, the most luxurious space Grant had been in to date.

Several uniformed attendants stood waiting around the room. None of them appeared to be armed. "Good morning, Mr. Cochrin. I am Wassim," said a dignified man with a middle eastern accent who seemed to be in charge. "Our deepest condolences for the loss of your friend Mr. Hantwick. We understand that he was a person of exceptional courage and intelligence."

"Yes—yes he was," said Grant, tearing up a bit.

Attendants directed Grant and the entire team to posh chairs and couches. Tadd and Lissa were reeling from the traumatic events of the morning, although they were starting to feel strangely distant, as if in another world. The two stared at a central low table holding bowls of assorted fruits and plates piled with unusual pastries, uncharacteristically hesitant to touch anything. "It's okay kids," said Grant. "Eat something—it'll make you feel better."

Attendants offered strong coffee and dark mint tea served in small glasses. This was clearly not traditional American cuisine. Sara recognized it as middle-eastern.

"Our flight will take about two hours today," explained Wassim. "After we are underway we will offer a late lunch, as it is currently six hours later at your destination. You have suffered a great loss, so please relax and restore yourselves. Should you have any remaining pain or discomfort from your earlier experience, a medical doctor is available."

McGwynn looked over his shoulder to see a woman in a white uniform standing behind him.

"We will arrive about 6:00 in the evening."

"Where?" asked Tadd, beginning to regain his precociousness.

"Tadd!" said Dana.

Wassim grinned. "Why, Tunisia, of course."

4.

With the exception of Tadd and Lissa, most of the team were unable to eat. Sara convinced Emilia to take a couple of glasses of the sweet, dark tea, which seemed to calm her.

The craft covered the five thousand miles from Cincinnati to the city of Tunis in less than two hours. Graviton plasma technology eliminated bumps and motion from the cabin. Again, large transparent portals opened in the wall, allowing the astonished team to see the passing land, ocean and clouds. At seventy five thousand feet, the sky above was black.

By the time they arrived, several of the team had fallen asleep in their plush chairs.

Wassim announced their impending arrival and pointed out the sparkling white buildings of Carthage and the Mediterranean beyond as they made a pass over the city. He offered the team hot, moist towels, and invited them to freshen up in the luxuriously appointed restrooms.

This time the portals remained transparent as the craft settled onto the tarmac. Two long, white vans and a contingent of navy-blue uniformed motorcycle police were lined up, ready to move. Owen and McGwynn noticed they were riding far more advanced machines than the antiques popular among raptors back in the American Wilderness.

"What's all that about?" asked Dana, looking out on the tarmac. "I have no idea why we're here or what's going to happen to us."

"You know as much as I do," said Grant, grimly.

"Looks like they're waiting for some dignitary. Maybe a senator or someone. Certainly not us. I don't know what to make of all this excessively polite, top-drawer treatment, but I expect we'll be ushered into an armored truck and taken to a high security prison. I would guess they're going to make an example of us." Grant lowered his voice further. "No matter what happens, let's try to stay together. Remember, I love you, and I'll do everything to protect you and the kids. Please forgive me for how this has turned out."

"No forgiveness is needed," whispered Dana. "We're in this together."

"Please remain seated for a few minutes," instructed Wassim, "while Mr. Hantwick's remains are transferred to the hearse."

From under the aircraft emerged a coffin draped with the flag of the Federation and surrounded by some twenty navy-blue uniformed guards. Six of them loaded the coffin into the back of one of the white vans as the rest of the guards saluted.

The entire team stared in astonishment and sadness. "You may now exit the ship," instructed Wassim. "Please—let us have the Cochrins exit last, with Mr. Cochrin at the back." As they descended the escalator in the bright Tunisian sun, their eyes adjusted to see more uniformed guards lining a path from the escalator to the second van. The guards saluted as the team walked between them.

Dana turned to her husband. "Is this some kind of awful joke?"

"Just roll with it," said Grant. "We'll soon find out."

As soon as the team was seated in the plush van, the entire procession of vehicles took off, speeding toward the airport gate and out onto the palm-tree-lined avenue, sirens blaring.

"Where are you taking us?" Grant asked a black-suited man seated in the van with them.

"That will soon become clear," smiled the man. "In the meantime I will point out some of the features of Tunis and Carthage as we make our way across the city. By the way, I am Houssem, your *aide-de-camp*."

"What?" responded Grant. "I don't even know what that is."

Traffic on busy side streets stopped to make way for the speeding entourage. Pedestrians stared and waved. Tadd and Lissa, not knowing what else to do, waved back. "Kids, let's not do that," said Grant quietly.

"Oh, it's quite appropriate, I assure you, Mr. Cochrin," said Houssem. The kids looked at their dad for permission, he nodded reluctantly and they continued waving. If this was to be their last moments of wonder and excitement, he wouldn't rob them of it.

They slowed as they turned on an avenue between stately buildings fronted by Corinthian columns. A gleaming, domed structure towered ahead. "That is the Capitol Building—the capitol of the world!" Houssem informed the awestruck team.

They made a left turn in front of the Capitol Building and entered a large, semi-circular driveway of another building, not quite as large as the capitol. It was topped by a tower with huge windows. "Welcome to the Presidential Palace," said Houssem.

As the hearse carrying Bryan's body headed off to another destination, the team walked toward the entrance, flanked by saluting guards. Attendants followed with the team's backpacks loaded on a brass luggage cart.

"I will show you to your quarters. Don't worry about a thing—your closets are stocked with fresh, stylish clothing matched to your respective sizes," said Houssem, while motioning commands to servants who were scurrying around. "Valets and maids in your rooms will help you freshen up and select appropriate attire for the occasion."

"What occasion?" asked Lissa, with large eyes.

"The reception, of course," answered Houssem. "Precisely two hours from now."

5.

Houssem led the team to a spacious elevator that would transport them up to a dining and reception room in the tower. None of the men on the team had ever donned a tie, much less a suit, much less a white suit—the color of formal wear in Federation culture. They barely recognized their own reflections in the hallway mirrors. The suits seemed stiff and confining, despite the personal tailoring that had been provided. McGwynn tugged at his collar. The tie was making it difficult to breathe. At least he still had his three long braids.

On the other hand, Dana, Sara, Emilia and Lissa, while still in shock over Bryan, found themselves escaping into the elegance of their sleek white dresses. A small army of hairdressers and cosmeticians labored over them, and seamstresses performed last-minute alterations for a perfect fit.

Sara had attended many receptions and dinners at New Harvard, but she had never been prepared like this. Lissa stopped in front of each mirror, posing and adjusting curls. Even Emilia was a bit distracted from her grief. She remembered the semi-formal events at Lastdays University, and Prophet Nordwyn's lavish dinner parties where she had served, but they were nothing compared to this.

But beyond all this, the team was still in the dark as to why this was happening. What were they being set up for? Sara couldn't help but recall ancient cultures where victims were treated royally prior to being sacrificed. Perhaps this was some sort of political sacrifice.

They exited the elevator, and in a hallway, Houssem arranged them in a line with Mr. and Mrs. Cochrin first. Emilia was showing some distress. McGwynn offered her his arm and she took it, smiling at him and wiping away a tear. Waiters opened the double doors and the team proceeded forward, with their names announced as they entered.

The circular room was surrounded by tall windows, revealing a spectacular view of Carthage, Tunis and the Mediterranean Sea in the distance. The sun had just set and lights were winking on around the city. A long table with some twenty settings dominated the room. Along one side of the room stood about ten men and women. Houssem directed the team toward the first man, over six feet tall, solidly built, with wavy grey hair, exuding power. He grinned and extended his hand to Grant, who took a few seconds to recognize the face he had seen so many times in pictures and holovideos.

"May I introduce His Excellency, World Federation President Mehdi Kazdaghli," said Houssem.

Incredulously, Grant and Dana shook his hand and mumbled something about being pleased to meet him.

President Kazdaghli laughed and put his hand on Grant's shoulder. "Grant! I feel like I know you. And here you are in the flesh, my brother. I am—all of us here are—overwhelmed to be in your presence, and I mean that for all your team. The only pall cast on this occasion is the absence of our dear friend Bryan, may he rest in glory. And Emilia, you have my deepest sympathies." A tear fell from the president's eye. The other men and women in the reception line stared at the floor and seemed moved. "If only our ship had been a few minutes earlier—but our surveillance did not see the raptors hiding in the forest until it was too late. Bryan is indeed a fallen hero and will be honored with a full state funeral."

The team nodded their heads, at the same time completely confused. The Feds had been watching them? For how long? And why would the Federation bestow such an honor on someone considered an outlaw—or for that matter, on the entire team?

The president introduced the others in the line, including Security Director Aymen Jugurtha, Surveillance Specialist Firas Echebbi and two members of the Foremost Council, including Secretary Schroeder. It struck Grant that this was a relatively small group—members of the president's staff and inner circle. As far as Grant could tell, there were no senators from the Grand Council and no justices from the Great Court.

Lissa had arrived in front of the president, who boomed, "My dear, sweet Lissa! How lovely you look! Much better than you did in the truck with the pig, eh?"

Lissa looked a little confused, then flashed a lopsided grin. "He wasn't really my type."

"Lissa!" scolded Dana. But everyone in the reception line and the team laughed. Even Lissa.

"Tadd!" said the president. "I know you have many pointed questions to ask, and my staff and I will do our best to answer them!"

Uncharacteristically, Tadd was speechless.

"Owen!" shouted Mehdi. "You must, at the first available opportunity, come see my collection of mid-twentieth-century muscle cars. We'll go for a ride through the desert in a 1966 427 Turbo Jet Stingray!"

Sara had arrived in front of the president. "Sara—

I know you are itching to explore my library. You will be astounded. But more about that later."

At dinner, Grant and Dana were seated next to President Mehdi and first lady Mrs. Syrine Kazdaghli, an elegant woman with the hard eyes of a political professional.

"You didn't know we were watching, did you?" said the president.

"*Watching* us? No... Excuse me, Excellency, I don't understand..."

"Yes. Nearly all the way. Bryan figured it out, because his company made those brilliant little wasp-drones that were following you everywhere. But he never told you. Don't worry, we respected your private moments, but otherwise, every word and action has been monitored and recorded. Hour by hour, day by day my staff has watched your incredible journey. And we have watched you change and learn, my friends."

The team stopped eating and stared at President Kazdaghli, as the reality sank in.

"So," said blurted Dana, "you have more than enough evidence to convict us. Where do we go now? Back to a work camp? Or to be executed? Are you mocking us with this one last party?"

The president looked aghast. "Oh, my dear Dana—no, no, no!"

"How could they be expected to think otherwise, since you have not yet informed them, my love?" asked Mrs. Kazdaghli.

"You are correct as always, my sweet," said Mehdi. He turned to the team, who listened intently. "Let me set this all in context. Some years ago, it came to my attention that one of our archivists had discovered complete files of the Bible, along with an entire library of works on Christian theology and history. By law they should have been destroyed, but I was curious. Already having some education in history, philosophy and religion, I secretly acquired the forbidden files and read the Bible. Then I read works on Christian history and theology. I read the early church fathers. I read St. Augustine, St. Thomas Aquinas, Martin Luther, C.S. Lewis, Karl Barth, N.T. Wright. Over time, I came to believe and I became a Christian—a follower of Jesus. Others joined me—my lovely wife, members of my staff here with us tonight, even some members of the Foremost Council—all secretly Christians."

The team was dumbfounded, but as the president talked, it began to dawn on the team what this revelation could mean for the world. Things could be different. The work camps could be a thing of the past, but the team tried not to anticipate their place in the transformation.

"At the same time," continued the president, "it has become increasingly evident that the Federation policy against all religion is not working. Humans do not function well in a metaphysical vacuum. And if we were honest, we would admit that even atheism is a form of religion. As I told the Foremost Council, forbidding religion to humans (ironically even irreligious humans) is like removing a bone from the mouth of a dog, without first offering the dog something to replace the bone—otherwise you risk a nasty bite. The materialistic Federation Values have not proven to be an adequate system to replace religion, any more than national socialism or Marxism had in the past. We are increasingly plagued with religious unrest—Muslims and Hindus rioting. Only in the Western Hemisphere have we been relatively free of such things. I believe it is because of the Christian heritage, however secularized."

Grant's head was spinning. The events of the day

were already too much for him, and now this bomb-shell. Although in one sense it seemed like positive news…so far.

"Pour Grant another glass of wine," ordered President Kazdaghli. "He is looking like he needs it." Everyone at the table laughed.

"We have developed a plan to re-introduce Christianity to the world," said the president. "It goes without saying that there'll be opposition, yet we're confident that we can overcome it. The Foremost Council is on board. Even those members who are not yet Christian concede to the plan's wisdom, because it will increase the stability, providing it is properly managed."

"That's incredible!" said Grant. "But why are you sharing this with us? And, not to complain, why are you treating us like celebrities—and why on earth have you watched us for the last two months?"

"Because you are part of our plan," said the president.

"I don't understand," said Grant.

"Obviously there are no Christian institutions left in the Safe Zones. So a few months ago we began surveilling the work camps. Ironically, our quest was identical to yours. We were looking for believers practicing a pure and exemplary form of Christianity. Since there are no Bibles extant, we honestly did not expect to find anyone who was practicing the faith I had seen in the New Testament. So we expanded our search to the American Wilderness, and you know first-hand what a circus that is. As I read Christian history, it seemed difficult to find any historical institutions or groups who were practicing biblical Christianity without some bizarre aberrations."

Sara nodded her head enthusiastically in agreement.

"It was a great conundrum," continued the president.

"Why do Christian institutions inevitably go awry? Is an infinitely powerful Supreme Being powerless to keep such institutions on the straight and narrow? Why does God allow them to stray and become abusive of his people? Why did Christ allow the Federation to crush Christianity, perhaps more so than other world religions? The only answer I could see was that God allows any human governance free will and accordingly, the possibility of failure. Therefore, it would seem that the fundamental solution to the institutional problem is excellence in leadership. Indeed, divinely inspired leadership."

"Yes, I can see…" began Grant.

"But, back to the original question—where would we find such leadership? We were at a loss. But then the most incredible thing happened. I received word from an old friend living in the region previously known as North Dakota. Durward Alder is his name."

The team gasped in disbelief. "Durward? That's impossible," said Grant. "He isn't a fan of the Federation, to put it diplomatically."

"Really?" said President Kazdaghli with a wry smile. "Durward is quite a character. I believe he himself advised you that people 'ain't always what they seem to be' in the Wilderness. More accurately, Durward was not a fan of the draconian policies of my predecessor, and to be honest, perhaps my policies when I first took over. But he certainly *didn't* tell you that we served together in the Federation Security Forces when we were young. I have kept in touch with him over the years. He is a Christian, was aware of your quest, and advised us that you and your team would bear watching."

"And that's when you sent in the drones?" asked Dana.

"Yes, and the rest is history—thoroughly documented! Even now our editors are at work, turning your story into an epic holographic feature that will be viewed and experienced in iCap by people around the world. It will be legendary. Someday soon we will gather you all in our theater and re-live the highlights of your journey—perhaps incorporating your comments into the feature. But right now we have *other fish to fry*, to use an old Americanism, with Christian overtones."

"What fish would those be?" asked Grant.

"We want to establish a new, worldwide church. Someone must lead it. We want a supreme patriarch whose Christianity is pure and simple—who has experienced life—whose faith has been tried and tested by adversity. A person of strength and humility."

"Good luck with that," said Grant. "We've been looking all over the place and haven't found such a person yet."

"Grant," said the president, "*you* are that person. You and your team will lead this church. You will become the supreme patriarch and pastor of the world!"

Suddenly the team felt disoriented. Grant frowned. "That's totally ridiculous. I mean with all due respect...I just don't think I'm able to...we don't...."

"Now, now," said the president. "We knew you would refuse initially. We knew that a position with this kind of power is the very last thing you would want."

"You thought right," said Grant.

"You were impelled to escape from the camp, even obsessive about it, but it seemed like you never really wanted to *lead* your group in the full sense of the word. A bit indecisive at the beginning, eh? But you learned, you learned. Which is precisely one of the major reasons you qualify for the position, because you don't crave power."

"No, no. I just don't think this will work…and if you're going to do it anyway, I think that you need to look for someone more qualified to…"

President Kazdaghli leaned into Grant's face. "Of course it will work. And tell me—who is more qualified? What school or seminary would we search to find someone? There are no genuine Christian schools or seminaries. You and your team will build them! We have seen your determination, your selfless love—not only for one another, but for those you have met along the way. We have seen you speak the truth to your own peril. We have seen your reliance on Christ in real situations. Further, you and your team carry scant cultural baggage compared to the various Wilderness groups—and even when compared to historical Christendom. I believe in the early twenty-first century, they called that a *none*—a Christ-follower who is not affiliated with any denomination." Kazdaghli laughed. "As my Phoenician ancestors were seafarers, I might say that your ship of Christianity has no barnacles clinging to it."

Grant buried his face in his hands.

"Let me *sweeten the pot*, to use another old Americanism," continued Kazdghli. "You and your friends need never, ever again worry about food, clothing or shelter. All of you will have the finest homes here in Carthage, and vacation homes wherever you want— Boston, Minot, you name it. Dana will be matriarch of the church. Lissa and Tadd will be exemplary young people, traveling the world and speaking to millions. Owen and McGwynn will be prelates, ministering to people the world over—and by the way, McGwynn, your talents will be essential in converting the gangs that control much of the Wilderness as the Federation assimilates it into the Safe Zones. And I wonder what kind of magnificent music you will come up with, eh?

Sara and Emilia—you will establish a new university and seminary, where the true history and tenets of Christianity will be taught, and thousands of pastors will be trained. We will build churches to rival the greatest Christian edifices of history. Grant—or should I say *Your Holiness*—you will preach the simple way of Christ in the most magnificent cathedral ever built!"

Grant turned toward the team and could see that they were pondering the implications of all this.

"Let me add," said Mrs. Kazdaghli, "that we will supply capable staff to carry out your work, who will see to administration. You need only direct and inspire."

No one said anything for a while. Then the president spoke again. "The political reality is this—even the most moral atheism does not keep the people in line as completely as the idea of an all-seeing God, whose wrath is mitigated by a loving Son. The promise of reward or punishment in an afterlife simply produces better, more compliant citizens."

Grant studied the president. While not at all in alignment with the words of the *remnant*, "blessed are the meek" in Grant's opinion, his statement was probably a good description of the way things work humanly. It was also an alarming window into President Kazdaghli's motive, "inheriting the earth." Yet at the same time, he seemed to be a sincere man. But was he truly a Christian? Grant was confused.

"Grant," smiled Kazdaghli. "You are suddenly looking about thirty years older. Do not let this weigh on you. It is a wonderful thing I am asking. And after all you have been through today, we are certainly not expecting an instant answer. Please, return to your quarters, relax, perhaps de-stress in your spa. Sleep on it. Pray about it. Discuss it amongst yourselves. Call my office in the morning and we will talk further. But remember, my brothers and sisters, this is not merely a request from me—it is a *calling from God*. How else can you interpret the miracle of your grandparents' Bible?

"How do you know about that?" asked Grant.

"Remember our drones," answered the president.

"Oh, yeah. I keep forgetting," said Grant. "Are you sure you didn't have something to do with that *miracle*?"

"Grant, I assure you, absolutely not. Even the Federation with all its sophisticated technology would be hard pressed to engineer such a coincidence," affirmed the President. "It is nothing less than a sign, even to us!"

Despite being in a lavish room and in the most comfortable bed they had ever experienced, Grant and Dana were sleepless that night. And no wonder.

6.

Early the next morning, Grant knocked on Sara's door. He wanted her perspective on things.

"He's certainly persuasive, isn't he?" said Sara.

"No kidding," said Grant. "First he wows us by treating us like royalty. And then he lays the Christianization plan on us. It's just too much to process. He makes it sound like a worldwide revival. And really, I should be happy about authentic Christianity being openly accepted. I should be delighted that I can play a major role in it. But something's not right."

"Kazdaghli may believe himself to be a genuine Christian, but he has also discovered the political value of Christendom," said Sara. "Some eighteen hundred years ago, the Roman Emperor Constantine did pretty much the same thing. His empire was plagued with religious unrest, much of it coming from Christians. When he became a nominal Christian himself, and subsequently made Christianity an acceptable faith within the empire, he gained immense political leverage. Further, he presided over church councils, effectively making himself the ultimate ecclesiastical authority."

"Hmm. Was he a real Christian or was he just a political opportunist? Or is it possible to be both? Was Constantine sincere—was he truly following Christ or was he using Christianity to achieve his own ends?" asked Grant.

"Sincere? What does that even mean?" said Sara. "That's something only God can judge. Whether Constantine was sincere or not, his decisions allowed Christianity to flourish."

"Maybe," said Grant. "But did it transform Christianity for the better or the worse?"

"The more you think about it, the more complex it gets, doesn't it?" said Sara. "What are you going to do?"

"I don't know yet."

After conversations with the rest of the team, Grant was still undecided. He returned to his room and sat down on the couch with his wife. An attendant had taken the kids off to enjoy the palace's water park.

"You know, Dana, the one thing I'm afraid to ask is—what happens to us if we refuse? But beyond that, what would happen to the world? Would they find someone else to be pastor of the world? Maybe an opportunist who would become some kind of antichrist?"

"Good question," said Dana. "And if we accept, we could make a huge difference. We could be God's instruments to spread the authentic message of Jesus. In time we could even clean up all that crazy stuff in the Wilderness."

Grant nodded his head. "But if the message of Jesus is institutionalized and standardized and codified, will it still be genuine, or will it become corrupt? And why would I be the only human exception to the old axiom that *absolute power corrupts absolutely*?"

Dana thought for a while. "Honey, I don't think I can add anything to what you just said. We're on the same page. Whatever you decide, I'll support it."

"I can't tell you how much I appreciate that, dear," said Grant. "You know, it's ironic that both our team and President Kazdaghli's have been driven by same quest—to find genuine Christianity. For different reasons, but still…"

"Maybe every Christ-follower does this at some point in their life," said Dana. "But now I'm wondering if that's what it's all about. I'm starting to think it's about *being* more than *searching*. And maybe that's what we were supposed to find at the end of the quest.

As Grant entered the elevator, he reflected—the quest had not at all ended in the way he expected. Dana would have all the security she ever wanted but certainly not in the way she envisioned it. If he accepted, would he be doing it to serve God or for the immense power and prestige? Already he could see Tadd and Lissa anticipating instant celebrity.

Was this a calling or a replay of Jesus' wilderness temptation? Or are both elements always present in any spiritual endeavor? And exactly what would the team's simple faith look like after it had been institutionalized? Is it even possible to institutionalize genuine faith?

Servants opened the ornate double doors to the president's office. If Grant was uncertain, the President was not.

"Good morning, *Your Holiness*!" beamed President Kazdaghli, rising from the chair behind his immense desk. The greeting made Grant wince, and Kazdaghli noticed. "It takes a little getting used to, doesn't it? But before you say anything, I have a couple of thoughts I would like to offer."

"I'm listening, Excellency," said Grant.

"First of all, I wanted to clarify that we did not destroy Lexington. We merely extracted the contraband technology, along with Abbot McFallow, Mother Shirley and some of their staff. They are in a safe place. You may wish to talk with them soon."

"That's...I'm really happy to hear that," said Grant.

"I thought you would be," said the president, "lest you doubt our sincerity. Additionally, I wanted to point out that under our proposal, the law banning *religion* will not change, so much as the way it is *interpreted*. Just the other evening, while you were camped near Charleston, I heard you put it so well. You said, 'Christianity does not function well as a religion. It is simply an active trust in Christ.' That was inspired, Grant. Imagine a chance to establish Christianity without the religion!"

Grant was taken aback. The phrase sounded appealing, yet in practice this would be a forced Christianity. So how would the president's proposal differ from the inquisitions, crusades, pogroms and witch trials that characterized most of history when there was no separation of church and state. "That's not really what I..." began Grant.

President Kazdaghli held up his hand. "Let me tell you a story, Grant. Long ago, back in fourth-century Italy, there lived a powerful and popular politician named Ambrose. In the city of Milan, there happened to be a conflict over the election of a bishop. Ambrose decided to step in to resolve the conflict. To his great surprise, the people called for his election to the post. Not even baptized, he flatly refused. He was elected anyway, and went into hiding. Only when the emper-or supported his appointment did he resign himself to accepting it. Within a week, he was baptized, ordained and consecrated as Bishop of Milan—and went on to become one of the great historic fathers of the church."

"I don't know what to say," said Grant. "Look, I'm just a geologist. I can tell you where to drill for oil. That's what I do. And I'm a Christ-follower. Other than that, I've taken this little group across the North Amer-ican Wilderness, but I really don't have the adminis-trative skills necessary to run a big institution."

"Grant, Grant, Grant," said the President. "You for-get that I have access to the records of your service in the work camp. You are, in fact, a splendid administrator, in addition to being a scientist with a well-disciplined mind. And your journey has taught you leadership. Let me tell you another story, just in case what you say about your administrative deficiency is true, which it isn't. Back in the seventh century in the ancient city of Nineveh, there was an ascetic Christian named Isaac. They decided to ordain him a bishop—and suddenly he found himself mired in administrative duties. He hated it. After five months he quit and returned to the life of an ascetic hermit."

Grant looked quizzically at the President. "I don't understand how that should encourage me to accept your offer."

Kazdaghli laughed. "It is a bit of a strange story, isn't it? My point is that unlike Isaac, you won't have to wor-ry about administrative duties. You will be given the most skilled administrators. As my lovely wife explained last night, your job will be to provide spiritual direc-tion and inspiration for your new worldwide Chris-tian flock. Grant—think of it! You will be the *second most influential person on earth.*"

That kind of power was the last thing Grant wanted. But such power could lead to a resurgence—a great reawakening—of Christian faith around the world. And what would accepting this power mean about his own faith?

Both Grant and Kazdaghli were quiet for a while. The morning sun was shining though the huge windows and spreading across President Kazdaghli's desk, illuminating his personal white leather-bound Bible. The rays of the sun were brilliantly reflected by the second prominently displayed memento—a gleaming silver model of a Federation warship.

Grant finally broke the silence. "Give us one more day, Excellency. I promise I will give you my answer tomorrow morning."

Kazdaghli arose, reached across the desk, and warmly clasped Grant's hands between both of his. "Splendid. I know you will make the right decision. The world awaits."

As Grant exited Kazdaghli's brightly lit office into the darkened hallway leading to the elevator, he flashed back months ago to Minot—crawling on their knees through that dark tunnel—escaping from confinement, yet giving up security, in the hope of finding a new, free life.

Suddenly, for the sake of God, his family, his friends and the entire world, it was clear to Grant what he had to do.

A couple of years ago my publisher Greg Albrecht and I started discussing *dystopianism*—a future world that is generally worse than the one we currently inhabit. It seems that everyone has created movies, miniseries and books dealing with grim dystopian themes. Not wanting to be left behind, Christian publishers have offered their own dystopian takes over the years, with, among many other things, a series of novels and films about life under an antichrist in a post-rapture world, right before Jesus returns. Sometimes I think these stories were designed to terrorize people into getting right with God, and I can't see they've left a positive legacy.

Thinking beyond well-trodden paths, we wondered what a dystopian world might look like if an apocalypse came and went and Jesus didn't return along with it? After all, the Bible does say that he *won't* return when we expect. What would the world be like? What would religious institutions, if any, look like? Could things get any crazier than they are today? Weeks and months went by as I added flesh to the skeletal outline.

We live on the precariously thin crust of a planet that is always in transition. As if tectonic, climatic and ecological perils that are built into the world weren't enough, we insist on being our own worst threat of extinction. Despite our intelligence and creativity, we as a species are collectively and individually insane, and are headed toward annihilation (sure, that may sound a bit negative, but I am certain of divine intervention, which has already happened, actually).

Still, with all these threats, the way in which the near future will play out is hard to predict. Any one book has to narrow its focus—and *The Remnant* deals with a challenge and a complex set of issues that we could easily find ourselves facing in the coming decades.

Into this setting, using character-driven writing, I

placed *The Remnant* characters. Rather than creating a plot and forcing the characters into it, I like to develop the characters, and then imagine how they might interact, which in turn drives much of the sequence of events. This is probably a more complicated way to work, as unbridled characters will inevitably lead a writer to more than a few dead ends and rewrites. But I think it leads to more interesting turns in a story.

Yet this is why a second, third and fourth set of eyes is essential. And why I am thankful for my outspoken wife Kaye who brought several inconsistencies to my attention, for Laura Urista who, in addition to scheduling the production of the book and formatting the text, authenticated the North Dakota dialect (she lived there *doncha know*), for Katie McCoach, who made major improvements in character development and interaction, for Dr. Brad Jersak who weighed in on issues of pace and plausibility, as well as offering historical and theological insight, for Adria Holub for her thorough copy-editing, for Marv Wegner's brilliant graphic design and cover—and for Greg Albrecht, who helped develop the concept and shepherded the development of *The Remnant*. In addition, Dennis Warkentin adroitly manages promotion and fulfillment.

I must also thank profusely many of my family, friends and acquaintances, in addition to a few composers, musicians and even preachers for names I have borrowed and echoes of character that I have referenced. While it goes without saying that some historical figures are real, no character represents any real person, as such.

Finally, as J.S. Bach wrote at the end of most of his compositions—*S.D.G.*—*Soli Deo Gloria*. I am sure all who have collaborated with me in this project would agree with him—*Glory goes to God alone for this work.*

Monte Wolverton, Easter Sunday, 2016

What will Grant Cochrin decide to do?

Grant is facing a huge dilemma. Will he throw his instincts out the window and agree to become the "second most influential person on earth"—accepting the title of "His Holiness" offered by World President Mehdi Kazdaghli? Could this prestigious title enable Grant to proclaim authentic Christianity?

On the other hand, Grant deeply distrusts religious institutionalism. Will he turn down the offer, and attempt to return to the Wilderness—risking himself, his family and friends being sent to another work camp, or a prison—or much worse?

What would you do if you were Grant? We invite you to visit our Facebook page—*The Remnant*, CWRpress—and share what you think Grant and the team will do—or should do. Or you can email your thoughts to us at info@ptm.org, or send a letter to us at: *The Remnant*, CWRpress, Pasadena, CA 91129.

If we decide to publish a sequel, and we receive your perspectives, ideas and opinions before June 1, 2017, we may incorporate them in the sequel.

If you're reading this in or after late 2018, then the sequel to *The Remnant* may have been published and you can discover the answers by reading it!

If you're reading this in the 22nd century, in a religious detention camp...well...you're living the sequel!

www.ingramcontent.com/pod-product-compliance
Lightning Source LLC
Chambersburg PA
CBHW070853250626
47159CB00003B/1049